To Trust a Duke

Soldiers & Soulmates
Book 3

Alexa Aston

Text by Alexa Aston
Cover by Wicked Smart Designs

Dragonblade Publishing, Inc. is an imprint of Kathryn Le Veque Novels, Inc.
P.O. Box 23
Moreno Valley, CA 92556
ceo@dragonbladepublishing.com

Produced in the United States of America

First Edition March 2020
Trade Paperback Edition

The characters and events portrayed in this book are fictitious. Any similarity to real persons, living or dead, is purely coincidental and not intended by the author.

ARE YOU SIGNED UP FOR DRAGONBLADE'S BLOG?

You'll get the latest news and information on exclusive giveaways, exclusive excerpts, coming releases, sales, free books, cover reveals and more.

Check out our complete list of authors, too!

No spam, no junk. That's a promise!

Sign Up Here

www.dragonbladepublishing.com

Dearest Reader;

Thank you for your support of a small press. At Dragonblade Publishing, we strive to bring you the highest quality Historical Romance from some of the best authors in the business. Without your support, there is no 'us', so we sincerely hope you adore these stories and find some new favorite authors along the way.

Happy Reading!

CEO, Dragonblade Publishing

Additional Dragonblade books by Author Alexa Aston

Second Sons of London Series
Educated By The Earl
Debating With The Duke
Empowered By The Earl
Made for the Marquess
Dubious about the Duke
Valued by the Viscount
Meant for the Marquess

Dukes Done Wrong Series
Discouraging the Duke
Deflecting the Duke
Disrupting the Duke
Delighting the Duke
Destiny with a Duke

Dukes of Distinction Series
Duke of Renown
Duke of Charm
Duke of Disrepute
Duke of Arrogance
Duke of Honor

The St. Clairs Series
Devoted to the Duke
Midnight with the Marquess
Embracing the Earl
Defending the Duke
Suddenly a St. Clair
Starlight Night (Novella)
The Twelve Days of Love (Novella)

Soldiers & Soulmates Series
To Heal an Earl
To Tame a Rogue
To Trust a Duke
To Save a Love
To Win a Widow

Yuletide at Gillingham (Novella)

The Lyon's Den Series
The Lyon's Lady Love

King's Cousins Series
The Pawn
The Heir
The Bastard

Medieval Runaway Wives
Song of the Heart
A Promise of Tomorrow
Destined for Love

Knights of Honor Series
Word of Honor
Marked by Honor
Code of Honor
Journey to Honor
Heart of Honor
Bold in Honor
Love and Honor
Gift of Honor
Path to Honor
Return to Honor

Pirates of Britannia Series
God of the Seas

De Wolfe Pack: The Series
Rise of de Wolfe

The de Wolfes of Esterley Castle
Diana
Derek
Thea

Also from Alexa Aston
The Bridge to Love

PROLOGUE

Dunbury—May 1808

ASHLYN CLARKE AWOKE with a start, her cheeks damp with tears. She'd dreamed again of that fateful night.

And how one kiss had changed the course of her life.

Falling asleep would be impossible so she used the bedsheet to dry her face and remained in bed. Her thoughts drifted to five years ago. At eighteen, she'd been on the cusp of her first London Season and already eagerly trying out her dancing skills at the local weekly assembly. A regiment newly stationed in the area had attended the week before and its soldiers and officers were back again. Ashlyn had danced with several of the men, including a young, handsome officer named Daniel Clarke.

After a lively reel, Clarke had fetched them each a cup of punch and then they'd strolled just outside the assembly rooms to catch their breaths and a bit of fresh air. He'd told her of his suspicion that Britain would soon declare war on France and his reluctance to go. He then asked her for a kiss, saying he'd never given one before. Ashlyn hadn't seen any harm in the gesture and had obliged him. The kiss had been brief and very innocent.

Then her world came crashing down.

Her stepmother, jealous of the close relationship Ashlyn had with her father, appeared from nowhere. She raised such a fuss it brought several others outside, including Ashlyn's father. Her stepmother insisted marriage was the only thing that would save

Ashlyn's reputation and her father reluctantly agreed.

The banns were read and three weeks later, she pledged herself to Daniel Clarke and then spent one night with him. They'd both fumbled about, trying to consummate the marriage, neither of them knowing what to do. She found the experience painful and unfulfilling, not to mention embarrassing.

The next day, Daniel left with his regiment for additional training while Ashlyn was packed into a carriage. As the vehicle drove away, she saw the triumphant smile on her stepmother's face. She arrived two days later at Dunbury, home to the Earl of Dunwood, Daniel's older brother. She explained that she'd married Daniel and he'd sent her to his childhood home as his regiment shipped out. Ashlyn found herself living among strangers—and soon found herself with child.

She smoothed the bedclothes, thoughts of Gregory filling her mind. Her son, now four, was the only good thing to have come from the brief physical encounter with Daniel, who still remained a stranger to her. His letters came sporadically and gave her no sense of who he was as a man. She worried about the day he finally came home to her. She didn't know his favorite food or color. If he enjoyed sports or music. Where he'd gone to school. She couldn't even remember whether his eyes were blue or green.

The door opened and Dilly sailed in. Her lady's maid was usually full of gossip. Ashlyn knew she shouldn't encourage Dilly but she was lonely. Her in-laws, whom she'd never felt comfortable around, spent a majority of their year in London and were there now for the Season. She never went with them, not feeling right about dancing until the wee hours of the morning while her husband faced danger every day of his life. Because of that, she and Gregory remained at Dunbury and had created a life separate from the others. Their time together, along with the hours she volunteered tutoring local boys at the nearby parsonage, gave her purpose in life.

Ashlyn rose and washed as Dilly set out her clothing for the day. She could tell by the maid's eyes that she had news to share.

"Lord and Lady Dunwood returned late last evening, my lady," Dilly began.

Surprise filled her. "They are at Dunbury? Why, the Season is barely a month old."

"The earl is very sick," her servant explained. "The pneumonia. His London doctor told him to get back to the country and fresh air."

"I'm sorry to hear that."

"All below stairs are saying he'll die. That he already looked like death warmed over," Dilly continued. "Lady Dunwood is beside herself. She's worried the earl will go and then she won't be in charge of the household anymore. *You* would be the new countess."

Ashlyn froze. Lord Dunwood only had one daughter, Eliza, a horribly spoiled brat who was three years older than Gregory and bullied him whenever she could. Ashlyn was always relieved when the Dunwoods left for London and hoped they would stay a good while so that Lady Eliza would be gone from the household. With no son to inherit, though, the earldom would fall to Daniel in the event his brother died. She wondered if her husband would come home from war if that occurred.

Maintaining her composure, she said, "We shouldn't speak of such matters, Dilly."

The maid sniffed. "Everyone in the household hopes you'll become Lady Dunwood soon, my lady. You are kind to all and never have a cross word for anyone. Lady Dunwood constantly causes problems."

She frowned at Dilly and the servant finally fell silent, putting the finishing touches on Ashlyn's hair.

"I'll tidy up here, my lady. You go have your breakfast."

Making her way downstairs, Ashlyn entered the small dining room and was surprised to find her sister-in-law present.

She took a seat and said, "I've just been informed that Lord Dunwood is ill. Please let me know if there's anything I may do for him. Or you."

The countess glared at her. "Don't pretend to be nice to me. I know what you're thinking. You wish for my husband to die so that yours becomes Dunwood. Where will that leave me?" Bursting into tears, the older woman fled the room.

Her accusation stunned Ashlyn. She'd never thought of Daniel inheriting the title and estate. Even if he did, he would never turn out his sister-in-law and niece. Ashlyn might not know much about her husband of five years but she believed him to be a gentleman in every sense of the word.

She picked at her breakfast and decided to go to the nursery, where Gregory would be finishing his meal. They'd spotted a new group of ducklings on their walk around the lake yesterday and her boy was eager to visit them again.

The nursery was empty when she arrived. Dishes for Gregory and Eliza's breakfast had yet to be cleared. She went to Gregory's room and found his nursery governess there picking up his toys.

"If you're looking for Master Gregory, he went with Lady Eliza and her governess," the old woman said.

"Where were they going?" Ashlyn didn't like the idea of Gregory in his cousin's company.

"I couldn't say, my lady."

She left, unhappy with the nursery governess for allowing Gregory to leave her sight. Though Ashlyn had never specifically said her son was not to be in his cousin's company, everyone in the household knew what a terror Eliza was and how jealous she was of her young cousin.

Downstairs, she asked the footman in the foyer if he'd seen her son.

"Yes, my lady. Master Gregory was with Lady Eliza and her governess. They were going to the kitchen, I believe."

"Thank you."

Making her way there, she found the governess having a cup of tea and a scone, laughing and gossiping with the cook.

"Where is my son?" she demanded.

"Oh, he and Lady Eliza went to play."

Ashlyn frowned. "Where? And why aren't you with them?"

"Lady Eliza had a special game she wanted to play with her cousin. I thought they would be fine on their own for a little while. Lady Dunwood encourages her daughter to be independent. Watching after her young cousin encourages this."

"You're wrong about that," she snapped. "Lady Dunwood doesn't seem to care what her daughter does—or whom she does it to."

Anger sizzled through her as she left the kitchen. She regretted her indiscreet words but the governess should know better than to leave her charge alone, especially with a boy as young as Gregory. Eliza had started a fire recently. She'd been caught mistreating one of the barn cats. She'd broken a vase and blamed Gregory for it. Ashlyn longed to discipline the girl but had been given strict instructions that she wasn't to involve herself in any way regarding Eliza.

Returning to the foyer, she enlisted the footman to help her search for the children.

"I'll take this floor," she told him. "You may start in the basement."

"Yes, my lady."

She worried about the special game Eliza sought to play. The last time the girl had played alone with Gregory, it had been a game of hide and seek—with Eliza locking Gregory in the basement. Eliza had calmly returned to her governess and gone about her lessons while Ashlyn had panicked for several hours when her son couldn't be found. Eliza finally admitted with a sly smile that Gregory could possibly be in the basement. Ashlyn rushed there and found him, cold and frightened. Of course, nothing had been done to keep Eliza from playing her games.

Gregory had promised her never to go to the basement again, which is why she started her search on this floor. Sending the footman was a precaution.

The children weren't in either parlor so she went to Dunwood's study and found the door locked. Moving away, she heard a high-pitched wail and then a scream—from within the room.

Pounding on the door, Ashlyn cried, "Open up at once!"

No one came. She beat on the door again and the butler appeared.

"Find the key for this lock," she ordered and continued beating the heel of her hands against the wood.

The butler returned with the housekeeper, who pulled a ring from her apron pocket. It held dozens of keys and Ashlyn panicked, knowing it would take forever to figure out which one unlocked this door.

She turned to bang on the door again when she heard the lock thrown. Eliza opened the door, her face red as tears streamed down it. Her eyes widened as she caught sight of Ashlyn.

"I didn't mean to. He wanted to be a soldier. Like his papa."

Ashlyn pushed the girl from the doorway and rushed inside. Her footsteps faltered the moment she saw Gregory lying on the ground, blood soaking his chest. A sword rested on the ground beside him.

"Call for the doctor!" she shouted and ran to her son.

Falling to her knees, she lifted his head to her lap and cradled it. Blood bubbled from his lips.

"It hurts, Mama," he murmured.

Helplessness swept through her, knowing she could do nothing to save him. "I know, my sweet boy. I know. Don't talk."

She stroked his hair, choking back sobs, and watched the light fade from his eyes.

"No!" she cried, hugging his still body to hers.

They finally pried her from him an hour later.

Ashlyn wished she were the one dead.

ASHLYN DRAGGED HERSELF from the bed, fighting the urge to return and bury herself in it. Gregory had sat in his grave two weeks now. He wouldn't be coming back.

Neither would the Earl of Dunwood.

Her brother-in-law succumbed to his pneumonia the day after Gregory's death. She'd sat in the church with two coffins at the front, one large and one small. The clergyman spent most of his time singing the praises of Dunwood, a man who spent little time at his country estate and probably hadn't known the names of most of the servants and local people who attended his funeral. Gregory was mentioned only as an afterthought, which hurt Ashlyn more than she could ever have imagined. The light of her life had been snuffed out.

All thanks to Lady Eliza.

The girl claimed they'd been playing at being soldiers. She'd even removed her father's pistols from their case, though she hadn't known how to load them. They'd played with the guns until she'd grown bored and then she'd removed the sword which hung from the wall, a weapon of some past family member. Eliza said she'd only held it out to show Gregory and that her cousin had wanted to hold it, charging toward her to take it away. Instead, he'd run straight into it.

Or so Eliza repeated every time she was asked about the so-called accident.

Everyone fawned over the girl and remarked upon the tragedy, believing the lies she told. Only Ashlyn knew the truth. That Eliza had deliberately stabbed her cousin and killed him. The girl and her mother had now gone to London, where they could be surrounded by friends. Ashlyn hadn't known if she could look upon either of them and was grateful for their departure.

Mark Clarke, a second cousin to Daniel, had come and taken charge of the family. She barely remembered meeting him at the funeral and had taken to her bed once Gregory and his uncle had been buried. Clarke had visited her twice, sharing that he'd written to Daniel, informing him he was the new Earl of

Dunwood and requesting he sell his commission and come home to his family.

Today, she roused herself. If Daniel was coming home, she didn't need to be one of the problems he faced. Already, Dilly had told Ashlyn of whispered rumors that the previous earl had squandered much of the family fortune at the London gaming tables. Daniel might be returning to an impossible situation.

She could help if necessary. Before her wedding five years ago, her father had given Ashlyn a tidy sum, to be spent as she chose. He warned her never to tell her new husband of it since men controlled all property and monies of their wives. He'd given her the name of a solicitor who would see the funds held for her use. It had been her plan to save the funds for Gregory's education. With her only child gone, she no longer cared about the sum. If the rumors proved true, though, she would give Daniel the money to help the estate survive.

Dilly brought Ashlyn a mug of hot tea, her eyes wide at seeing her mistress up and about.

"Have water brought for a bath," she instructed the maid.

Ashlyn drank the tea, the liquid warming her. Soon, servants brought buckets of heated water and she sank into the tub. Dilly washed Ashlyn's hair and scrubbed her thoroughly. For the first time in two weeks, she felt almost human. Inside, though, a vast emptiness lingered. She supposed it would always be with her. A darkness that would never catch the light. Gregory had been her light. Her reason for living. Daniel would never be able to understand that. He'd never laid eyes upon his son. Never known the joy of hearing Gregory speak his first words or seeing that first smile.

It hit her that with Daniel now holding the title, he would want other children. Ashlyn couldn't bear the thought of another boy replacing Gregory. How could she birth another child? Give her heart away as she had before? Yet she would not be able to deny her husband his rights over her body. The thought of lying with him again turned her stomach.

She pushed the thought aside. One thing at a time.

She found Cousin Mark in the small dining room, still at breakfast, a newspaper spread in front of him. If he was surprised to finally see her up and about, he hid it well.

"Good morning, Lady Dunwood. It's good to see you."

Taking a seat, she said, "I want you to know I appreciate you being here. For taking care of everything when I was indisposed."

"You've suffered a great loss, my lady. It's understandable that it will take time for you to recover."

Ashlyn never would but she didn't correct him. He'd been very helpful and there was no need to hurt him.

He rose and retrieved a stack of letters from a nearby table and said, "These have come for you if you're ready to read them."

The thought of reading through condolences left her with a sour stomach but it needed to be done.

"Thank you. I'll read through and answer them today."

Cousin Mark looked at her with concern. "Take your time. There's no rush."

"No. I want to. It will give me something to do."

She pushed an egg about her plate and finally gave up, taking the letters with her to what had been the Countess of Dunwood's correspondence room. It was where letters were answered and menus planned. Though the room was now hers, Ashlyn felt like an imposter sitting at the desk.

Each page essentially said the same thing. The writers conveyed their sorrow for her loss. She tired of the same trite phrases written again and again and dreaded the thought of answering each one in a similar manner.

The final letter caught her attention because it looked worn, as if it had traveled a great distance. She opened it and before reading the contents, looked to the bottom of the page. It was signed by a Lieutenant-Colonel Baker. She knew the name from Daniel's letters. Baker was his commanding officer, a man Daniel had written of frequently.

With dread, her eyes rose to the top of the page.

Dear Mrs. Clarke –

It is with great sorrow that I write to you of the passing of your husband, Lieutenant Daniel Clarke. Lieutenant Clarke had been under my command these past two years and I found him to be a thoughtful, dedicated officer. He will be sorely missed among his men and fellow officers.

He was not lost in battle but grew weak from dysentery, a disease that runs rampant among our troops. I've arranged for Lieutenant Clarke's body to be returned to England so that he may be buried among his family members.

My deepest sympathies go to you and your son, Mrs. Clarke.

Sincerely,
Lt. Col. Reid Baker

The letter fell from her hand.

CHAPTER ONE

Gillingham—February 1811

COLONEL REID BAKER was finally going home to England after nearly a decade as an officer in the king's army—all thanks to his childhood friends, Danforth Grayson and Burke Nicholson.

Gray left the Peninsular Wars first, selling his commission to act as guardian to his orphaned nieces and nephew. When his sickly nephew died, Gray became the Earl of Crampton, wedding Lady Charlotte Nott, the children's governess. Burke had followed Gray home a year later, returning with his right eye missing. He'd taken up a new role as a spy for the War Department, bringing a ring of high-placed government traitors to justice and marrying his fellow spy, Lady Gemma Covington, in the process.

It was hard to imagine his two closest friends as husbands, much less ones who were lucky enough to make love matches. Gray had always been a loner who'd been struck hard by the losses of his men in battle. Thanks to Charlotte, Gray's emotional wounds had healed, and the couple had one son, as well as custody of Gray's two nieces. Burke, a third son and notorious womanizer who'd refused to enter the church, had joined Reid and Gray as army officers after they'd left university, thirsting for adventure. In gratitude for Burke exposing the circle of traitors, the crown awarded the extraordinary spy an earldom, and

Gemma would give birth to their first child in June.

These men, the brothers of his heart, now lived on their country estates in Kent, close to Reid's family home, Gillingham. Urgent letters from Burke and Gray finally convinced Reid he needed to come back to England. The pair had visited the Duke of Gilford at his wife's insistence, and they revealed to Reid he must end his war career and take up his responsibilities to his family because Gilford was now bedridden and had one foot in the grave.

As a marquess and heir apparent to a dukedom, Reid had no need to go to war in the first place. Few men of his rank did. Yet from the time he was young, he'd felt an immense sense of patriotism and the desire to make a difference in the world. When Bonaparte sucked England into his bloody wars, Reid relished the idea of helping defeat the enemy. A natural leader, he needed to fix problems and produce results. His intelligence and confidence had led to him rising to rank of colonel in the decade he served his country.

A part of him, though, had simply wanted to escape. His father had wed again when Reid was eighteen, having been a widower for fifteen years. The new duchess was only a year older than Reid himself and she quickly produced two boys for the duke. By entering the army, he gave his father time to enjoy his second family without a reminder of the first one. And if Reid succumbed in battle, Gilford still had an heir and a spare.

His father rarely wrote to him, only a few times a year, and none during the past two years. The duchess had flooded Reid with letters for the better part of a year, imploring him to return, but he'd ignored them, too caught up in his war duties. He answered tersely, telling Dalinda that he would be home when Bonaparte met defeat and not before. She'd finally quit pestering him.

Then he received lengthy letters from both Gray and Burke, who'd gone to visit his father at Dalinda's insistence. The Duke of Gilford had been as a father to both boys and the pair had spent several holidays at Gillingham throughout their school and university years. Both described the duke's faltering health and how Reid was needed at home to manage all the properties and finances. Gray, in particular, urged Reid to hurry if he wanted to see his father alive.

That had spurred him into action. He was already weary of war and ready for the green of England again, not having realized he was homesick after almost ten years abroad. He'd done more than his duty to king and country and now needed to see to his own family. If his father were as critically ill as the others said, then the estate and holdings would have been neglected. Reid's responsibilities now were to his family. He quickly sold out and caught the first ship home.

He saw the village of Gillbrook appear on the horizon from his spot atop the mail coach, which had proven to be the fastest way to reach Kent once his ship landed on the southern coast of England. His heart beat a bit faster, knowing how close he was to seeing where he'd grown up and eager to know his half-brothers, who were ten and twelve.

Within ten minutes, they'd arrived at Gillbrook. Reid was the lone passenger who disembarked, carrying only his satchel. It contained a spare uniform and a few odds and ends, including his razor and comb. After he alighted, the driver wished him well and took off, keeping to his schedule. Reid's gaze swept across the familiar buildings. Though the hamlet looked prosperous, with neatly painted buildings and wares on display in shop windows, he saw not a soul walking the streets or emerging from any store or abode. Considering it was a quarter past ten in the morning, surprise filled him as he wondered where everyone might be.

Pushing the mystery aside, he decided to walk to Gillingham, which was a mere two miles from Gillbrook. It felt good to stretch his legs, though he tugged his cloak about him as a cold winter wind cut through him. He set a brisk pace and arrived home shortly before eleven. As he reached the front door, he realized he had no key and hadn't for years. Playing visitor, he rapped loudly on the door, wondering if he'd even know any of the staff. Surely, Mr. Bellows, the longtime Gilford butler, and Mrs. Paul, the housekeeper, would still be employed. He chuckled, thinking of the aptly named Mrs. Cook, their cook, who'd married Cook, the head gardener. They should also be at Gillingham.

When no one answered, Reid impatiently tried the door and found it unlocked. No footman appeared as he came through the foyer and wandered up the stairs. The drawing room was empty, as were two small parlors and the library. He made his way to his father's bedchamber and also found no one there. If the duke was so ill, wouldn't he be in bed? Reid hoped Dalinda hadn't convinced Gray and Burke to write falsehoods in order to get Reid home. Knowing his friends, he didn't feel that possible.

He dropped his satchel in his old room and came back downstairs, his stomach rumbling. Going to the kitchen, he saw several servants rushing about as Mrs. Cook issued orders. An incredible amount of food had been prepared and was being placed upon trays. Had he stumbled upon a party?

Reid managed to keep a footman from plowing into him, holding the man about the shoulders and then sliding past him. He went straight to the cook.

"Mrs. Cook, what is going on?"

The kitchen went silent. He felt a dozen pairs of eyes on him.

The Gillingham cook clapped her hands. "Go on! Get about your work!" she demanded, and the staff hustled to do her bidding. She turned back to him, giving him a warm smile, as she bobbed a curtsey.

"It's nice to see you after all this time, Your Grace."

Her words struck Reid as a bullet to the heart. There would be only one reason for Mrs. Cook to address him as she had.

The Duke of Gilford was dead.

"My father . . ." he began and then swallowed hard.

Sympathy filled her eyes. "Gone, Your Grace. Two days ago. Everyone in the household and a large portion of Gillbrook is at the funeral now. If you hurry, you might be able to see the burial, then the mourners will come back here."

"Thank you."

Though he still had the dust of the road covering him, Reid hurried from the house. The chapel lay half a mile away, with the graveyard in between. He took off running and only paused when he spied a large group gathered around a gravesite. Slowing to a walk, he joined the mourners at the rear before making his way along the edges until he reached the front, seeing both Gray and Burke there, along with whom he supposed were their wives.

Reverend Jackson acknowledged Reid with a brief nod as he continued reading from the twenty-third Psalm, a favorite of the duke's. No one else noted his presence, their heads bowed in prayer, except for two boys standing on both sides of his stepmother. Dalinda looked as beautiful as ever in her widow's weeds, dark brown hair framing her pale skin. Tears streamed down her cheeks, her grief obvious.

Her two sons eyed Reid suspiciously. Neither seemed to grieve in the least. He frowned at them but both stared back defiantly, as if daring him to call them out. Somehow, it didn't surprise him. Dalinda had always struck him as a bit scattered. She wouldn't be much of a disciplinarian. If his father had been too ill to deal with his sons, their mother probably ignored any misbehavior.

That would have to change.

The clergyman had gone into a prayer following his reading and now brought it to a close. Those gathered raised their heads and he sensed the shock run through the crowd as they noted his presence. By now, though, Reid's focus was on his father's pine coffin. It was hard to believe the man who'd always appeared larger than life had come to an end, his remains residing in the coffin. He took a step forward and placed his palm on its surface, his throat thick with unshed tears.

After a moment, he looked to Reverend Jackson and nodded. The clergyman thanked those present for their attendance and invited everyone back to Gillingham for refreshments.

Reid turned away, his eyes downcast as his hand remained on the casket. He sensed the crowd moving away.

"Goodbye, Father," he said softly and stepped away.

He saw only his stepmother and half-brothers had stayed behind. The boys openly glared at him now as Dalinda came toward him.

He took her hands. "I'm sorry for your loss, Dalinda."

She sniffed and more tears cascaded down her cheeks. "He was such a good man. I will miss him very much."

"We all will." Reid paused. "I assume these are my half-brothers." He looked at the pair. "I haven't seen you since you were in the nursery."

"We haven't been in the nursery in years," Arthur, the older one said snidely. "And we haven't missed you at all."

"No, we haven't," echoed Harry, the younger one.

He waited a moment, seeing if their mother would correct them, but she kept silent.

"It seems I will be responsible for more than running Gillingham," he said curtly. "I suppose part of my tasks will be teaching you two some manners."

Arthur sneered at him as Dalinda said, "Oh, Reid, they are so upset now over their father's death. There's no need to discipline them now."

"I disagree. Good manners are never held to a certain time or place but should always be in evidence. Grief over a parent's death is no excuse for ill behavior."

"Why did you have to come back?" Harry demanded. "We were fine without you. Nobody wants you here."

Reid knelt in order to be eye-level with them. "The duke was my father, too. I spent over twenty years with him before I went to war. I am very sad at his passing—and I'm saddened that my half-brothers are so disrespectful, right at his gravesite."

"You can't tell us what to do," Arthur said stubbornly, his chin jutting out.

He rose and glared down at them. "Actually, Arthur, I can," he said abruptly. "I am the new Duke of Gilford—and what I say is the law around here. Wipe the sneers off your faces. If you can't look sad, then put a bland expression on your faces. Each of you take one of your mother's arms and we shall return to the house. Many people there wish to offer all of us their condolences. Accept their words graciously and thank them.

"Is that understood?"

His strident tone conveyed his immense displeasure with them. Both boys cowed. But they did step to their mother's sides and helped her back to the house without a word. She started to speak but his look cut her off. He would need to talk with her at length later regarding discipline.

Once they arrived back at the house, Reid separated from them. He made sure to circulate throughout the drawing room, speaking to everyone briefly and thanking each for their attendance. He received condolences from the town mayor down to the footmen who waited upon the group.

One woman whom he wasn't acquainted with introduced herself. She emitted a sense of tremendous confidence, though she was almost a foot shorter than he was. Her lively, amethyst eyes were the most unusual he'd ever encountered and only added to her great beauty. Reid felt drawn to her in a way he couldn't describe.

"I am Lady Dunwood, Your Grace. New to the neighborhood these past three years but very sad to see your father go. The duke was a kind, gracious man. He will be sorely missed for his wit and humility."

"Thank you, Lady Dunwood. Father will always be the best man I know, no matter how many more gentlemen I encounter during my lifetime."

He knew of no Lord Dunwood in the area but realized he'd been away nearly ten years. Before he could ask her about her family and where she lived, the local doctor and his wife interrupted and he spoke with them. By the time he finished accepting their condolences, Lady Dunwood had disappeared from his elbow. He searched the room and determined she was gone.

He finally had time to speak to his friends. Both Burke and Gray gave him strong handshakes and bear hugs, and he turned to be introduced to their wives.

"Though we've never met, I feel as if I already know you both," Reid told them. "Your husbands have written glowingly about you."

"Are you certain they wrote the letters themselves, Your Grace? Gemma and I might have dictated what they were to write so you would have a delightful impression of us. I'm Charlotte, by the way." She offered Reid her hand and he kissed it, already taken with Gray's countess.

"Burke's handwriting leaves much to be desired," the other wife said. "I'm Gemma and very pleased to meet you, Your Grace."

He kissed her hand and proclaimed, "No, none of that. You are Gemma and Charlotte and I am Reid. I am also the man who knows more about these two scoundrels than they ever could remember. If you want to know who your husbands truly are, I am more than happy to be at your service and reveal their pasts."

"Oh, I knew I would like you," Charlotte proclaimed, sliding her arm through his.

"Get your own Miss Nott," Gray proclaimed, pulling his wife back to his side and laughing good-naturedly.

Reid knew Gray called Charlotte by her governess name at times. He could see by the glow in their eyes that the couple was deeply in love. The same held for Burke, whose arm had slid around his wife's waist. The look that passed between them almost knocked the breath from Reid, so potent with love—and desire.

"I'm sorry we're meeting under such sad circumstances," he told them. "Once things have calmed down and I have a better idea of my new responsibilities, I hope the four of you will return to Gillingham for a week or so in order for us to become better acquainted."

"That would be lovely," Gemma said. "Though you shouldn't wait too long, Reid." She patted her belly. "Our baby will arrive in late June."

"I'll make it soon, Gemma." He looked to Charlotte. "And bring young Viscount Warren and the girls when you come."

They spoke a few more minutes and then the two couples departed to return to their own estates, making them the last of the mourners to leave. Reid found himself tired and still hungry since he hadn't bothered eating anything from the trays that had circulated through the crowd.

Dalinda came to him and immediately said, "They are good boys, Reid. Merely high-spirited."

"They were both rude and incredibly obnoxious," he declared. "There's no excuse for such ill behavior. Father would be appalled."

"Well, he wasn't around to guide them the last two years," she said, anger sparking in her eyes.

Pity filled him, knowing she'd lost her husband, one she seemed to have truly loved.

"I know you've done the best you could, Dalinda, especially with Father being so ill. I'm sorry it took me as long as it did to end my service to the crown and return home. I'm here now and ready to help you in rearing the boys. They need a mother's love but a firm, male hand will also be important."

"I won't have you beat them, Reid," she declared. "They are just boys."

"They are—but they're closer to being men than you'd care to admit. Are they at Eton together? Or somewhere else? Tell me a little of their schooling and background. I want to get to know them better, not only as their guardian but as family."

She hesitated.

"Dalinda, is something wrong?"

She began wringing her hands. "They were at school. In fact, they've been to three schools. No, four."

Concern filled him. "Why so many? Did they have a difficult time adjusting to being away from home? Some boys do, you know."

"No, they . . . well, they . . ."

"Spit it out, Woman!"

"They've been asked to leave every school they've attended," Dalinda wailed. "You've got to help them, Reid. I don't know what to do with them. They're unruly. I cannot control them any longer. It's hopeless. You're going to have to handle them now because I don't know how."

It was not the homecoming Reid had hoped for.

CHAPTER TWO

ASHLYN READIED HERSELF for the day. She pulled her hair into its usual chignon, an easy style for her to manage on her own. When she'd left Dunbury, she hadn't taken Dilly with her, not wanting any reminders of her time there. Though Mark Clarke, the new Earl of Dunwood, offered Ashlyn the dower's house, she'd refused. He'd settled a nice sum upon her for giving up the residence. That, along with what her father had secretly provided, proved enough for Ashlyn to start her own school. Dunwood Academy now operated from a rented property in Kent, with four instructors and between ten and twelve students in attendance at any given time.

She'd been drawn to establishing a school due to her love for her son and wanting to find a way to honor Gregory. Knowing she could never give her heart again as she had to her boy, she'd decided never to wed. Instead, she made herself useful in the lives of other boys, troubled or lonely ones who needed special attention. That's why she enrolled only a select few so that each pupil would have ample care, both academically and emotionally. While most of her students' parents paid their enrollment and boarding fees, one pupil was the recipient of the Gregory Clarke scholarship. Ashlyn liked to think Gregory would be proud of what she and her staff accomplished each day with the pupils in their charge.

She arrived in the large dining room and saw most of her

tutors going through the buffet Mrs. Clayton had set up. Ashlyn employed no butler or footmen and so the housekeeper was responsible for placing Mrs. George's dishes out for each meal. Ashlyn thought it more collegial for her tutors and pupils to serve themselves. She met with her staff each morning during this first meal so they could discuss their students and the various upcoming lessons. After half an hour, the instructors left to prepare for the day and she dined with the boys.

Taking her place at the head of the table, Mrs. Clayton brought a cup of tea.

"Good morning, Lady Dunwood," the housekeeper said, her face ever cheery as she set the cup down. "Two sugars and cream, just as you prefer."

"Thank you, Mrs. Clayton. Is Mrs. George preparing the baked chicken later today?"

"She is, my lady."

"Good. I so enjoyed the spices she used last time."

The four men had finished filling their plates and taken a spot. Mr. Selleck began, noting which literature would be studied this week and that the language focus would be on Latin and French. Mr. Peterson spoke next. The bald, rotund man was the opposite of the tall and thin Selleck and taught arithmetic, logic, and economics.

Short and stout Mr. Butler followed, noting his emphasis would be on famous philosophers during his ancient history lessons this week. It would go hand-in-hand with the lectures he intended to give on religion.

Finally, the drawing master, Mr. Phillips, spoke his piece. The tall, elegant instructor also taught the boys how to play various musical instruments and helped Ashlyn with dancing lessons, as well. The pair also worked with each student individually on social etiquette and conversation. She believed being able to speak comfortably on a variety of subjects would help her boys attain success in their future schooling and later in life.

"It sounds as if everyone has a busy week planned," she noted. "I did want to mention that we are still at ten students since the Easton boys left. If you know of any worthwhile pupils that could assume their places, please let me know. If that's all, I will see you later in the day."

Ashlyn had a habit of dropping in on classes. She wanted to keep not only the boys but their tutors on their toes. She also enjoyed taking part in the lessons and seeing the boys' progress firsthand.

The men left and Betty and Louise, the two maids, quickly cleared their dishes away as Mrs. Clayton and Mrs. George brought in chafing dishes for the next round. One of the things which had surprised Ashlyn most was how much growing boys ate. Her pupils ranged from seven to thirteen and though they were different ages and sizes, every one of them possessed a voracious appetite.

Edward, the scholarship student, indicated for her to go first through the line and she thanked him. She was pleased he was becoming more comfortable at the academy. The son of a local farmer, the side of his face was marred by a large purple birthmark. Edward's father had shared with Ashlyn how his son had been teased unmercifully his entire life and stared at by strangers, both young and old. Fortunately, she had created an atmosphere of acceptance at Dunwood Academy and believed her boys had accepted Edward—and that Edward was slowly coming around from his shyness. He was brilliant at both mathematics and music and she'd witnessed him tutor several boys in complicated equations, drilling down and explaining to them in simple, everyday language. She had high hopes of him winning a spot at Eton or another strong public school and going from there to university. Her secret wish was that he might one day return to Dunwood Academy as an instructor.

As they all gathered around the table, she made sure the maids had placed a penny beside the silverware for each boy. Seeing they all had one, she looked to the far end of the table.

"Peter, why don't you start us off and give the penny for your thoughts?"

Ashlyn had begun the practice at breakfast each morning, having each boy share whatever he wished without judgment. Once each boy had spent his penny and contributed to the discussion, the conversation was opened for anyone to speak. This way, everyone had a say and no one was left out. It also kept certain boys from dominating the conversation. They would think carefully before spending their penny, not wanting to be shut out from speaking.

The shy student grinned and tossed his penny into the jar in the center of the table. Cheers broke out since Peter sat the furthest away from the jar. Though no penalty occurred if a boy's toss missed, an extra biscuit at teatime was awarded to those whose penny made it inside the jar. Ashlyn had the students rotate on a daily basis so no one had an unfair advantage by always claiming the closest seats to the jar.

"I spent time with Mr. Jarrett yesterday in the stables caring for Maymorn. I got to feel her belly and the kicks from the foal inside her."

She was pleased Peter had put two complete sentences together. When he'd arrived a month ago, he was so shy that he couldn't string two words together.

From there, the boys spoke up on their own. William told of a passage he'd translated and how much easier Latin seemed to him now that he was at Dunwood Academy. She was pleased he shared the tidbit without his usual arrogance and bragging. Samuel, who was very intelligent but liked to be left to himself, spoke about his fencing lesson yesterday. The boys listened attentively to one another as they ate and once each coin had been spent, they broke into smaller conversations. She looked at her pupils with pride, knowing each boy was progressing in different ways.

The clock chimed and they looked to her expectantly.

"I hope that you enjoy a marvelous day and have good things to share with one another tomorrow morning—if not before.

You're dismissed."

Each boy pushed back his chair and returned it to its place before picking up the used dishes and silverware and returning them to a cart Mrs. George had wheeled out. Ashlyn believed it important that her boys be courteous to all. Since she kept a minimum of servants, the boys contributed in small ways to the household. Collecting their dishes was one of them.

As they filed out, telling her goodbye, Mrs. Clayton approached her.

"You have a visitor, Lady Dunwood."

"I wasn't expecting anyone," she said, frowning. "I have bookkeeping to attend to."

"It's the Duke of Gilford, my lady. He said it's most urgent. I took him to your study and he awaits you there."

Ashlyn felt color flood her face. "Very well. Thank you, Mrs. Clayton."

She left the room and hesitated a moment. She longed to check her appearance in a mirror but refused to go upstairs to do so. Meeting the new duke at his father's funeral a few days earlier had left quite an impression on her. Immediately, she'd been attracted to his height. His good looks. The thick, dark brown hair and eyes the color of melted chocolate.

And that bloody uniform.

It's what had led her to dance with Daniel. He'd looked so handsome in his regimental colors. Look where that had gotten her. A forced marriage of one night. Years of loneliness living among strangers. Her dead boy.

No, Ashlyn would have to be on guard around the Duke of Gilford. She would see what he wanted and get rid of him quickly. She didn't need any disruptions in her life. It ran on an even keel. No ups. No downs. Just the way she preferred things.

She arrived at her study. The door was already open. Gilford, still wearing his officer's uniform, stood looking out a window, his hands clasped behind his back. Ashlyn swallowed and entered the room.

"How may I help you, Your Grace?"

REID WAITED FOR Lady Dunwood in the small, neat study. He was eager to speak to her again. She'd made quite an impression on him during their brief conversation after his father's funeral. He'd learned from Bellows that the dowager countess was a war widow who'd opened Dunwood Academy in a rented property three miles to the east of Gillingham. Though the establishment was less than three years old, it had a reputation for helping troubled boys work through their problems and gain admission to more traditional schools.

He only hoped she had room for his wayward half-brothers.

As he'd met with various staff members at Gillingham, he'd heard numerous stories of the boys' behavior the last few years. Harry and Arthur had placed toads in the beds of all the footmen. They had hidden the key used to wind the household's clocks, causing every one to come to a standstill. They had switched Cook's sugar for salt, resulting in a disastrous dinner party. They had even told two of the maids about the ghost which walked the halls, causing both to quit out of fright. Mrs. Paul had forced the servants to return and made Harry and Arthur confess how they'd made the ghost up. It seemed the more his father's health declined, the more Dalinda had indulged the boys and let them run wild. In a way, he couldn't blame her. From all reports, she'd been a devoted wife, nursing her husband in his illness, even though that meant neglecting her boys. Without a man's steady hand, the pair did as they chose—and most of their choices proved to be unwise.

"How may I help you, Your Grace?" a voice asked.

Reid turned from the window and saw Lady Dunwood, looking lovely in a gown of sky blue. Her golden hair was swept from her face, highlighting her high cheekbones and delicate nose. As he moved to greet her, once again those deep, amethyst eyes drew him in.

She curtseyed to him and he took her hand. He hadn't done so before and a jolt hit him. She must have experienced the same for her eyes widened. She recovered quickly, though, her features returning to her usual calm, placid look as he released her hand.

"Thank you for seeing me, Lady Dunwood. I have a pressing matter to discuss with you."

She indicated a chair and took one herself. Reid seated himself and then said, "I'm told you are the solution to my very difficult problem."

Color rose in her cheeks, turning her ivory skin a soft rose. "And what problem would that be, Your Grace?"

"My much younger half-brothers."

Understanding lit her eyes. "I see. You wish for them to attend Dunwood Academy."

"It's a distinct possibility. I'd like to meet your instructors, of course. Discuss the curriculum." He sighed. "And warn you of the immense challenge you would be taking on if you accept them."

"How are they challenging?"

"It seems my stepmother devoted the majority of her time to my father during his last two years. His illness was time-consuming. That left Harry, who is now ten, and Arthur, who is twelve, on their own—without much discipline." He paused. "I'm afraid they've been asked to leave four different schools, due to their unruly behavior."

She smiled and Reid's heart turned over. "That is exactly the type of boy we specialize in helping, Your Grace. Boys who need extra guidance and attention. Some are withdrawn. Some are overbearing and arrogant. Others have had difficulty fitting in at traditional schools."

"My half-brothers are rude and sullen. I haven't a clue as to their academic progress."

"That is easily established. And I do have two openings that recently occurred so if you choose to send them to Dunwood Academy, they could start immediately."

"Tell me about your offerings."

She ran through the names of the various tutors and what subjects they taught and how she frequently visited classes to keep both instructors and pupils sharp.

"While we offer all the traditional courses you would expect, we expect greater participation from our young students. They are actively involved in lessons, both in small groups and on an individual basis. It helps us cater to their needs and also come to know each boy better."

Reid reflected on his education. "It's a bit different from my own schooling. I rarely said a word. Even in university. My tutors treated me as a sieve which they opened and poured in a fountain of their own knowledge for me to soak up—and then regurgitate during exams."

"The tutors do give some lectures but they also employ the Socratic Method. Would you like to visit a few classrooms now and see for yourself?"

"I'd like that very much."

They left her study and visited several rooms. He heard conversations in French and saw boys helping one another with Latin verb conjugation and translations then a mathematics lesson where the lone pupil actively asked questions. Mr. Peterson scribbled equations on a blackboard and then sat next to the lad as he worked out answers on his slate. The history tutor was concluding a more traditional lesson by lecturing to a pair but then upon completion, he had the two students take the roles of different philosophers. The boys conversed in character, adopting the philosophy of their assigned man.

As they left the room, Reid said, "That was very unique. And challenging for each boy."

"Yes. They had to not only know the basic tenets of each philosopher but have a deep understanding as to how he would stand on more modern issues," the countess said.

"I'm suitably impressed."

"Oh, there's more for you to see," she said airily as the clock chimed and boys filtered out, going different directions. "Come along."

They went to a large drawing room, where two boys were already present, along with an elegantly dressed man.

"Mr. Phillips, this is His Grace, the Duke of Gilford."

The tutor bowed. "A pleasure, Your Grace. Are you touring the academy? You won't find a better place if you have a boy who needs a stellar education."

"I'm looking for a suitable school for my half-brothers."

"We would be happy to have them here," Phillips said. "If you'll excuse me?"

"Certainly," Reid said.

He watched as the tutor started one boy on a watercolor painting, demonstrating a certain type of brushstroke. He left the student to practice and then went to the other one, who'd been warming up with a violin.

"Mr. Phillips also helps me teach dance and social etiquette," Lady Dunwood said.

"I can see how well-rounded instruction is."

She laughed. The rich, throaty sound struck something within Reid, making him want to say something witty in order to make her laugh so he could hear the sound again.

"My boys also learn to press their own clothes and are taught how to sew on a button. You never know when those skills might come in handy."

Reid thought of his former batman, Anderson, whom he'd already sent for to serve as his valet. The man had been with Reid for more than five years and had told him he'd be happy to return to England to serve him there. Anderson was handy with a needle and thread and it made Reid wonder where he'd learned the skill.

"Let's go outside," Lady Dunwood suggested. "You'll want to see the grounds."

They left the drawing room and moved downstairs. She

headed straight for the door, stopping only to lift a shawl hanging from a hook and wrapping it about her.

"Wait. Do you not need a hat?" He'd never seen a woman leave a house without wearing one.

"Hats are a nuisance. When it's a day of sunshine, sometimes Mrs. Clayton persuades me to take a parasol to shade my face. Otherwise, I only wear them when I go into town or to some social occasion where they're required."

He found this woman refreshing. Not only was she incredibly beautiful, but she was friendly and unpretentious.

"At least let me get the door for you since I see no footman about."

"Oh, I don't employ any. Nor do I have a butler."

Her words took him aback. He couldn't imagine how a household ran without either. "Why not?"

"They're really unnecessary. It's not as if I receive social calls. I am headmistress of a school. My time is taken up with bookkeeping and working with my boys. I do have a housekeeper and two maids, along with a cook." She chuckled. "I should have two cooks with what all these boys and men eat. But as for other staff, they're not needed."

Opening the door, Reid followed her out and offered her his arm. She looked at him blankly for a moment and then took it. The warmth of her hand resting there did something odd to his insides.

"You see, I'm a bit out of practice as far as having a gentleman escort me about goes."

"And yet you teach etiquette," he teased.

She burst out laughing, deep from her belly. The rich, full noise drew him to her even more.

"I suppose I should practice what I preach," she said, a glint of mischief in her eyes. "I hope this hasn't lessened your opinion of my school."

"Not in the least. I'm sure the admirable Mr. Phillips steps in when you stumble in matters of social customs."

"You're a troublemaker," she said, approval in her voice. "I quite like them."

"Drawn to scamps, are you?"

She sobered. "They need love and attention as much as the next boy. Sometimes much more than those very good boys who do nothing out of the norm and are always trying to please their elders." She paused. "Let's go to the stables."

"Oh, so you give riding lessons?"

"Yes. And you see that field over there?" She pointed. "The boys play sports there. I find exercising the mind as well as the body makes for a happy, satisfied, and—dare I say it—tired boy at the end of the day."

"And exhausted boys are ones who cause less trouble?" he asked.

"My secret is out," she said playfully.

Reid longed to know all of this woman's secrets.

Chapter Three

ASHLYN CONTINUED HER tour with the Duke of Gilford, finding herself relaxed and elated at the same time. She was in her element talking about the school and her boys. What they studied and what their routines were like. She enjoyed showing the duke every aspect of the school and hoped he would decide to send the wayward boys to her. She'd noticed them at the funeral, looking belligerent, and wondered how they were feeling about their father's death. She knew she could help them.

But who would help her?

Despite maintaining her usual aura of calm efficiency while speaking to Gilford, her insides were churning as if she rode out a storm at sea. Masses of butterflies had taken flight, beating against her insides as if they yearned to be free. Ashlyn found it hard to breathe normally, especially with her hand resting upon the duke's sleeve, his solid arm like a rock beneath her fingertips.

She chided herself for feeling giddy as a schoolgirl coming across her crush unexpectedly. These idiotic feelings weren't real. She was merely in the company of an extremely attractive man, which was a rare occurrence. She'd never made her come-out to Polite Society, where she would have been exposed to gentlemen of all ages. She'd spent years buried in the country, raising Gregory and volunteering at the parsonage helping young boys with reading, writing, and simple arithmetic instead of attending London Seasons. Her daily life now revolved around her pupils.

Though Mr. Phillips would be considered handsome, she'd never viewed him as a man, merely one of her staff members who was quite capable in his position.

It shouldn't surprise her that she would find Gilford so appealing, especially with her experience regarding men being so limited. The duke's good looks, charm, and regal bearing would assure that women clamored for his attention wherever he went. She told herself it was perfectly acceptable that she should think him handsome, because he was. If he chose to send Arthur and Harry to Dunwood Academy, she would have to meet with him upon occasion regarding the boys' progress. It would be important to rein in the incredibly intense feelings she experienced in his presence. The old adage *"out of sight, out of mind"* would apply in this instance. If she wasn't around him, she wouldn't be so consumed with thoughts of him.

Or so she told herself.

As they headed toward the stables, a part of her yearned for all the things she'd missed out on by being forced to wed Daniel at such a young age. She would have danced with men such as Gilford. Gone for carriage drives and ridden in Rotten Row. Attended musicales and garden parties in the company of many gentlemen. Ashlyn understood a part of her social growth and maturation had been stunted by being isolated as she had been for so long.

She would put aside these frivolous feelings. She had to—else she might act on them—and what a disaster that would be. Imagine how Gilford might react if she gave in to temptation and did what she wanted to do.

Kiss him.

They arrived at the stables just as Jarrett came out with Edward. The boy led Maymorn, walking slowly as he talked to the pregnant mare.

"Good morning, Mr. Jarrett. Master Edward. This is the Duke of Gilford, come to visit Dunwood Academy in order to see if it might be the place for his brothers to attend." Reid noted that she didn't call the boys his half-brothers even though he had made it clear that is what they were.

Both the groom and boy bowed to the duke, who surprisingly offered his hand to each. Ashlyn looked on with pride at the confidence Edward showed in meeting a new person. As for Gilford, he didn't react to the large firemark obscuring the boy's face.

"That's a right pretty horse you have there, Master Edward," the duke told the child, who lit up.

"Maymorn is going to have a foal," Edward exclaimed. "Mr. Jarrett is letting me take her to the pasture for some exercise. It's good for a mother to walk around with the foal inside her."

Gilford nodded approvingly. "I'm quite fond of horses myself."

"Mr. Jarrett knows everything about horses," bragged Edward. "I'm learning lots."

"I'm sure you are." The duke turned to Jarrett. "How many horses do you stable?"

Ashlyn listened as the men talked about the various mounts and how the groom and Mr. Selleck gave the boys riding lessons.

"They learn to muck out the stalls, too," Jarrett said with a wink. "Master Peter is inside doing so now."

Gilford looked puzzled. "You say the *students* do the mucking?"

"That's right, Your Grace. Lady Dunwood only has me in the stables. No other groomsmen. The boys learn to care for the horses, from feeding and grooming to cleaning up after them."

He turned to her. "You did say you taught some unusual skills."

"Being responsible for the care of animals is an important lesson to learn," she said. "As a tenant, my landlord won't allow dogs so the boys care for the horses, as well as a few goats and pigs."

"The pigs smell something awful," Edward remarked. "But they are as good-natured as the goats. We have cats, too, to keep the mice away."

Gilford smiled. "It sounds like you have everything important here at Dunwood. That could be very advantageous to my half-brothers."

Edward nodded solemnly. "We do, Your Grace. We learn from books but other places, as well. Lady Dunwood even has Mrs. George give us cooking lessons. You should taste one of my plum tarts."

"Best we get along, Master Edward," Jarrett said. "Maymorn needs to stretch her legs now and you still have two stalls to muck."

The boy offered his hand to the duke and Ashlyn's heart soared. "It was a pleasure to meet you, Your Grace. I hope you'll allow your half-brothers to come here."

"I'll give it strong consideration, Master Edward. Thank you for your hearty endorsement."

The groom and pupil led the mare away. Gilford turned to her.

"He's had the port-wine stain since birth?"

"Yes. Edward holds the Gregory Clarke scholarship position. He's the son of a local farmer who's brilliant at playing five instruments and gifted in mathematics. My hope is he'll land a scholarship at a good public school and move on to university."

"He seemed a bright, thoughtful lad."

"You should have seen him when he first arrived several months ago. Quiet as a lamb. He'd been judged harshly by all who met him because of his appearance."

"I know from my own school days that boys can be bullies. How did they take to Edward?"

"Quite well. I spoke with them as a group and then with each one individually before Edward came to us. Many of them have their own problems. It's made them more aware that others have troubles, as well. I'm proud to say we've never had an incidence of bullying."

"None?" he questioned. "I find that very hard to believe, Lady

Dunwood. You might not be aware of any bullying but I assure you that it goes on behind closed doors when no adults are around. It's the way of English schools. Older boys bully younger ones. Bigger ones bully the smaller boys."

The headmistress gave him a withering look. "You are wrong in that regard, Your Grace. I guarantee you that it does not occur here."

"Then I'm afraid I should never enroll Arthur and Harry because I'm sure they wouldn't fit into such an idealized place."

She frowned. "No, I hope you do. I would love to work with them, as would my staff."

"And when they do misbehave?" he challenged. "And though I've only met them, I guarantee you they will. What is the usual punishment?"

"I talk to them, of course."

The duke frowned. "You . . . talk to them. And then thrash them?"

She glared at him. "I would never resort to physical violence. Usually, a simple conversation does the trick. Of course, I'll withhold sweets for a week in dire cases but I really don't have many instances of that."

The intense look he gave Ashlyn caused her to shiver.

"Talking is all you do." He shook his head in disbelief. "Talking."

"Yes. It's what I did with my own son. Of course, Gregory was a very good boy so there was little to correct him about."

"Was?" he asked softly.

Ashlyn nodded, her throat growing thick. "Yes. He passed when he was four."

Sympathy filled the duke's eyes and he took her hands. "I am most sorry, my lady. I'd been told you lost your husband in the war. To have lost your child, as well, must have been heart-wrenching."

For a moment, Ashlyn couldn't speak. She was aware of her small hands in his large, rough ones. The sense of comfort and security that gesture brought. She gazed down at them joined together. In losing both her son and husband, no one had offered her physical comfort, though she'd longed for a soothing embrace. Beyond a polite handshake, she'd had no physical contact with anyone for a very long time.

Until this man.

Gently, she pulled her hands from his and said, "It was a trying time. They both passed within a short time of one another. That's when I decided to start the academy."

"And you named the scholarship after your son?"

"I did. Edward will hold it until he moves on. My hope is one day he'll return to teach at Dunwood Academy."

The duke studied her for a moment. "You plan to keep at this that long?"

"This is my life now, Your Grace."

"You are still young, Lady Dunwood. Surely, you'll wed again and have children."

"Never," she said, more vehemently than she should have, judging by his arched brows. Tempering her tone, she added, "These neglected boys are my life's work, Your Grace. I wouldn't think of abandoning them."

"Not even for children of your own?" he pressed.

"No. I had my one, perfect boy. I have no interest in wedding, much less having another child. I've dedicated my life to the pupils at Dunwood Academy." She smiled brightly, pushing down the raw emotions that threatened to surface. "Have you decided whether or not to entrust Arthur and Harry to me and my staff?"

"I have one more person to speak with before I come to my decision," the duke said. "Mr. Jarrett mentioned a boy mucking the stables. I want to talk with him."

"Peter?" she asked, wondering why he would single out one pupil whom he didn't know. "Come to the stables with me and I'll introduce you."

"No, my lady," Gilford said. "You've been with me every step of the way this morning. I'd like to meet Peter on my own."

CHAPTER FOUR

REID LEFT THE very perplexed Lady Dunwood and entered the stables. The sweet scent of hay filled his nostrils, combined with the smell of horseflesh. He paused at a couple of stalls and rubbed a few noses before finding the boy he searched for, shoveling manure into a heap.

"Are you Master Peter?" he asked, thinking the lad about eight or nine.

A ginger-colored head bobbed up. The freckled face scrunched up in curiosity. "Who might you be, Sir?"

He'd been impressed with the other lad's manners and had wanted to test another boy, away from his headmistress. Reid also had a few questions that he thought a pupil would answer more honestly without the lady's presence.

"I'm the Duke of Gilford," he said easily.

The boy looked slightly taken aback being in the presence of a duke but quickly recovered. He propped his shovel against the wall and came toward Reid before making a smooth bow.

With an earnest look, he said, "I am Peter Bryland, Viscount Marlowe, Your Grace." He pulled his work glove off and held out a hand but withdrew it a moment later. "I'd offer to shake your hand but I'm not sure a duke would care to shake with someone who's been mucking a stall."

He gave Reid a cheeky grin and Reid found himself liking this boy quite a bit.

"May I ask why you're doing physical labor, Lord Marlowe?"

The boy frowned. "Please, Your Grace, call me Master Peter."

"Why wouldn't I call you by your title?"

"We don't use them here," he explained. "Not every boy who comes to study at Dunwood Academy has one. Some are second or third sons. One pupil is the son of a farmer. Lady Dunwood likes all of her boys to be on equal footing. We're all addressed the same—and we dress the same, as well." He grinned. "At least when we're in the classroom."

"Yes, I toured a few classes earlier. I heard you conversing as Plato with another pupil being Epicurus."

Peter's eyes lit up. "That was ever so much fun. Mr. Butler has us do that on occasion."

"Do you enjoy your studies here?"

The boy nodded. "Very much. Mr. Selleck teaches more languages than at my former school. And Mr. Peterson exposes us to economics, not just mathematics. The coursework is difficult but our tutors are excellent. When they're not available, I can always find another boy to help me understand something. Drake always helps me conjugate difficult verbs and Edward is adept in explaining numbers."

"I don't know Drake but I did meet Edward outside with Mr. Jarrett," he said carefully, wanting to get the boy's true opinion of Edward and the firemark he bore on his face. He was convinced the other boys gave Edward a hard time, despite what Lady Dunwood seemed to believe.

"Mr. Jarrett gives us riding lessons. He also helps with sports."

"And what do you think of Edward?"

Peter looked puzzled. "I just told you. He's excellent at mathematics. And music. You should hear him play the cello and pianoforte. He's taken up the harp recently and already plays it better than Mr. Phillips. Edward is probably my closest friend here, along with William."

"Why do you like Edward? And William?" Reid pressed.

He shrugged. "William and I came around the same time. We just get along. Edward is very funny. And nice. At my other school, people weren't very nice to me. My brother was there with me." A shadow crossed Peter's face. "I love him but he does everything well. All the tutors and other boys compared me to him and made fun of me because I wasn't very good at sports or academics."

"You think that's changed at Dunwood Academy?"

"Yes," Peter said eagerly. "Lady Dunwood only takes on a handful of boys each term. She works with us on what we need to get better at. I'm shy but I'll bet you didn't know that, Your Grace."

Reid laughed. "I would have never guessed so, Master Peter."

"That's because I didn't have confidence. Lady Dunwood has helped me see what I'm good at. The things I'm not good at? I just practice more now. I'm much better now at kicking and throwing a ball." He paused. "My brother has dark hair and blue eyes. He's very handsome. I used to get teased all the time because of my freckles. Boys would hold me down and try to wipe them off. They called me horrible names and kicked me."

"Bullies are in every school, Master Peter," Reid said gently. "You just have to learn how to stand up to them."

The boy shook his head. "They're not here. Everyone is kind. Oh, a few boys act up some when they first arrive but Lady Dunwood will have a talking to them and set them straight."

"So you're no longer bullied for your freckles? Or Edward for his firemark?"

"No," the boy said and Reid saw he spoke truthfully. "I don't even see Edward's firemark when I look at him. I see Edward instead."

He was astonished. And fearful of Arthur and Harry upsetting the wonderful balance at this school.

"Well, thank you for speaking with me, Master Peter."

The boy looked at him curiously. "Do you have a son you'll send here, Your Grace?"

"I'm not married but I do have two younger half-brothers. They are ten and twelve. I'm looking for the right school for them."

"Send them here," Peter said with confidence. Then he leaned in, lowering his voice. "Even if they are full of mischief. Lady Dunwood will see they fit in. All the boys here will."

The boy's words convinced Reid. "Look for Arthur and Harry Baker soon."

"I will," Peter said with enthusiasm.

"You're still here, Your Grace?"

Reid turned and saw Edward standing there. "Yes, Master Edward. I've been learning about Dunwood Academy from a pupil's point of view. Your friend here has convinced me that my half-brothers should go here and to no other place."

"You won't be sorry you sent them here," Edward said. "This is a good place."

He only hoped Arthur and Harry wouldn't be cruel to the boy before him. He doubted they had it in them to look past Edward's firemark as the others had.

"I think it will take them time to adjust to the way things are done here," he said evenly.

"Oh, they're troublemakers, are they?" Edward said. "Don't worry, Your Grace. Lady Dunwood doesn't put up with nonsense. She'll give them one of her talking-to's." He grimaced. "You don't want one of those. Once you've had one, you know to walk a straight and narrow path."

Reid still didn't see how a tongue lashing was enough to straighten out certain boys but he'd decided to give this place a chance.

"I wish you boys a good day," he said cheerily.

"We were happy to make your acquaintance, Your Grace," Peter piped up.

As Reid left, he heard Edward thanking Peter for mucking out one of the stalls that should have been his to do. Shaking his head, he wondered about a place that might turn troubled youths into model students.

He returned to the house, cutting through the kitchen on purpose. He'd always thought you could learn a lot from a kitchen. A woman looked up from chopping vegetables.

"Might I help you, my lord?"

"I'm going to send my two half-brothers here and just wanted to see how your kitchen was organized."

"I'm Mrs. George. And as you can see, I keep the place spotless." She chuckled. "That is, until it's time for one of the boy's cooking lesson. They get a bit messy but they're good lads and always clean up after themselves."

"What do you have them make?" he asked, curious about this part of their learning.

"My boys learn to wash and chop vegetables. They can make several kinds of soups. Boil meat. Make fruit compotes and tarts. Even bake bread."

"Bread, you say?"

"Yes, my lord."

"Well, thank you, Mrs. George."

Reid left the kitchen and returned to the study, hoping to find Lady Dunwood there. The door was open and he glanced in, seeing she sat at her desk, a slight crease on her brow. She worried her bottom lip as she tapped a pencil against the desk. A shot of lust swept through him. He longed to take that full, bottom lip between his own teeth.

And much, much more.

It troubled him when she'd said she wouldn't wed again. He wondered if her marriage had been unsuccessful. It was hard knowing, since she was a war widow and relatively new to the neighborhood, how long she'd been wed before her husband went to war. The thought she'd lost both a husband and her only child must have made her want to close herself off from giving affection. Yet she seemed to do so readily—even fiercely—where her pupils were concerned.

As he watched her begin scribbling with the pencil, Reid

thought he'd need to wed himself. As the new duke, it was his obligation to carry on the line and provide an heir. He'd experienced a bit of jealousy, seeing how satisfied Gray and Burke seemed with their wives, and he longed for the same. He doubted he'd make a love match as his two friends had but he hoped he could find a woman who would be an interesting companion, one he could respect and build a life with. Someone like Lady Dunwood.

Or . . . maybe Lady Dunwood herself.

The dowager countess was beautiful and intelligent. Not a girl straight from the schoolroom but a mature woman, probably in her mid-twenties. Though Reid had no knowledge of the women in the neighborhood, having been gone for so long, he decided he couldn't do better than marrying a woman of Lady Dunwood's breeding and confidence. He'd always enjoyed a challenge.

Convincing this woman to wed him would be the ultimate challenge. He smiled to himself, already eager to begin the game.

He rapped on the doorframe and she looked up, those fascinating, amethyst eyes immediately drawing him in.

"Did you learn all you needed to from Master Peter?" she inquired, pursing her lips a bit.

"I did. Enough to ask if you have the strength and fortitude to take on my wayward half-brothers. I'm afraid after seeing your boys that my two will disrupt the harmony at Dunwood Academy."

Her brilliant smile made his heart skip a beat. "I look forward to having Arthur and Harry become a part of us. I'm always up for a challenge, Your Grace."

So am I, Lady Dunwood.

ASHLYN DRESSED WITH more care than usual, choosing a violet gown that was a favorite of hers. She told herself it was because she liked it—but she knew she wore it for the Duke of Gilford. The gown's shade brought out the color of her eyes and for some idiotic reason, she wanted to impress Gilford. Rationally, she told herself it was totally unnecessary. He'd already committed to sending Arthur and Harry to Dunwood Academy. He'd done so because he'd been pleased at what he'd seen at the school.

Not for what its headmistress wore.

Still, she took her time, dabbing on a bit of perfume which she only used for special occasions, and making sure every hair was in place. Glancing at herself in her hand mirror, she knew she looked her best.

At the first breakfast with her staff, she tried to calm the butterflies in her stomach and sipped tea as her tutors loaded their plates. Once they all were seated and eating, she cleared her throat.

"We have two new students who will arrive this morning. Arthur is aged twelve. His younger brother, Harry, is ten. Their father was the previous Duke of Gilford, who recently passed away. Unfortunately, they suffered from a bit of neglect because he was so ill, resulting in rather poor behavior on their parts."

Mr. Selleck asked, "Is this your polite way, Lady Dunwood, of telling us they're hellions?"

"It's possible," she replied. "They have been asked to leave a few schools. Four, I believe."

Mr. Butler snorted. "That would be a record for even a Dunwood Academy pupil."

"Do you know anything of their academic background?" Mr. Peterson inquired.

Ashlyn bit back a smile. Her practical mathematics instructor always thought of academics first.

"I don't, Mr. Peterson. As usual, I will meet with the pair and ascertain as much information as I can from them. They might be unwilling to be open with me at this point, due to their recent loss and fragile emotional state. Still, I'll get a writing sample from both and then the four of you can do your own evaluations during the day, as well. We can meet after dinner and discuss over a sherry where they should be placed and what their strengths and weaknesses are."

After finishing the meal, the men filed out, swiftly followed by her ten boys who entered the room and filled their plates. Once they'd spent their pennies in sharing their thoughts, Ashlyn addressed the group.

"This morning we have two new pupils arriving."

A surge of excitement swept through the room with her announcement. The mention of new students coming always did.

"They are two brothers, Arthur and Harry, ages twelve and ten."

Immediately, she noticed Drake's reaction. The boy looked startled and then dropped his eyes to his plate. She would speak to him after the meal and see what had him out of sorts, although she decided it was because he was acquainted with the pair. Ashlyn hoped this wouldn't be a setback for Drake. He'd arrived with a pronounced stutter but it had lessened in the months he'd been with her. Now, it only emerged when he was distressed.

"Some of you have lost a parent and know how difficult that can be. Arthur and Harry recently lost their own father and it's proving difficult for them to adjust to. Their new guardian, the Duke of Gilford, is their older brother. He's been away fighting for His Majesty's Army for many years so they've been confronted with a stranger who's now in charge of them."

Ashlyn paused, letting the boys absorb her words.

"Because of that, they will need help adjusting to our ways at Dunwood Academy. I know each of you will help them in this endeavor."

Quickly, she explained which rooms the boys would be placed in. She'd decided to separate them so they would be forced to meet others and not cling to one another.

"Be sure to show them around the school," she continued. "Help them get situated. Tell them a little about yourselves but don't press them to do the same. They'll open up when they feel comfortable doing so."

She rose and the boys followed suit. "William and Drake, I'd like to see you briefly. The rest of you are dismissed."

All the boys took their dishes to the waiting tray and the two she'd asked to stay behind came to her.

She addressed William first, wanting to speak to Drake alone. She hadn't wanted him singled out, which was why she'd also asked William to remain behind.

"William, I must say that Mr. Peterson was praising your efforts to me. He said your last examination showed remarkable progress. I wanted to tell you how proud I am of you and that I will write to your father today to share this good report."

The boy blushed. "Thank you, my lady. I did have some help, though. Edward walked me through several equations. I didn't understand them before when Mr. Peterson presented them but somehow Edward made it right in my mind and I could see how to solve them."

"Edward is very generous with his time. I'm glad he was able to help you but don't give him all the credit. You are the one who succeeded in learning the material. Run along and join your classmates."

"Yes, my lady," William said, his face beet red. Even the tips of his ears were bright red.

Once he left the room, she turned to Drake. "What's troubling you today, Drake?"

He shuffled his feet uncomfortably, his eyes downcast. "I-I-I am f-fine, m-m-my lady."

"No, you aren't, else you wouldn't be lying to me."

His head shot up and she saw the misery on his face, guessing at the problem.

"You know Arthur and Harry from your previous school, don't you?"

He nodded. "I d-do. Harry's not so b-b-bad if you g-get him away from his brother, b-but he's a b-b-bad apple when Arthur's around." The boy shuddered. "Arthur is b-big for his age and p-p-p-picks on everyone. I d-don't think he likes anyone and n-n-n-o one likes him."

Ashlyn placed a hand on Drake's shoulder. "I know this must be difficult for you. Do you think we can help them make a change?"

He frowned. "I hope so. I-I like it here. I d-don't want them spoiling things f-f-for the rest of us."

She squeezed his shoulder reassuringly. "If there's any trouble, you know you're to come to me at once, don't you?"

"Yes, m-my lady."

"I'll do my best to help these boys blend in."

She hugged Drake and hoped her words and gesture comforted him. She was also glad she'd placed Arthur in a different room from Drake.

"Harry is in your room. Will that be all right?"

Drake nodded. "I'll try m-my best, Lady Dunwood."

"That's all I ever ask for."

After he left, she wondered about how the newcomers would affect the stability and harmony of Dunwood Academy and prayed that she would have the wisdom to guide them in the right direction. Especially since the Duke of Gilford, who'd commanded who knew how many soldiers, seemed to face defeat at the hands of two young boys. Ashlyn tossed back her shoulders and stood a little taller. She'd told the duke she was up to this challenge. Her word meant a great deal to her, as did her charges. She wouldn't let any boy under her watch suffer needlessly. She hoped she would be able to make a difference and help Arthur and Harry see their true potential.

"My lady, the ducal carriage has arrived," Mrs. Clayton said, interrupting Ashlyn's thoughts.

"Very well. I'll go meet it now."

Ashlyn threw her shawl about her and exited through the front door just as the Duke of Gilford left his grand vehicle. He still wore his officer's uniform, making his shoulders look impossibly broad, while his muscular legs seemed a mile long. He must be an inch or two over six feet. She guessed he'd arrived home from the war with nothing else to wear and couldn't raid his father's bureau since the previous duke had been a good three or four inches shorter. She only wished the man would get himself to a tailor soon. Looking at him in uniform made her feel giddy.

And that wouldn't do.

"Good morning, Lady Dunwood," he greeted and then handed down a woman. She had dark brown hair and wore a frazzled look. Ashlyn knew her to be the boy's mother and the widow of the previous duke.

After the dowager duchess came her new pupils. Arthur was tall for his age and wore a sullen look. Harry, on the other hand, looked a bit bewildered.

"Good morning, Your Grace," Ashlyn said. "I can't thank you enough for entrusting your boys to my care." She turned to her new pupils and waited to be introduced.

"These are my half-brothers, Lord Arthur and Lord Harold, known as Harry. I've discussed with them how they'll leave their titles at the door," the duke said.

"I don't see why," mumbled Arthur.

Harry bowed to her and Arthur reluctantly followed suit. Harry offered his hand and she shook it.

"It's always nice to add a phrase to a handshake," Ashlyn said, beginning their lessons right away. "Something such as that it's nice to meet the other person."

Harry gave her his hand again and as they shook, he proclaimed, "It's very nice to meet you, Lady Dunwood."

"The pleasure is mine, Master Harry," she replied and watched him glow. Turning to Arthur, she extended her hand and he shook it without saying a word.

"I'm happy to have you at Dunwood Academy," she said, filling the void. "I've told my staff and the other boys of your arrival. Everyone is most eager to meet you."

Arthur shrugged, while Harry looked hopeful. It reinforced

her decision to separate the two. Ashlyn looked to the dowager duchess.

"I think it best if you don't come in, Your Grace. Say your goodbyes now," Ashlyn urged.

The teary-eyed mother embraced her youngest. "Be good," she urged Harry, kissing the top of his head as the boy flung his arms around her.

She reached out to a silent Arthur and hugged him, the boy's arms remaining by his side. He pulled away, avoiding her kiss, and looked at Ashlyn expectantly.

"You must also tell your brother goodbye," she encouraged.

Arthur's eyes cut to Gilford and back to her. They flared with anger. "He's my half-brother."

She held the boy's gaze and firmly said, "You're still to tell him goodbye. Good manners dictate acknowledging everyone present, and relations, in particular. Even those you aren't comfortable or friendly with."

Arthur glared her a moment and then turned away. "Goodbye, Gilford," he said hastily, crossing his arms once his duty was done.

"Goodbye, Reid," Harry added.

"Learn all you can," the duke urged. "Easter is in mid-April this year. We'll see you then for your holidays."

"That long?" the mother moaned.

"You are welcome to visit before then, my lady," Ashlyn assured the woman, "but please let me know beforehand by message. The boys have busy days ahead of them, filled with learning in and beyond the classroom. We don't want them disrupted from their new schedule. Let's give it a month and then you may call."

"All right," she agreed, her mouth trembling.

By now, the coachman had placed two valises on the ground and Ashlyn said, "Take your valises and wait for me in the foyer."

Arthur sneered. "That's a footman's job, carting about luggage."

"We have no footmen at Dunwood Academy," she said smoothly. "*You* are the footman. Take your valise inside and wait. Is that understood?"

Her firm tone left no doubt. Both boys lifted their cases and took them inside.

Once they disappeared, the duke whistled. "You've gotten them to do more than I have. I wish you the best, Lady Dunwood. And if they prove too much for you, send them back."

"They're good boys," their mother interjected.

"They are," Ashlyn agreed. "Goodness is buried within them. I'm the excavator who will dig it out of them."

Her Grace looked uncertain but the duke roared with laughter.

With a wink, he said, "Good luck to you. Or perhaps I should wish my half-brothers good luck—because I believe they've met their match."

CHAPTER FIVE

ASHLYN WATCHED THE duke's carriage drive away and stiffened her resolve. She had her work cut out for her with these two new charges.

Entering the foyer, she saw Arthur sitting atop his valise while Harry turned in a slow circle, taking everything in.

"Leave your cases to the right of the stairs. You may take them up later when you settle into your rooms. For now, I'd like you to accompany me to my study."

She turned and walked away, guessing Arthur made a face because Harry failed at stifling a giggle. Ashlyn opened the door and ushered them in, moving to a small sitting area. Arthur sat, uninvited. She stared daggers at him. He frowned as he rose to his feet.

"Besides academics, you will take classes in dance and the arts, as well as social conversation. That includes manners. Good manners," she emphasized, letting her stern words soak in. "A gentleman always waits for an invitation to sit before he does so. And," she added, "he waits until all ladies are seated before he even thinks about sitting."

Ashlyn paused and then said, "Please, take a seat, Master Arthur. Master Harry."

She did so and the boys followed. Harry's eyes were round. Arthur's narrowed—and were wary.

"Ten boys are currently enrolled at Dunwood Academy. I

never accept any more than twelve during a term. That ensures each boy receives ample individual attention from the instructors and me."

"Is it true all the boys here are troublemakers?" Arthur asked. "That's what I heard one of our groomsmen say."

"I would use troubled instead of troublemakers," she said carefully. "Every pupil here has gone to a different school at one time or another. You see, everyone has problems, Arthur. Even the titled and wealthy, though not all of our students are from wealth. Some are of the upper class but their fathers have come close to bankruptcy. Others have lost a parent, just as you and Harry have. Some have been picked on for their looks or speech."

She looked at Arthur. "No one is perfect. Dunwood boys realize that and support one another. They help each other with their problems. They never—ever—make fun of one another."

"Never?" asked Harry, obviously surprised by her words.

"Never," Ashlyn said firmly. "It's not acceptable at any time to do so. We are better when we come together. It's good to recognize our differences and support one another. No one is bullied here—and no one does any bullying."

"Will you expel them if they do?" challenged Arthur.

"No," she said calmly and observed that her response puzzled him.

"Do you thrash them?" he asked.

"No. But I do speak with the offending boy and get to the root of the problem. As I said, this is a place where you won't be judged, Arthur. You will also not judge others. You will say nice things or nothing at all. Boys here help one another with their assignments, be it translating Latin to Greek or proving a certain theorem right or wrong. There are also riding lessons and sports. Some boys aren't as athletic as others but that doesn't stop them from playing and enjoying games."

"Why don't you have footmen?" Harry asked.

"Because it's important to do for yourself and not always have someone waiting upon you."

Ashlyn explained the physical chores the boys were responsible for, including the care of various animals. While Harry looked excited by the prospect, Arthur raised his objections.

"You're saying we not only curry the horses and feed them but we muck their stalls?" he asked with distaste.

"Yes. You'll also learn to cook simple dishes and care for your own clothes, pressing them and sewing on buttons that come loose or fall off."

Arthur snorted. "It sounds as if we are slaves. You shouldn't be paid tuition. You should be paying the pupils for taking care of the place."

"There are far worse things you could be doing," she said evenly. "Gardening, for instance. Pulling weeds. Planting flowers and cutting grass. And laundry. Washing clothes is backbreaking work. I don't require those things but you will gain a healthy respect for the people who do those tasks for you."

"What if I don't want to do all of this?" Arthur asked, testing her. "Will you send me home to Gillingham?"

"No. You will stay here and learn. That is the agreement we've entered."

Arthur looked astonished. "I didn't agree to anything."

"No, you didn't," Ashlyn said. "It was you mother and brother who believed you could learn here. Our classes are unique compared to most schools. I think you should give our program a try before you try to leave. In fact, I'll strike a bargain with you both. Easter is in seven weeks. That is when you'll be given a two-week holiday. Stay until then, doing all that I ask, and then if you choose to leave in April, I'll be agreeable."

Doubt flashed in Arthur's eyes. "So, you're saying if we don't like it after seven weeks, we can leave. No questions asked."

"Not from me," Ashlyn said cheerily. "Of course, you'll have your mother and brother to answer to. By then, you will have learned some of the art of polite conversation and be able to break the news to them in an appropriate manner. For now, though, you'll stay. You'll be open to our education methods.

You won't make fun of any other students or gang up on anyone. You'll give me your best. That's all I ask."

"Yes, Lady Dunwood," Harry said quickly.

Ashlyn decided that the younger boy had merely gone along with his older brother's antics and that he truly wished to be good.

"What do you say, Arthur? You have a clean slate. I don't care if you've been a rascal in the past. Today is a new day. A fresh start. You can be whomever you wish to be."

"All right," he grumbled. "I'll try."

"Remember you're not only trying. You're trying your best. That's a lot to live up to. Sometimes you'll succeed but sometimes you'll fail. We learn as much from our failures as we do our successes."

Again, his brow wrinkled as he mulled over her words.

"Let's start by hearing a little about your previous schooling. Not the schools themselves. I'm not interested in where you went. I want to know what you learned."

She spent an hour quizzing them aloud, getting them to talk about their experiences. Harry seemed drawn to writing and languages and adored history. Arthur was more practical and admitted that he enjoyed numbers and Latin. Neither boy had any prior experience with art or music, so she told them they would start by drawing with charcoal and advance to different paints. That seemed to please Arthur.

"You'll also choose a musical instrument to learn. Mr. Phillips will give you a choice but if you're drawn to mathematics, you might enjoy the pianoforte."

"You said something about sports," Arthur said.

"Yes. We play every day the weather is good. Kicking balls. Learning archery. Playing lawn tennis."

"And riding?" Harry asked hopefully.

"Yes. Mr. Jarrett is head of our stables. He and Mr. Selleck teach riding."

Ashlyn asked each boy about how long he'd ridden and the

type of horse he preferred. She also had them write on a few topics in order to gain a sample from them. Mr. Selleck would use it to ascertain their reading level and pass that along to the other tutors.

Once they'd completed the assignment, she said, "I think it's time to see your dormitory. There are four boys to a room."

Leading them from the study, she had them carry their valises upstairs. Arthur seemed a little put out by being separated from his brother but Harry appeared enthused by the opportunity to be on his own. She then gave them a tour of the house and they watched a few classes in action. They said little but she could see they were impressed by what they observed. She made sure in each room to introduce them to the other boys and instructor.

They entered the drawing room, where Mr. Phillips sat with Drake, who played the violin. The moment the boy saw them, he stopped playing. Ashlyn glanced to Arthur and saw he recognized Drake from their previous school.

Drake rose and moved his bow from his right to left hand. "H-hello, Arthur. H-H-Harry." He held out a hand.

Arthur took it first. "Hello, Drake. Do you like it here?"

The boy nodded.

Harry shook hands after that and Mr. Phillips had Drake continue to practice while he discussed which instruments his new pupils would attempt to learn. They both decided on the pianoforte and the music teacher nodded in satisfaction.

Ashlyn then led them to a common room, where students gathered to study and talk. Samuel and Edward were there. She took a deep breath, knowing this would be a huge hurdle.

"Boys, come here a moment. I have our new students with me."

She sensed Harry stiffen beside her as Edward, who'd been looking down at a page, turned toward them. Before, only the left side of his face was visible. Looking straight on, his port-wine stain was obvious. He rose and came across the room with Samuel.

The boys made their own introductions without her help and she was pleased with the newcomers' responses.

"I like to be left alone," Samuel said in his blunt manner. "Lady Dunwood says that is fine sometimes. I do participate in classes. And I'm very good at sports."

"I like sports, too," Harry said in a friendly manner. "Maybe I can be on your team."

"Does it hurt?" Arthur asked, looking at Edward.

Ashlyn kept from cringing, trusting Edward to be mature and lead the way.

"About as much as freckles would," the boy replied easily. "The only thing that ever hurts is when others make fun of me for it. I was born this way. It will never go away. I've accepted it. I hope you will, too."

"Oh," said Arthur. "Did you fight anyone who made fun of you?"

Edward grinned. "I wanted to but Papa said I couldn't fight the entire world. He told me not to waste my time and energy on people who were so small-minded."

"And no one here really cares?" Arthur persisted, obviously fascinated.

"No. It may have been hard for others when I first came," he shared. "I'm accepted now for who I am." Grinning, he added, "I'm the best in the school at mathematics. Every boy has come to me for help. Once they got to know me and saw I'm a regular chap, it hasn't been a problem." He paused. "Will you have a problem with it, Arthur?"

The boy considered it a moment. "I don't think so," he said. "But what you will have trouble with is when I prove *I'm* the best with numbers at Dunwood Academy—not you."

Ashlyn was afraid a few fists would be thrown, then all four boys laughed heartily.

In that moment, she believed Edward had done the impossible.

He'd won over Arthur.

"If you could, Edward, I have a few things to do now. Would you take Arthur and Harry outside? I'd like them to see the playing field and the stables. Have Mr. Jarrett speak with them so he knows which mount will be best for them on this afternoon's ride."

"We get to ride today?" Harry asked, his face lighting up.

"We ride several afternoons a week," Samuel said. "May I go, too, Lady Dunwood?"

She beamed, knowing this was true progress. Samuel rarely wanted to be around the other boys.

"Yes, I think that would be a splendid idea. Once you're done, please stop by my study again."

"Yes, Lady Dunwood," both Arthur and Harry said in unison.

She watched the four leave and a warmth spread through her. They weren't perfect. Missteps would occur along the way. But Ashlyn was convinced that she'd made huge inroads with these new pupils.

Returning to her study, she read through what the pair had written this morning and then wrote up her own observations. She would share these with her tutors this evening as they discussed what would be best for the two. Half an hour later, a knock sounded at the door and she bade them to enter.

Harry nearly bounced off the walls, his enthusiasm contagious. Arthur was more reserved but still seemed like a much different lad than the sullen one who'd arrived this morning. She asked them a few questions about the horses and consulted her schedule, telling them when they'd start caring for the animals outside and noting they'd always have another boy with them to show them the ropes.

"You may go to your rooms upstairs now," she told them. "I've had the maids place three uniforms on your beds for you so that you'll be dressed as the other boys from now on."

"When do we eat, Lady Dunwood?" Harry asked.

She reviewed with them when mealtimes occurred and when they were to wash and dress. Making their beds each morning was also a part of their new routine. Neither boy complained as she mentioned this. Another sign of progress.

"Do you have any more questions?"

"No, my lady," both responded.

"Then you're dismissed."

As they left, Harry said, "I told you, Arthur Baker. This is going to be a great place."

The door closed and Ashlyn smiled to herself, lifting her pencil again. Then she tapped it against the desktop, something bothering her. She couldn't put her finger on it.

Until it hit her.

Baker. Harry had called his brother Arthur Baker. She realized she hadn't heard the boys' surname before. Then she recalled them saying goodbye this morning. While Arthur referred to the duke by his title, Harry had called the duke Reid.

Reid Baker.

The pencil stilled.

Reid Baker had been Daniel's commander. The officer who'd notified her of her husband's death.

Surely, it was a coincidence.

But how many Reid Bakers were ranking officers in His Majesty's Army?

Ashlyn's gut told her only one existed. Should she tell Gilford that Daniel had been under his command? How could she even bring up such a subject when she never spoke of her husband to anyone? Once the duke had determined to send his brothers to Dunwood Academy and they'd made arrangements for the boys to begin today, he'd made mention of being away at war for years, ever since university. She doubted with all the men under him that Gilford would remember a young officer who'd perished not from his battle wounds but from dysentery.

Still, knowing this man had been over Daniel left her uneasy. She was already self-conscious in the duke's company. This made everything ten times worse.

Ashlyn determined never to speak of Daniel in the duke's presence.

CHAPTER SIX

REID CAME IN after a long day out on the estate and told Anderson he needed a bath. The calendar might say mid-March but Reid was chilled to the bone. He'd spent the last two weeks since dropping his half-brothers off at Dunwood Academy become familiar again with Gillingham. He'd ridden to every corner of the property, meeting up with tenants he'd known since he was a boy and acquainting himself with new ones who'd come. He was saddened to hear about the loss of a few good men he'd known, farmers who'd been salt of the earth types who'd been kind to Reid whenever he rode about with his father.

He'd also spent time with his estate manager and poured over the ledgers for hours at a time, seeing how profitable Gillingham had been over the years he'd been away. He wouldn't participate in the upcoming London Season because he still had too much to learn here, then he'd make his way across England to visit his other estates. As a duke, his holdings were vast and he wanted to familiarize himself, taking time to tour each property and become known to his staff.

Reid stripped off the clothes he'd worn and showed Anderson a tear in his coat, courtesy of an unwieldy fence that he'd helped repair. It felt good again to be out on the land, making improvements, seeing the crops and livestock, and trying out various horses in the stables. He'd finally settled on one to be exclusively his, a huge black of seventeen hands named Thunder.

"Your bath is ready, Your Grace," Anderson said.

Reid climbed into the copper tub, one his father had used and his father before him. He scrunched down, eyes closed in contentment for a few minutes before he scrubbed himself and rinsed. Toweling off, he allowed his valet to dress him, glad he was finally rid of the uniforms he'd worn for a decade. Anderson had taken his measurements and then rode off to London, selecting a wardrobe for Reid. Having been a valet to an earl before his army days, the man knew how a gentleman should dress. He'd brought back a few outfits upon his return to Gillingham and told Reid the remainder of his wardrobe would arrive soon. Based upon what he now wore, Reid could tell Anderson had an eye for quality materials and a sense of style. It affirmed his decision to bring his batman to England and he hoped they'd be together for many years to come.

Anderson adjusted the cravat and then nodded in satisfaction. "You're fit to dine with Viscount Martin and his daughters."

Reid scowled. Although he'd enjoyed renewing friendships with a few gentlemen in the neighborhood, he dreaded tonight's dinner. Dalinda wouldn't be present, having left Gillingham to visit her brother and sister-in-law. Reid hadn't even known she had any siblings and wondered why this brother hadn't attended the duke's funeral. His stepmother explained that Dez's wife had just given birth to their first child and she hadn't wanted him to leave Anna alone.

Dalinda had left yesterday to visit the couple at their country estate in Surrey and before she left, she'd let slip that Viscount Martin had two daughters of marriageable age. He realized as an eligible duke that was the chief reason Martin had issued the dinner invitation. Besides wanting to spend more time on his various properties, Reid avoided the upcoming Season because of pushy mamas of girls making their come-outs. The women would clamor for his attention. He had no interest in the Marriage Mart, chiefly because he'd made up his mind. His wife would be Lady Dunwood or no one.

At this point, he was entirely too busy to pursue the dowager countess and it didn't matter anyway. She'd proclaimed she wouldn't wed again, which meant she wasn't going to be swept off her feet by some gentleman. She'd be busy as headmistress of her school. That gave him ample time to accomplish what he needed—and then work on making her his. Besides, he wasn't in any hurry.

Or was he?

Reid decided it was time to ask his friends to come to Gillingham for a week. He wanted to show Burke and Gray his property and seek their advice on a few matters, especially since both were now earls with estates of their own. He also wanted to get to know Gemma and Charlotte better. The little conversation he'd had with the women at his father's funeral let him know they were not only beautiful but savvy. If the four came for a visit, it would allow Reid the chance to ask Lady Dunwood to tea. He was desperate for his friends' opinions of her. It had been far too long since he'd been around gentlewomen and he needed to know if his evaluation of Lady Dunwood was correct. If she held up to their scrutiny, especially the two wives' opinions, he would proceed with his plan to wed her.

Though he'd rather have ridden on horseback, Reid took his carriage to the viscount's manor house. Lord Martin greeted him and Reid remembered how his father had enjoyed the viscount's company—but the viscountess was another matter. She'd behaved erratically over the years, especially after the birth of her younger daughter. Before he left for university, Lady Martin had been sent to a madhouse. For all he knew, she remained there.

The viscount led him to the drawing room, where two young women rose.

"Your Grace, may I present to you my girls?" He indicated the plain one on the left, short of stature but with a decent figure. "This is Lady Edith, who is twenty and my older child."

She swept into a graceful curtsey. "Your Grace. It's very nice to meet you."

Reid took her gloved hand and kissed it. "It is lovely to meet you, Lady Edith."

"And this is Lady Eden, my younger girl, who'll have her first Season come April. She recently turned eighteen."

The beauty with the large bosom and tiny waist curtseyed and then eyed him hungrily, as if she might be a dog who hadn't been fed for three days. Her eyes were bright and her smile alluring.

"Your Grace," she purred. "I'm delighted to make your acquaintance."

The butler called them into dinner and after half an hour, Reid wished he could claim a headache and leave. Lady Edith had proven to be intelligent and quite witty. If he hadn't already decided upon Lady Dunwood for a wife, he would have considered this country miss to be his duchess. What had him grinding his teeth, though, was her sister. Lady Eden had openly flirted with him, saying outrageous, inappropriate things. He'd never been more uncomfortable in mixed company. Every time her father or sister tried to steer the conversation in other directions, Lady Eden continued her flirtation.

Finally, the many courses came to an end and the women left the men to their port.

Lord Martin looked at him solemnly. "Would you consider saving me a Season and taking Eden off my hands?" the viscount pleaded.

His request took Reid aback. "I must politely decline, Martin." He left it at that, not wanting to name the dozen or more reasons Eden Martin was unsuitable to be his duchess.

The viscount sighed. "I had to try. Madness in a family tree is not ideal when you have two daughters to marry off."

The viscount's frank words gave him pause. "Do you believe either touched by Lady Martin's madness?"

"Not Edith. She's calm and sweet. Would you consider wedding her?"

"Not at this time," Reid said, his firm tone, closing the door to that request.

Martin shrugged. "I understand."

"I will need to wed," he continued. "I am actually looking for a more mature woman when I do. After all, I'm thirty. I don't want a girl straight from the schoolroom."

"You may not need to go to London for the Season," Lord Martin said. He named a few eligible women in the neighborhood and finished by saying, "Of course, there's always Lady Dunwood. Though I doubt she'd be interested. Even if you are a duke."

"I have met her," Reid said neutrally, wondering what the viscount's opinion was of her. "Dunwood Academy was recommended to me. I've placed Arthur and Harry there."

Lord Martin chuckled. "I've heard those boys have become a handful. Kicked out of several schools. Well, Lady Dunwood is known for taking on troubled lads. I hope she will settle those two down. I know your father would have been upset to see how they've turned out."

"Let's hope they are still young enough that I can help mold their characters—along with Lady Dunwood's careful guidance, of course."

"She's helped several boys," Lord Martin said. "I sat with her at a dinner a few months ago. She's very committed to her school. Told me it's her life's work when I asked if she planned to wed again. Seems she's married to a school and a dozen boys instead of doing the proper thing and wedding a man. A beautiful woman but a bit too independent for my taste."

Her independence was one of her most attractive features. One that Reid thought would help make her an excellent duchess. Lady Dunwood wouldn't be swayed by others' opinions. She would lead the way with her own.

"Shall we join my daughters?" Lord Martin asked.

Reid endured another hour at the manor house. While Lady Edith played the pianoforte well and had a passable voice, her sister made mistake after mistake as she played and screeched like a chicken.

When she finished playing and they politely applauded, Lord Martin asked, "Do you ever practice, Eden?"

"Not if I can help it," the girl said saucily, looking at Reid and licking her lips seductively. "There are so many other things to practice beyond playing music, Papa."

"I must be returning home," he said and stood abruptly.

Lord Martin and both his girls wished him goodnight, walking outside with him. The wind gusted and Reid urged them to return inside as he waited for his carriage.

"Come again soon," Viscount Martin called before he closed the door.

Reid didn't think so. The man was decent but a bit boring. He felt sorry for Lady Edith being stuck in that household and hoped some gentleman would see her worth during the upcoming Season. She was even slightly pretty when she smiled.

A giggle sounded and he whipped around, seeing Lady Eden before him.

"I've wanted to be alone with you all night," she declared before throwing her arms about him and kissing him on the mouth.

Shock ran through him at her bold move, quickly replaced by fear. If Lord Martin opened the door looking for her and saw them in an embrace, he would demand they wed.

Quickly, Reid tore his mouth from hers and gripped her shoulders, pushing her away and holding her at arms' length.

"Never do that again," he growled.

Mischief lit her eyes. "Isn't this the way to land a duke?"

"Not this duke. Now—or ever."

Her bottom lip thrust out in a pout. "I know you think I'm pretty. You kept looking at me during dinner. I knew you wanted to kiss me."

"I only looked at you when you spoke and that was out of politeness. I never wanted to kiss you."

He heard the sound of the carriage coming around but kept

his hands firmly on her shoulders, afraid she'd fling herself back into his arms if he didn't.

"You're lying," she said, low and angry.

"I have no reason to lie to you, Lady Eden."

"I'll tell Papa you kissed me," she said defiantly. "He'll insist we wed."

"And I'll tell him otherwise." Reid paused. "I'm a duke. No one crosses a duke. Lord Martin will believe me—not you, my lady."

The carriage came to a halt behind them.

"I want to wed you," she said fiercely.

"You don't even know me."

An eerie gleam came into her eyes. "I want to be a duchess. I want to be in your bed. I want you, Your Grace. You don't know it yet but you'll decide you want me, too."

He released her and was grateful she stayed in place. "Goodnight, Lady Eden."

Turning, he saw the steps already in place and the door open. Reid bounded into the vehicle and fell back against the cushions. Quickly, the coach took off.

His breathing evened out and he knew that had been a narrow escape. Lady Eden was definitely touched by her mother's madness. He would need to stay far from her.

Else he'd be saddled to her for life.

The thought of living with her for decades caused him to shudder. Especially if she became with child and passed along the madness in her blood.

Reid swore he'd never have the Martins to Gillingham and would refuse any further invitations from Lord Martin. Unfortunately, there would be social occasions in the neighborhood where they both might be in attendance.

It only confirmed his resolve to place a ring on Lady Dunwood's finger.

When he arrived back at Gillingham, he made his way to his study and dashed off two quick notes, one to Gray and the other to Burke, urging them to bring their wives and in Gray's case, his children. He wrote both, explaining he sought their advice on a number of issues.

Including marriage.

If that didn't get his lifelong friends to Gillingham in a rush, Reid didn't know what would.

Chapter Seven

Ashlyn spent a good portion of her day organizing her accounts and seeing what bills needed to be paid. She charged forty pounds sterling for a boy to attend the academy and another forty for the room and board. As much as her students ate, she thought she should increase the fees covering meals. She'd taken on much of the responsibility of running Dunwood's household when she'd wed Daniel because her brother-in-law and his wife spent a good portion of their year in London. When the countess was home, she couldn't be bothered with mundane affairs. Beyond approving weekly menus, the rest had fallen to Ashlyn to handle. Since she'd spent so many years as her father's shadow and had buried herself in the estate's ledgers, she had a good working knowledge of money. Her experience in such varied areas had come in handy in beginning her own school and making sure it remained prosperous.

Glancing at the clock, she saw it was too late in the afternoon to go to town and see that all of the merchants were paid in person. It was something she liked to do and believed kept a spirit of goodwill between her and those in town.

Tea would be served in an hour. It would do her good to stretch her legs some before then. She went to the foyer and tossed a shawl about her shoulders and set out. She began walking down the lane that led to the house, disappointed that the day was cloudy and gloomy. It looked as if it might storm within the hour and she thought it better to turn around when she spied a rider approaching in the distance. No one was expected and she paused, curious as to who came to call. Other than set appointments with parents of her students, visitors were rare.

Her breath hitched when she recognized the Duke of Gilford riding a large black horse. He was the last person she wished to see. The man had dominated her thoughts ever since he'd deposited her new students with her. Ashlyn found herself idly wondering what he was doing several times a day and chided herself for letting her attention wander. What was worse was she also thought of him at night when she crawled into bed. It seemed almost sinful to think of him then, especially as she felt vulnerable in her night rail. She imagined what it would be like to have him take her hands again. To stroke her hair. To kiss her.

To bed her.

Her one night with Daniel had been frustrating. With both of them being virgins, neither had really known what to do or how to do it, much less well. Her stepmother hadn't prepared Ashlyn in the least, while Daniel only had hearsay to go on, bits of conversations he'd overheard from fellow soldiers. When they consummated their union, it had been messy and painful. She'd even bled, which made her angry at him and brought her to tears. Daniel told her it was something he'd heard happened to women when they coupled with a man. She knew he was misinformed and explained to him that women bled every month, with no man being involved in the process at all. The cramps sometimes hurt but nothing like the way she'd been torn apart by her new husband.

They'd spent the rest of the night on opposite sides of the bed, facing away from one another. In the morning, Daniel had apologized to her and promised he'd learn how to do things right for when he returned. He'd tried to kiss her but Ashlyn had turned her head away so that his lips only grazed her cheek. She'd wanted nothing more to do with him.

At least something good had come from that horrible experience. She'd had Gregory. Ashlyn would have endured the fires of Hell itself to have the little time she'd been given with her son. Gregory had been all goodness and light, perfect in every way. Losing him had broken something in her. She knew she'd closed off her emotions after his death. Her pupils were a poor substitute for her dead child but she'd learn to eventually open enough of her heart to give them some tenderness and attention. There was a limit to how much she could give, though, and it certainly didn't include having feelings for the Duke of Gilford.

His mount came to a halt a few feet from her and he swung his long legs from the saddle.

"Good afternoon, Lady Dunwood," he said with a smile that made him far too handsome for his own good. His dark brown hair was windblown from his ride and his face slightly tanned. He must have spent a good deal of time outdoors since she'd last seen him.

"Good afternoon, Your Grace. What brings you here?"

"I've come for two reasons. May I walk with you?"

"Certainly."

Ashlyn turned back toward the house and he fell into step beside her, holding the reins so the horse trailed behind them. His nearness brought those bloody butterflies back to her stomach. She even caught a whiff of the cologne he wore, something woodsy that tempted her to lean closer and inhale more deeply.

They walked in companionable silence for a few minutes and as they reached the house, she led him back to the stables so he could leave his horse.

The duke said, "I'd like to see my half-brothers if I could. I know you suggested to Dalinda that we wait longer but I've had second thoughts. I don't want them to think I abandoned them here."

"That can be arranged," she told him. "I think they've done quite well. Harry is a darling and so easy to get along with."

"My Harry?" he asked, his face full of surprise. "And what of

Arthur?"

"Would it surprise you to find Arthur has settled in better than either of us would have expected?"

He gave her a dubious look. "I doubt that. Speak plainly, Lady Dunwood. No need to sugarcoat the truth."

"That is the truth, Your Grace. Oh, he had a bump or two but nothing that wasn't easily resolved. In fact, I think Arthur has the makings of being a fine leader."

He looked as if she'd punched him in the gut—and she couldn't help but laugh. Soon, he joined in with her.

"We're talking about Arthur Baker, my half-brother? The surly lad with a huge chip on his shoulder."

"I assure you the chip has been chiseled away," Ashlyn confided. "I think both boys were lonely. I'm sure their parents loved them but with the duke being so ill and the duchess spending all of her time nursing him, Arthur and Harry were neglected. I think they acted out to gain attention and when that didn't work, they acted even worse."

Gilford nodded slowly. "It seems you're right. I know the staff has told me they weren't awful until the past few years. That would coincide with the beginning of my father's illness."

They reached the stables and the entire group of students emerged, along with Mr. Selleck.

"Boys, His Grace, the Duke of Gilford, has come for a short visit," Ashlyn announced.

"Hello, Your Grace," twelve boys greeted in unison, along with Mr. Selleck's deeper voice. The tutor added, "We've just come from our afternoon ride, Your Grace. Master Arthur and Master Harry have the makings of fine horsemen."

"I am happy to hear that," the nobleman replied.

"The rest of you go wash up. Teatime will be in forty-five minutes," she said.

All the boys left with Mr. Selleck except for Arthur and Harry, who remained behind.

"I will leave you to your visit. You're welcomed to join us for tea, Your Grace."

"Thank you. I'll walk with the boys for half an hour and then we'll join you."

"Can Lady Dunwood walk with us, Gilford?" Arthur asked.

The duke nodded. "She may if she has time to do so. And remember, Arthur, you may call me Reid. It's perfectly fine for family to address me as such."

"Thank you, sir," Arthur said. "Reid it will be."

The duke's eyes met hers, his astonishment evident.

Mr. Jarrett appeared. "Here, Your Grace, I'll take your horse."

Gilford handed it over and the four of them set out. As they strolled, he asked several questions about what the boys had studied over the past two weeks and seemed pleased by their answers.

"Have you given Lady Dunwood or any of your tutors any problems?" The duke glanced from Arthur to Harry and back again.

"I haven't," Harry piped up. "But Arthur got a talking-to," he revealed.

"What did you do, Arthur?" the duke asked sternly.

"It doesn't matter what I did," Arthur said, a sharp tone in his words. He glanced to her and said more softly, "That's what Lady Dunwood said when she spoke to me. It's in the past and I've apologized for what I did. And I know not to do it again." He met his uncle's gaze. "I don't ever want Lady Dunwood to be angry with me again."

"Have you made any friends?" the duke inquired. "I know it's harder to do when you already have a brother with you. He becomes your fallback and makes it not as necessary to put yourself out there."

"We like everyone here," Harry said sincerely. "They're quite nice. I like Jeremy the best. He's a year younger and the best rider and athlete here. Everyone wants to play on his team. Peter's in the bed next to mine. He really helped me settle in."

"The fellow with the ginger hair and freckles? Yes, I've met him. He seems a good lad," the duke said. "What about you, Arthur?"

The boy shrugged. "It's like Harry said. With only ten others here, it's easy to get to know everyone. I like Drake a lot. I knew him at another school. We weren't friends there but we are now. And Edward is probably my closest friend."

Gilford looked thoughtful. "I may have met him. Which one is he?"

Ashlyn knew the duke tested Arthur, wanting to hear how Arthur described his new friend.

"He's very tall, Reid. The tallest boy here. Edward knows mathematics better than anyone. That's probably why we get along because I like numbers, too."

"Does he have blond hair?" the duke asked.

"No. It's very black and he has blue eyes. He's funny. And he knows how to fart whenever he wants."

She looked sternly at Arthur and he quickly apologized. Glancing at Gilford, she saw he was pleased.

"We should head back to the house in order to give you time to wash before tea. Run ahead. We'll meet you in the drawing room," she ordered.

The brothers took off. The duke touched her arm. Goosebumps sprang up on her flesh.

"You are a miracle worker, Lady Dunwood," Gilford marveled. "I wouldn't have thought it possible to bring both of those boys to heel in such a short amount of time."

"As I mentioned, I think they were merely lacking in attention. Once they received it, they didn't need to seek it out in ways that were harmful to themselves or others. All my boys get plenty of attention. Plus, they are kept very busy with their studies."

"And worn out through physical activity," the duke said lightly with a smile. "I do remember your secret and will put it into play when they come home during their Easter break."

"I think it's a lesson all parents learn. I did so with Gregory. He was a bundle of energy. You'll learn the same once you wed and have children of your own."

"May I ask a little more about Edward's background? You said his father was a local farmer."

"Yes. He has a younger sister. His mother passed away last year. His father works very hard. Edward takes after him and has an excellent work ethic."

"You mentioned you had hopes of Edward landing a scholarship at a public school."

"I feel he can. He's much too bright to spend the rest of his life behind a plow. Not to belittle a plowman, but I feel Edward has more to offer the world. A scholarship is paramount, though, for him to continue his studies."

The duke said, "If he doesn't earn a scholarship, I will see that he receives an education."

Ashlyn gasped. "But you barely know him, Your Grace."

"If Arthur's made friends with Edward and doesn't even mention his firemark, then the boy is more than intelligent. He's got depth to him. Arthur is seeing Edward for who he is. That speaks volumes to me. I insist. Please keep it in mind."

"I will," she said shakily, her throat thick with emotion. "That is a very generous offer."

He shrugged. "As a duke, I want to put my position to good use. Funding a worthy local boy's education is a small gesture on my part but it would mean a great deal to Edward and his family."

Gilford took her arm. "Come, let's go in to tea. I find myself famished."

Ashlyn walked back in a daze. They went to the drawing room and it filled quickly with pupils and tutors.

"Tea is held shortly after the boys play their sports or ride. I find this is the time they are their hungriest. They have a light meal a few hours later to tide them over until breakfast. This is also a time we practice manners and conversation."

"I'm happy to participate. My manners may be a little rusty. Tea was not a daily practice on the battlefield and good, decent conversation was often lacking. Still, I'll try my best."

He gave her a winning smile and her heart turned over.

Ashlyn kept quiet for the next hour as she watched her boys interact with one another and the Duke of Gilford. He proved to be charming and attentive to each boy, drawing them and their tutors out. By the end of the hour, she'd learned things about everyone present that she hadn't known.

"Thank you for such a pleasant teatime," she told everyone. "I will see you later."

The group filed out, shaking hands with Gilford before they left. Harry, the last one present, gave the duke a brief hug and then rushed out, a huge grin on his face.

"You were certainly an entertaining guest," she remarked. "Thank you for spending time getting to know each boy. They will be singing your praises. I don't know how to thank you."

"I do," he said, a slow smile spreading across his handsome, tanned face. "You can return the favor and come to tea at Gillingham tomorrow. I have friends staying with me and I want them to meet you. I think you'd like them very much. And you can stay for dinner, as well."

Ashlyn hesitated. "I hate to be away from the boys for so long."

"Isn't tomorrow Saturday? A half-day?"

"Yes," she admitted. "We only do studies in the morning. The boys are free the remainder of the day. I like to be nearby, though, in case I'm needed."

"Don't you attend dinners with others in the neighborhood sometimes?"

"Well, yes, though I don't socialize much," she said nervously, not wanting to be in this man's company.

And yet wishing to at the same time.

"Then it's settled. You'll come to tea. Stay for dinner. I won't take no for an answer, Lady Dunwood. After all, I am a duke. No one has the audacity to tell me no."

"You haven't been a duke very long," she reminded him.

"No, but I was a colonel. At that rank, very few people told me what to do because there weren't that many men above me. Becoming a duke hasn't been much of a stretch," he teased.

When she hesitated, he said, "You don't have a choice, my lady. I will send my carriage for you at three o'clock tomorrow afternoon. You will be ready and you will come to Gillingham. Am I clear?"

Ashlyn resigned herself and said, "Very clear, Your Grace. I will see you for tea tomorrow afternoon."

CHAPTER EIGHT

ASHLYN WENT DOWNSTAIRS, a valise in hand. She set it by the door and found Mrs. Clayton.

"Remember that I won't be back until after dinner tonight. Much later because I'm sure the duke and his guests will dine later than we do here."

The housekeeper smiled. "Don't you worry about a thing, my lady. Mrs. George and I will see the boys fed."

"Mr. Butler is in charge, as usual, of making sure that they all get to bed at a decent hour," she added.

The students were divided into three bedrooms, with four boys sharing a room. Three of her staff saw that each room's occupants accomplished their set tasks—washing faces and hands, brushing teeth, and dressing for bed. Mr. Butler, who was a favorite of all, went to each room and bid the pupils goodnight, then all candles were extinguished.

"Go and enjoy yourself, my lady," Mrs. Clayton urged. "You don't get out nearly enough."

Ashlyn returned to the foyer. She shouldn't be this nervous. She went to dinner in the neighborhood upon occasion, which is how she'd met the former duke and duchess, and had even attended a Christmas party last year at Viscount Martin's residence. She also saw others at church every Sunday. Never had she been as agitated as she was now.

It was all because of Gilford. He was far too good-looking for his own good. All the physical activity from his army days had honed his body to perfection, something that she should never have noticed in the first place. It was hard not to do so, however. She'd thought once he stopped wearing his uniform that he would revert from god-like status to appearing merely mortal. Yesterday, though, he'd appeared for the first time in the perfectly tailored clothes of a gentleman of his rank. Unfortunately, his tailcoat had done nothing to hide his broad shoulders and his buckskin breeches, tucked into polished Hessians, only emphasized his muscular thighs and calves.

She wished she could have refused his invitation but hadn't wanted to seem churlish. Curiosity, too, caused her to agree because she wondered what his friends were like. Before Gilford's sudden arrival at his father's funeral, Ashlyn had only heard his name mentioned twice in passing, as the Marquess of Medford. He'd been gone at war so long that he was rarely spoken about in the village. Now, though, the one-time army officer was the Duke of Gilford, the most powerful man in the county.

And the best looking, by far.

Pinching herself, she murmured, "Stop thinking about him," under her breath. She would get through tea today and dinner tonight. She would be polite toward him but never directly address him. She planned to occupy her time by conversing with his friends instead. If she didn't speak to Gilford, she wouldn't have to look at him. And if she didn't look at him, she prayed her insides would keep from turning to jelly. Already in thinking about him, she found it hard to breathe.

The clock in the foyer chimed three. Ashlyn retrieved her case and opened the door. She saw the ducal coach coming to a stop in perfect timing. As she started toward it, the door flew open and out bounded the Duke of Gilford.

Bloody hell.

"What are you doing here?" she asked sharply.

He gave her a winning smile. The sun shone on his brown hair, lightening it somewhat. She had the urge to run her fingers through it, only causing her irritability to rise.

"I'm coming to get you for tea," he replied, closing the distance between them and taking the valise from her. He handed it to a footman.

"You told me you were sending your carriage," she said petulantly.

"And I did—with me in it. Don't grumble so," he said, trying to placate her.

Knowing she sounded childish, she softened her tone. "I only meant that you shouldn't have left your guests to fetch me. I could have ridden a few miles in a carriage by myself. In fact, I could easily have used my carriage to come to Gillingham. You didn't need to send yours."

The duke took her hand and that familiar jolt rippled through her at the touch. "And deny myself the pleasure of your company? I think not."

Was he flirting with her?

He helped her into the vehicle and she sank onto the luxurious cushion, a small *ah* escaping her lips. Much to her chagrin, he sat next to her, taking up most of the seat. Ashlyn scooted over but found he still dominated the space.

Reaching for the door, he closed it and turned to her. "I heard that little sigh. It is a nice interior, if I must say so myself. I find I'm enjoying all of the little luxuries since I've returned to England. Hot water to shave with every morning. Clean, pressed clothes. Delicious meals seasoned with love and skill. And a soft pillow and feathered mattress that almost seem sinful."

She thought him referring to his bed was the height of ill manners, especially since they were alone. She bit her lip to keep from correcting him. He was a duke, one of the few in the realm, not some schoolboy for her to chastise. She didn't want him to think her provoked.

And aroused. Thinking of him naked in that bed.

"You devoted a good number of years to His Majesty's service," she noted.

"I did. So did my friends, whom you'll soon meet."

"Tell me about them," she urged, hoping that would distract her from the images in her head.

"I met Gray and Burke on my first day at school. We were all seven years of age and away from home for the first time. We became inseparable, going to university together and then purchasing commissions as officers in the King's Army."

"I know why you sold out. Why did they?"

"Gray was the first to go. His brother and sister-in-law passed away, leaving three orphans behind. Gray went home to Gray Manor to become their guardian and see to the running of the estates for the new Earl of Crampton, who was but twelve. Unfortunately, the boy was sickly and passed away, making Gray the new earl."

"Where is his country estate?"

"About eleven miles from Gillingham. He's brought his wife, Charlotte, and their three children. The girls are his nieces and Viscount Warren, their son, is a few months shy of two years of age."

"And your other friend?"

"Burke was a third son and as wild as they come. He lost an eye in the war and sold out soon after."

"How terrible!" Ashlyn exclaimed.

"Burke wouldn't think so. He returned and went to work for the War Office as a spy. That's how he met Gemma, his wife. They're mad for each other. Gray and Charlotte, too, are a love match. For bringing down a network of traitors within the government, the crown awarded Burke the title of Earl of Weston."

"Oh, I've heard of him but haven't met him," she said. "His estate is Westbrook, is it not?"

"Yes. He's only three miles to the west of me. All in all, it's remarkable that the three of us wound up so close together in Kent, especially since neither Burke nor Gray ever expected to hold a title." Gilford paused. "They're good men and they've married even better women. I can't wait for you to meet them."

Ashlyn wondered why he would be so eager for her to meet his friends. Although she was a dowager countess, she didn't necessarily run in the same social circles as he did. She accepted very few invitations, preferring to remain at Dunwood Academy with her boys. As a duke, he would be welcomed anywhere he went, his presence sought after to make events successful.

The carriage began to slow and she realized they'd already arrived, an advantage to being so close to Gillingham. The duke guided her from the coach and escorted her inside, helping her remove her shawl and giving it to a footman. They went up the stairs and directly to the drawing room, where the two couples awaited them. All four rose as she and Gilford crossed the room to where they gathered around a fireplace. She noted the dowager duchess' absence and remembered that Gilford mentioned that she'd gone to her brother's for a visit.

"Lady Dunwood, I'd like to introduce you to my dear friends." He indicated the couple on his left. "This is Lord and Lady Crampton."

The earl had chestnut hair and startlingly blue eyes, while the countess had brown hair and vibrant green eyes. Both greeted her warmly.

"And here are Lord and Lady Weston," the duke continued.

The earl wore a silk eyepatch of black over his right eye, the same color as his hair. His lone gray eye looked at her with interest. His wife had abundant auburn hair and sparkling blue eyes. She also looked to be with child.

"I am pleased to meet you both," Ashlyn said. "I see congratulations are due."

Lady Weston smiled and patted her belly. "Our first rascal will arrive sometime in June."

Ashlyn laughed. "And you already know it to be a rascal, whether boy or girl?"

Lord Weston slipped an arm about his wife. "It's a given if it's a girl. My Gemma is very mischievous."

She swatted him playfully and told Ashlyn, "I would say the same about Burke. Any boy he had a hand in making will be a bit of a rogue."

"I'm hoping our first is a daughter," Weston added. "I expect she'll be a bit of a tyrant. The better to keep all of her brothers in line."

"If she is, she'll learn from me how best to keep Nicholson men in their places," the countess said.

"You think you know how to do so?" her husband asked, his voice low and seductive.

And then he kissed her soundly. Right there, in front of everyone.

Ashlyn fought back the gasp and merely stared.

Lord Crampton laughed and drew her attention away. "Those two are still practically newlyweds. They only wed last June. Wait until they're an old married couple like us." He pulled his wife close and gazed into her eyes. "How long, Miss Nott?"

"Two years and almost four months, Major," she replied smartly.

Then Lord Crampton kissed his wife, hard and swift. He broke the kiss and grinned shamelessly at her, like a naughty boy who'd been caught—and didn't care in the least.

Ashlyn felt her cheeks heating at these outrageous displays of affection. She'd never seen anyone kiss in public. She'd never even seen her own parents kiss in the privacy of their home. Kissing just wasn't done in front of others. She was embarrassed to even be in the same room where it occurred. And yet it brought about a touch of jealousy. She'd never been close to Daniel in this way. Never really comfortable with him in the short time they'd known one another. None of the few kisses they'd shared had been infused with the bold passion that she'd just witnessed between these two couples.

She sensed Gilford's eyes on her. She met the duke's gaze and he shrugged. "I told you. Both love matches. They're quite hopeless."

He began laughing and the two pairs joined in. Somehow, Ashlyn felt herself swept up in their laughter. She glanced back at the duke's friends wistfully, wishing she had friends such as these.

Lady Weston took her hand. "I apologize for my husband's outlandish behavior, Lady Dunwood, because he never will."

"And why should I?" Lord Weston asked playfully. "I'm never sorry for kissing my wife."

"Neither am I, Burke," Lord Crampton chimed in. "Miss Nott has been embarrassed a time or two when I've done so in public but she gets over it quickly."

"Why do you refer to your wife as Miss Nott?" Ashlyn inquired.

The earl gave her a devilish smile. "Because it was Miss Nott I fell madly in love with," he said simply. "I like to think back to those days of tumbling headfirst into love with her."

"I was governess to his nieces, Harriet and Jane," Lady Crampton explained. "When my father passed away, I was turned out from my own home by the new earl and had to make my way in the world." She looked fondly at her husband. "Gray teases me about having a bit of the governess still in me." She turned back to Ashlyn. "Reid tells us you run a local academy. I'd love to hear all about it."

"Why don't we all sit?" the duke suggested. "Tea will be here any moment."

The door opened and two footmen rolled in the teacarts. They settled themselves and Gilford said, "Since Dalinda is gone, would you do the honors of pouring out, Lady Dunwood?"

"Of course, Your Grace," she replied, busying herself as the others made up plates from the sandwiches and sweets that had been brought.

Once everyone had a cup in hand, Ashlyn told them a bit about Dunwood Academy and the various boys and their instructors.

"Lady Dunwood employs traditional methods of instruction alongside more unique ones," Gilford said. "I was fortunate enough to see some of the classes in action."

"What do you differently?" Lady Crampton asked. "I know Miss Wight, the girls' governess, would be interested. Harriet and Jane would be, too."

"I believe you learn more by active participation. So much of learning is passive. Take horseback riding, for instance. Before you get on a horse, you learn some of the basics. How to sit and hold your reins, for example. But nothing compares to actually being on the back of a horse and experiencing a ride. I feel learning is the same way. I push my students to become involved in their own learning."

"Give us some examples," Lord Weston urged. "This sounds fascinating."

Ashlyn did so, with the duke chiming in with examples of what he'd seen during his visit to the academy.

"Sounds a far cry from our schooldays," Lord Crampton said. "Even at university. How did you hit upon such an idea, Lady Dunwood?"

"I wanted to help special boys. Those who'd experienced trouble learning at other schools. Some of my boys do come to us with slight behavior problems."

"She's speaking of my half-brothers, just in case you weren't aware," the duke said.

"Through teaching my own very active son, I found he learned better—and faster—and retained things longer by becoming a part of learning."

"Oh, I didn't realize you had a son," Lady Weston said. "Is he at school with you or elsewhere?"

Ashlyn swallowed. "He passed away three years ago, my lady."

Lady Weston reached for her hand and squeezed it gently. "I'm so sorry," she said. "That must have been dreadful."

"It was the most difficult experience of my life," she admitted. "But I help other boys now. They have become as my own family."

"You should see the miracle she's wrought with Arthur and Harry. They left here surly and grumpy and yet a few weeks later, they are enthusiastic and well-mannered."

"Enough of Dunwood Academy. Please tell me more of yourselves."

Lady Weston smiled. "Yes, gentlemen. Tell us more." She looked to Ashlyn. "Charlotte and I love hearing about the three of them and their growing up years. They were quite something."

The rest of teatime passed pleasantly, with much laughter as the men told stories on one another from their youth and university years. She noticed they didn't speak of their time at war, though, and decided it must have been difficult.

The door opened and three children appeared, two older girls and a boy toddling behind them. A woman Ashlyn assumed was their governess followed them in.

"Lady Dunwood, I'd like you to meet my nieces, Lady Harriet and Lady Jane," said Lord Crampton.

The girls made their curtseys and greeted her.

He then scooped up the boy. "And this is Viscount Warren."

His son awarded a wet kiss to his father and the earl handed the boy to his mother, who said, "If you'll excuse us, we like to read with the children after tea each day."

"I'll go with you," Lord Weston said. "Gemma likes to lie down a bit after tea." He took her hand and brushed a kiss upon her fingers. "She tires easily these days." Looking to Ashlyn, he said, "We'll see you at dinner, Lady Dunwood."

The two couples and children left and she found herself alone with Lord Gilford.

"Would you care to see Gillingham?" he asked. "I'm quite proud of it."

"I'd be happy to take a tour, Your Grace," Ashlyn said.

The duke offered her his arm and she slid her hand into the crook, catching a whiff of his cologne. All through the witty banter of teatime, she'd been aware of him watching her. She sensed the growing attraction between them. Not just on her part, but his, as well. She wondered again what it would be like to be kissed by him, a man in the prime of his life. Licking her lips, she left the drawing room with him, telling herself this tour was merely a friendly gesture and a way to pass the time before dinner began.

Or not.

Chapter Nine

ASHLYN ENJOYED SEEING the parts of the house Gilford led her through, especially the gallery displaying portraits of the previous dukes and their families.

"You'll have to have your portrait painted now that you've gained the title," she suggested.

"I suppose I shall. I'll need to find an artist to make me appear strong and handsome, as my father was."

"You are strong and handsome," she said. "Quit fishing for compliments."

He waggled his eyebrow. "I'm glad you think so highly of me."

She snorted. "Looks don't matter to me, Your Grace. It's a person's character that makes him or her worthy."

The duke's gaze seemed to penetrate to her soul. "Then I will have to make sure you find mine worthy, my lady."

He took her arm and guided her downstairs. She had to think to breathe, being so near him.

"I'd show you more of the house but a few of the wings are closed and wouldn't be worth seeing."

"It is a rather large house. Will you ever open it up entirely?"

"I plan to once I fill it with children—and they fill it with their children."

"Do you have a lady in mind to help you in this venture?" she asked lightly, chiding herself for the personal question and yet eager to hear his response.

"Actually, I do," he replied, his lips twitching in amusement. "She is a very beautiful woman, both in her outward appearance and on the inside. She will make for a most excellent duchess."

His words cut her to the quick. They shouldn't have. He was a man in the prime of his life. A new duke, wealthy and powerful. Of course, he would want to wed and see that he had an heir.

Yet the thought of him with another woman made her eyes smart with tears. She glanced away and blinked several times, willing them not to fall. Now more than ever, she had to hide her growing feelings from him.

"Shall we go outside? I'd like for you to see my stables. I'm quite proud of the horseflesh at Gillingham."

"Certainly," she said.

As they left the house, he told her, "I wish we had more time. I'd take you riding about the estate and show it off, as well."

"I haven't ridden in years, Your Grace. It's probably best we don't."

"Why haven't you?" he asked, obviously baffled.

"I rode frequently as a child with my father. He had no sons and so took me about the estate with him as he talked with his tenants and saw to repairs. Then I married and didn't have much of an opportunity to ride where I lived."

"But you have many horses now and your students ride often."

"I don't ride with them," she revealed. "It's a time when the house is quiet and I see to other things. Meet with their tutors. See to paperwork and bills. Frankly, it's been so long since I've been on horseback, I may have forgotten how to ride."

He shook his head. "No one forgets how to ride, Lady Dunwood. You might need a lesson or two to refresh you but it would all come back."

"I suppose I could ask Mr. Jarrett to help me."

"No," the duke said quickly. "It would be awkward for him to instruct his employer in what to do."

Ashlyn didn't think so, knowing how determined and deliberate her groom was.

"I will take you out myself," Gilford proclaimed.

"What?" Ashlyn became flustered. "No, Your Grace. I cannot take up your valuable time. You have so many responsibilities."

"As do you, my lady," he said with a grin. "Riding is a pleasurable activity. You're denying yourself the enjoyment." He paused. "Everyone needs a little fun in their lives every now and then. Wouldn't you agree?"

By now, they'd entered the stables and she paused to stroke a horse who stuck its head from the stall because she didn't trust herself to answer the duke. Riding with him would be fun—but it wouldn't lead anywhere. He'd already told her he was going to ask someone to marry him. Ashlyn couldn't be around Gilford anymore.

Because she wanted him for herself.

She never would have thought it possible to dream of being with a man again physically. Not after her one night of limited experience with Daniel. No man had held her attention as Gilford did. He was smart and funny and curious about everything. It was imperative that she limit her interactions with him. She couldn't avoid him entirely, not with Arthur and Harry attending Dunwood Academy, but those would only be rare occasions in which they would meet. She needed distance from this man, as soon as possible, and would have it once this day ended.

"Thunder likes you," he said and reached up to join her as she stroked the magnificent black beast before them. "He's a devil to ride but I've always been up for a challenge."

His gaze met hers, heat in his eyes, and a frisson of desire rippled through her. For a moment, she could only stare at him before she forced herself to turn away.

"I should return to the house and prepare for dinner," she murmured.

"Of course. I'll escort you."

Gilford took her hand and tucked it through his arm. She

wanted to rip it away and run as fast as she could, never looking back. Instead, she strolled slowly back to the house, emotions churning as a maelstrom within her.

He took her up the stairs, saying, "I've had a room prepared for your use. Your valise was taken there. Charlotte and Gemma both offered the services of their abigail to you so you will have someone to help you dress for dinner."

They arrived at a door and he lifted her hand to his lips, pressing a tender kiss upon her knuckles. "I've enjoyed having you at Gillingham today, Lady Dunwood."

"Yes," she said breathlessly. "It was wonderful meeting your friends."

"They are more like family to me. I don't know what I would do without them."

Once more, he lifted her hand to his lips and brushed a kiss against her fingers. "I'll see you at dinner."

Gilford left and Ashlyn floated inside the bedchamber.

"You are mad," she told herself, the good feelings dissipating as she tried to ground herself in reality. "He is charming to everyone. You are no one special. He's being nice to you because you are helping him with his brothers. There's nothing more to it."

A basin of water sat nearby and she splashed cool water on her face, trying to calm herself. Drying her face, she turned and saw her evening gown draped across the bed, all the wrinkles pressed away. Her stockings and shoes were laid out beside it, along with her gloves. Moments later, a servant arrived and helped her to dress for dinner.

"You look lovely, my lady," the maid said. "The gown matches your eyes."

Ashlyn had chosen to bring a gown she rarely wore. It was the nicest one she owned, in a shade of deep purple. She never dressed for dinner at the academy, wearing the same gown from the day to the evening meal. Her instructors did the same and dinner was an understated affair, taking place shortly after her pupils dined together.

The maid took her downstairs so she wouldn't lose her way in the vast house and Ashlyn found she was the last to arrive. She saw the warm approval in Gilford's eyes and felt her cheeks heating.

Dinner was as pleasant as teatime had been, with many stories tossed about and much laughter had. Ashlyn couldn't remember when she'd enjoyed adult company so much. When it came time for the ladies to withdraw and leave the men to their port and cigars, she was surprised when they all rose from the table. Gilford came to her and escorted her from the dining room.

"Aren't you gentlemen staying after for your port and conversation?"

The duke chuckled. "Why? I've spent over two decades in Burke and Gray's company. I'd rather be with three beautiful women anytime."

They adjourned to the drawing room and Gilford urged Lady Crampton to sing and play for them. She readily agreed and Lord Crampton accompanied his wife to the far side of the room, sitting beside her on the bench before the pianoforte even though no music pages were in sight for him to turn. Ashlyn realized the earl merely wished to be near his wife as he slipped an arm about her waist as she began to play.

The music went on for half an hour and when it concluded, she applauded with enthusiasm.

"You play remarkably well, Lady Crampton, but your voice is that of an angel," she praised.

"I do enjoy music. I've taught Harriet and Jane to play. Harriet is more inclined to art but Jane is a serious musician. I think the time will soon come when she surpasses me."

Lord Crampton lifted his wife's hand and kissed her fingers. "Your fingers look quite tired, Charlotte. I think we should give them some rest after all that playing." He turned to the others. "If you'll excuse us?"

From the look in the earl's eyes, Ashlyn didn't think Lady

Crampton's fingers—or anything else—would be getting much rest.

"It was lovely meeting you, Lady Dunwood," Lady Crampton said. "I hope we can see each other soon."

As they left, Lord Weston rose and pulled his wife to her feet. "Gemma and I are also ready to call it a night," he proclaimed. "We were delighted to make your acquaintance, Lady Dunwood."

"Yes," Lady Weston echoed. "I would love for you to come to Westbrook sometime and stay for a few days." She rubbed her belly. "I know the time is coming when I won't get out much and will be eager for company. Please tell me you'll come."

"Perhaps for an afternoon, my lady," Ashlyn said, not wanting to be pinned down to a promise. "I rarely leave my boys."

The countess nodded wisely. "I will hold you to a visit, my lady. Goodnight to you both."

Once they left, Ashlyn started to speak up that it was time for her to go, as well, but the duke went to a table with crystal decanters and asked, "Would you like a sherry? Or a brandy, my lady?"

She shouldn't. She really shouldn't. But the thought of leaving him and driving away, never to have any time alone with him ever again made her reckless.

"A brandy would be lovely, Your Grace."

He poured the amber liquid into two glasses and joined her on the settee. Raising his glass, he said, "To friends—both old and new."

Ashlyn sipped the liquid, which burned a path from her tongue down her throat, pooling in her belly and spreading warmth throughout her.

But the heat that was already present before her first sip was due to the presence of the man beside her.

Gilford drained his tumbler. Hers still had brandy remaining but he lifted it from her fingers and set both aside. He continued to gaze at her intently until she grew so warm, she thought she might faint. The air crackled between them.

And then he brought his fingers to her cheek and stroked it gently.

His touch almost undid her.

Ashlyn sucked in a quick breath before all the air left the room. Both Gilford's hands cupped her face, his palms like fire against her flesh.

"Do you know how beautiful you are?" he asked softly.

She licked her lips nervously. "No. No one ever told me so."

His crooked smile caused her heart to skip a beat.

"Then everyone else is a fool."

He leaned toward her slowly, his hands keeping her in place as if he knew she would flee as a scared rabbit might from the hounds. Ashlyn's heart pounded against her ribs fiercely. She began trembling.

His lips paused just before they touched hers. "Are you afraid?"

"No," she whispered.

But she was. Afraid she would ignite if he kissed her. When he kissed her. Afraid of what she would feel. And how the hurt would never heal once he did. She wasn't the one meant for him. Another woman was. Yet in this moment, Ashlyn behaved totally out of character and threw caution to the wind.

She wanted him to kiss her. Touch her. Make her feel alive. For years, she'd bottled up all emotion within her. Until this man came along.

His lips still hovered just above hers. "I want to kiss you. Will you let me?" he asked.

Her reply was to bring her hands to his shoulders and pull him toward her.

Their lips collided and the sparks she feared did ignite. She wanted to gobble him up but he showed more restraint.

"Easy," he murmured against her mouth and she kept her hands on his shoulders but tried not to clutch him.

Slowly, he brushed his lips against hers, over and over, softly, tenderly. Ashlyn felt herself melting. Relaxing. Wanting. What, she didn't know, except that he knew how to give it to her.

Gradually, he increased the pressure and began kissing her with more ardor. His thumbs caressed her cheeks, his hands still holding her in place. She tightened her hold on his shoulders. The kisses became faster. Harder. Making her heart beat wildly.

And then his tongue brushed against her lips, back and forth across the seam.

She had no idea what he was doing or why he did it but she liked it. It became more insistent and he parted her lips. His tongue entered her mouth, sweeping along her tongue and teeth, bringing a delicious sense of warmth and excitement. Daniel hadn't done anything like this. Not even close.

His kiss grew more passionate, his fingers skimming along her jaw and then throat. One hand curled around the back of her neck as he pulled her to her feet. His other hand pressed against the small of her back, bringing her body against his. He was like a rock—solid, firm, unyielding. He sucked on her tongue, drawing it into his mouth and tentatively, she touched hers against his. A low, satisfied growl escaped him and, for the first time, Ashlyn felt a feminine power rising within her. His fingers splayed across her back, his hand moving up and down along her spine.

The kisses didn't cease. They grew deeper. More insistent. She felt herself growing dizzy. The place between her legs began throbbing fiercely, calling attention to itself. Sensations she'd never experienced trickled and then raced through her limbs.

Ashlyn didn't know when one kiss ended and another began. She breathed in Gilford, smelling and tasting his essence. He broke the kiss and his lips went to her throat, licking where her pulse throbbed. She whimpered and he drew her closer. His teeth grazed along her throat, bringing delightful shivers, then he nipped at her throat. She gasped. Then moaned. Her body melted into his. Her arms went around his neck, pulling him as close as she could. If she could find a way to burrow inside him, she would.

"What's your name?" he murmured against his throat.

She was in a fog and it took a moment to understand what he asked.

"Ashlyn," she managed to say as his tongue ran along her skin.

"Ashlyn," he echoed. "Ashlyn. It suits you."

His mouth found hers again and the kisses started anew. Without warning, he pulled her into his lap and they kissed until she was a mindless, quivering mess.

Finally, he pulled away, his forehead resting against hers.

"Ashlyn," he said roughly, "I think it's time you went home. Before something happens."

Something already had.

She'd gone and fallen head over heels in love with the Duke of Gilford.

Chapter Ten

REID HAD NEVER kissed a woman for as long as he had Lady Dunwood.

No. *Ashlyn.*

He'd never known another woman by that name. He'd never known any woman like her.

He rose from the chair and placed her on her feet. She swayed slightly and he clasped her elbows to support her.

"Let me call for the carriage."

He rang for a servant and a footman appeared almost immediately, Ashlyn's shawl in hand. She took it from him and wrapped it about her tightly, as if it were armor that would protect her from any further onslaughts.

"Have my carriage readied."

"It's already done, Your Grace. Waiting to take Lady Dunwood home. Her case has been packed and taken downstairs."

"Very good."

The footman disappeared and Reid took her arm. He escorted her outside and opened the coach's door, helping her inside—then climbed in after her and swung the door closed.

"What . . . are you doing?"

"Taking you home."

Not wanting to leave you.

"That isn't necessary, Your Grace."

"I brought you here and I'll see you safely home," he said

firmly, brokering no more protests.

"Actually, your driver got me here and is perfectly capable of seeing that I arrive at Dunwood Academy without any problem."

The vehicle started up.

"Too late," he quipped.

They rode to the end of the lane and he said, "Might I hold your hand? I promise I won't kiss you again this evening."

She pondered it a moment and then said, "All right," pulling her arm from beneath the shawl.

Reid tugged on her glove and placed it across his thigh.

"What are you doing now?" she demanded.

"I asked to hold your hand. Not your gloved hand."

Ashlyn pursed her lips. "You sound like one of my boys, quibbling over semantics."

He laced his fingers through hers. "Do you practice that?"

Her brow furrowed. "Practice what?"

"That terrifying headmistress look. I'm a grown man and you practically have me quaking in my boots."

He watched her suppress a smile. Where others would have laughed, she triumphed and kept a straight face. It was another thing he liked about her. Her determination.

And her mouth.

From the start of their kisses, her inexperience was obvious. She must have had one of those priggish husbands who determined a quick peck on the lips sufficed as a kiss before he went about his business. Ashlyn had been a fast learner, though. After her initial surprise, she'd more than matched him. Better than any other woman he'd kissed before. Satisfaction filled him. She would make for a great duchess and companion for him. It might not be the love match that his friends had found but Ashlyn would never be boring—in or out of bed. Since she didn't seem schooled in the art of love, he looked forward to teaching her all the ways he could please her and she could please him.

"I doubt anything terrifies you, Your Grace. You've been a soldier your entire adult life. You've seen things no one should see. I'm a simple woman who merely tries to keep a dozen young boys in line on a daily basis."

His thumb stroked her hand and he heard her breath hitch. "You are far from simple, Ashlyn."

"I'd prefer you call me Lady Dunwood," she said primly.

"And I'd prefer not to," he retorted. "I'm a duke. I do what I wish. What I'd like is for you to call me Reid."

They fell silent and he plotted a way to see her again. Though they were close neighbors, she remained tied to her school all hours of the day so there were no occasions to run into her at social gatherings. Then he hit upon a brilliant scheme, one that she couldn't refuse to participate in.

"I hope you'll attend my ball Saturday next," he began.

Her head whipped around. "What ball? I know of no ball."

"The invitations will be delivered tomorrow."

Her eyebrows arched. "Tomorrow is Sunday."

"Monday, then."

At least his secretary would have all tomorrow to prepare the invitations.

When she didn't speak, he said, "I've been away from home too long. While I've seen some of my neighbors since my return, I thought a ball to acquaint myself with all of my neighbors would be appropriate."

"Since we are already acquainted, Your Grace, I see no need to attend your ball. I've already spent most of this Saturday away from Dunwood Academy. I don't feel it necessary to come but I appreciate the invitation, all the same."

"This is very special ball, Ashlyn," Reid continued. "A country ball."

A crease formed on her lovely brow. "How is that different?" she asked guardedly.

"Have you never been to a country ball?"

"No."

"Well, not only will I invite all of my neighbors, but my tenants will also be welcome. I know many of them from growing up at Gillingham but some are new to me. My father used to hold a harvest ball each autumn once the crops had been gathered. That ball was strictly for our workers. I see this as a mixing of all classes."

"That's very kind of you to think of your tenants. I'm sure they'll enjoy coming to Gillingham and dancing the night away. I still don't see the need for my attendance."

Reid tried to keep a grin off his face as he'd already baited his hook. Now, it was time to reel her in.

"Oh, the ball invitation isn't merely for you. It includes your pupils."

Her eyes widened. "My pupils? I don't understand."

"Well, you have shared with me that part of your curriculum includes teaching your students the social graces. What better way for them to practice their dancing and conversational skills than in a social setting such as a ball? Especially one that is a bit more relaxed than a formal affair."

He let her mull over his words and saw that she tried to come up with an argument against coming.

And couldn't.

"Very well, Your Grace. I will be happy to accept your invitation on behalf of my students. Your country ball would be good practice for them." She paused a moment. "What is the dress for this type of event?"

Reid thought a moment. Since she rarely went out, seemingly only to dinner every now and then, she might not have a ball gown to wear. If he tried to provide one for her, she would refuse.

"It's very relaxed, Ashlyn," he said, loving her name on his tongue. "Your boys can wear their school uniforms. After all, my tenants, though dressed in their best church clothes, don't possess the finery of the upper classes." He let that soak in and then added, "As for you? This lovely gown you wore tonight would be more than appropriate."

He sensed her relax somewhat and congratulated himself on

jumping every hurdle she'd placed in his way.

"Are my tutors also invited? I would hate for them to be left out of the excitement."

"Do you always think of everyone else before yourself?"

She sniffed. "That's what women do, Your Grace."

"Reid," he prompted.

Ignoring him, she added, "They will be pleased to be included."

The carriage slowed and, with great reluctance, he released her hand. He took her glove and she held out her arm. Reid slipped it onto her hand and pulled it up her arm, his fingers grazing the soft flesh. The moment the vehicle stopped, he threw open the door and jumped down. He retrieved her case and placed it on the ground—and then reached for her. He might not be holding her hand any longer but he still itched to touch her.

Ashlyn came forward and his hands spanned her waist, bringing her to the ground. They lingered a moment and then he released her and placed her hand through the crook of his arm. A footman had already carried the small valise to the front door and retreated as they came toward the house.

Reid stopped as they reached the door and said, "Thank you for coming today and meeting my friends."

"They are quite lovely. You're fortunate to have their friendship."

"They're your friends now, Ashlyn."

That seemed to take her aback. "I suppose so."

"Prepare your students well for the ball," he said.

She gave him a haughty look. "They will be the best behaved there," she guaranteed.

He laughed. "I'm sure they will be. Hopefully, they'll have fun."

Taking her gloved hand, Reid lifted but didn't touch his lips to it. Instead, he bowed over it.

"I keep my promises, Ashlyn," he said softly.

With that, he released her hand and winked. He enjoyed

watching her jaw drop at the cheeky gesture and turned away quickly to hide his grin. He climbed back inside the carriage and it rolled away.

Now all he had to do was have his staff issue invitations and organize a ball in less than a week.

Reid couldn't wait to dance the first tune with his future wife in his arms.

ASHLYN ENTERED THE house, swirling with emotions, thankful all was quiet. She crept up the stairs, hoping she'd see no one because she felt on fire. She wouldn't be able to hide her upset.

She reached her bedchamber and closed the door, leaning against it for support.

What had happened tonight?

When she'd left Dunwood Academy hours ago, she'd known exactly who she was and what her life's purpose was. She was Lady Dunwood, headmistress of a small, thriving school for boys, happy to be living a good life filled with purpose. And now? She'd been reduced to a bundle of emotions, her body trembling with need for a man she barely knew.

Gilford's kiss had overwhelmed her at first, making Ashlyn realize Daniel had known only the bare rudiments of kissing. The duke had done things with his lips and tongue that brought out some deep, dark need within her. She'd lost all sense of time and place in his arms. Lost the sense of who she was. It was as if she'd shed her skin and a new Ashlyn had been reborn.

If that was what Gilford's kiss did, what more would happen to her if they went beyond a kiss?

She shuddered and went to undress, removing tonight's trappings and putting on her most comfortable night rail and warm dressing gown over it. Curling up in a chair, her feet tucked under her, Ashlyn contemplated how tonight had changed her.

And what she would do about it.

In truth, there was nothing she could do. The duke had already told her he had a bride in mind. She warred with herself, angry that he'd kissed her when he was planning to wed another woman. That she'd let him—and thoroughly enjoyed it. Ashlyn couldn't believe she was drawn to a man who would betray his future wife in such a manner. Moreover, she couldn't believe with a single kiss she'd become a woman who would participate in something so sordid. Yet her body called out for more from Gilford. She wanted his hands touching her in every intimate place. She wanted to explore his body, as well, in a brazen way she'd never thought of before.

It shocked her that she would even consider beginning an affair with him. That's what it would be between them, if she allowed it. Of course, society turned a blind eye to widows who chose to have an affair. They were deemed experienced. No one would say a thing. At least to her face. Behind her back, though, gossip would run rampant. She couldn't afford her reputation besmirched by a fraction. It was her livelihood and what brought new boys to her school. If she didn't have her academy, she would have nothing. Be nothing. Yet she feared she already was nothing without the Duke of Gilford. The thought of his kisses heated her blood. She knew he, too, had been moved by what had passed between them and meant to pursue her.

Ashlyn considered coupling with him one time. Just to see what it would be like. What she had missed out on by marrying another virgin. Gilford was obviously very experienced in the art of lovemaking. To be in his bed, even once, would be a thrilling experience.

She had to consider the consequences, though. She'd become with child after a single time with Daniel. The same could happen with the duke. Somehow, though, she determined he had the knowledge to prevent that from occurring. If he did, when could they come together? Certainly not at the ball he planned. She believed he'd made up the entire affair on the spot, slowly drawing her in by including her boys. She'd fallen for it, of course.

Just as she'd fallen for him.

Maybe she wasn't in love with the duke. Perhaps it was only lust. Ashlyn giggled at the thought. To think of her and lust going hand-in-hand was preposterous. She was a respectable war widow. Tonight, though, she'd learned underneath that thin veneer of respectability was a woman who felt deeply. Who desired something—someone—out of her reach. Who wanted one night in the bed of the most handsome, desirable man she would ever meet.

Ashlyn came to a decision. If Gilford asked, she would come to his bed for one night only. One night to fulfill her curiosity and reveal her utmost desires and satisfy these strange yearnings within her. A single coupling that would be what she lived on for the rest of her days.

If he asked. She wouldn't pursue him. It must be of his accord.

She climbed into bed and pulled the covers about her.

And prayed he might want her as much as she did him.

Chapter Eleven

Reid went down for a last breakfast with his friends, hoping to convince them to stay on another week. Gray and Charlotte were already seated, while Burke filled plates at the buffet for both him and Gemma.

"Good morning, Reid," they all called as he picked up a plate and loaded it with eggs and ham and four pieces of toast before taking a seat across from Gemma.

"You seem hungry today," she remarked. "Were you up late last night?"

"Lady Dunwood stayed on for a bit after the rest of you went to bed and then I saw her back to Dunwood Academy," he replied, images of Ashlyn burning into his mind. "What did you think of her?"

"I like her a great deal. My invitation for her to come and stay with Burke and me was heartfelt," Gemma said. "I fear she won't take me up on it, though."

"Why not?" Charlotte asked. "I found her delightful company and would have thought to ask her to come see us at Gray Manor if I hadn't been so distracted by this one." She playfully nudged Gray in the ribs with an elbow.

Her husband shrugged. "Can I help it if you're so easily distracted by me?" As he buttered a piece of toast, Gray added, "We all liked her, Reid. Very much."

"Very much," Burke echoed. "Now that we've met her, you

have our approval. Not that you needed it because by the looks you cast her way, you've already decided the matter." Burke paused. "My only question is if the lady in question knows your plans for her."

Reid laughed. "I gave her an indication last night."

Charlotte's eyes lit up. "You spoke to her?"

"Not exactly," he admitted and then grinned. "Unless if lips do the talking, that is. We did plenty of that."

Gemma gave him a wise look. "Kissing is a language all unto itself. I assume it was pleasant?"

Reid laughed. "Would you have wed Burke if his kisses had merely been pleasant?"

Gemma blushed. "No. I needed them to be all-consuming." She glanced to her earl. "And they continue to be."

"Let's just say I believe Lady Dunwood and I will suit quite nicely when the time comes."

"So you kissed her," Gray pressed. "Was that it?"

Reid eyed his friend. "It was more than enough. It was as if the earth moved and the skies thundered and shattered around us."

"Are you in love with her?" Burke asked quietly.

He considered the question. "No. I'm not. Not in the sense of the way you feel about Gemma or Gray feels about Charlotte. However, the physical attraction is there. Ashlyn is intelligent and confident. She will make for a wonderful duchess. I feel we'll have mutual respect between us and that we'll share a sense of family. That's good enough for me."

He watched as both couples exchanged marital glances and then focused on him.

"You four have cornered the market on love. I don't need or want it. It can become messy. I will enjoy having Ashlyn as my duchess. I will give her everything she could possibly dream of. We will be happy."

"At least you are using Christian names," Charlotte said lightly. "That's a start."

Reid didn't tell them that Ashlyn had refused to call him by his given name. He would change that. Sooner rather than later, he hoped.

"I know you were all set to leave this morning," he began. "But I want to try and change your minds."

"We can't stay," Gray said. "Burke and I have already given you all the advice you could ever need about running Gillingham. You were born for this role, Reid."

"I've got plenty to do at home," Burke protested. "You're on your own for now."

"Then promise me you'll return next Saturday for my country ball."

"What ball?" asked Gemma, looking puzzled. "This is the first you've mentioned of it to us."

He suppress a smile. "I only got the idea last night during the carriage ride back to Dunwood Academy."

Charlotte laughed. "You're looking for ways to be around Lady Dunwood. A country ball is a clever idea."

"I told her it was to acquaint myself with everyone in the neighborhood since I'd been gone so long," Reid said. "She refused my invitation, saying we were already acquainted."

Burke roared with laughter. "Oh, I do like her, Reid. Even more now. What I would have given to see you put in your place."

He explained how he'd enticed Ashlyn to come, telling her not only would his tenants be invited but asking her students to come to practice their conversation and dancing in public.

Gray nodded with approval. "You've always been clever, Reid. That was a good move."

"Lady Dunwood is not some chess piece to be moved around," his wife protested.

"I agree, Charlotte. Still, she needed more than a nudge. She told me when I enrolled Arthur and Harry at her school that she was dedicated to running it and had no plans to wed again. It's going to take some finesse to convince her to leave it behind."

"Why does she have to do that?" Charlotte argued as Gemma nodded her head furiously. "Why can't she be Duchess of Gilford and run her academy? You can't strip of her of the thing she loves most. She's devoting her life to those boys."

Reid had thought asking Ashlyn to be his duchess would be enough. Now, though, he saw Charlotte had a point. Ashlyn had created an entire life with purpose. Asking her to walk away from it would be unfair.

"I wouldn't ask her to give it up. Merely the day-to-day running of it. We're close by. She could visit every day if she chose. She could name one of her instructors as headmaster or even bring in another individual to run it."

"That's better," Gemma said. "You aren't going to win her over by taking away the thing she loves most. You may be handsome as sin and wealthier than Midas, Reid, but Lady Dunwood seems a proud, self-sufficient woman to me. She doesn't really need you or your title. She's built a good life for herself." She paused, a smile playing about her lips. "You're going to have to make yourself indispensable to her."

Reid nodded slowly, thinking Ashlyn was already that to him. "Thanks to both of you ladies for your advice. So, tell me—will you come back next Saturday for my ball? Even all of my tenants will attend."

Charlotte smiled warmly at him. "We wouldn't miss it for the world. I, for one, will be interested in seeing you and your servants pull something off so quickly."

He laughed. "I was a colonel for the King's Army, Miss Nott. If there's one thing I know how to do, it's to organize a large campaign on a moment's notice."

ASHLYN DROVE THE cart to Gillbrook after breakfast. She had several errands to run in the village, along with payments to make to various merchants. The day before had been blustery but today was sunny with only a nip of cool in the air. She enjoyed these trips to the local village, which was only five miles from Thornhill, the property she rented for her school. Though she wished she had more time to donate to worthy causes in the area, her time was taken up by running the academy.

She visited the grocer first, giving him a list from Mrs. George for next month's supplies, which would be delivered to the kitchen, though the grocer loaded her cart with staples such as sugar and flour while she was there. She called at the blacksmith's and asked him to come out to Dunwood Academy and take a look at one of the carriage wheels which concerned her.

"If you could do so before Saturday, I'd be grateful," Ashlyn said.

The smithy nodded, lifting a horse's hoof and hammering a shoe onto the animal. "Have you been invited to the duke's country ball, my lady?"

"Yes," she said. "So have my boys and their tutors. I want to make sure everyone arrives safe and sound. Are you going?"

He nodded. "Me and the missus. His Grace came around and passed out invitations himself this morning."

His words caused her to ask, "When was His Grace here?"

"Oh, a good hour or so ago. I'm sure he's done been 'round the entire village. It's been a long while since villagers were invited to Gillingham, the old duke being so sick and all. Don't worry, my lady. I'll come to see your carriage once I finish shoeing this horse. We'll get you and your boys to the ball."

"If I'm not back before you arrive, Mr. Jarrett will help you."

She told the smithy good day and went down her list, marking off each place she stopped, grateful that at each one she'd just seemed to miss the duke. One last stop at the sundry shop and her errands would be complete. Mr. Pippens, the owner of the sundry shop and town mayor, asked her to save a dance for him and she agreed. Ashlyn left the store with a few packages in hand and placed them in the cart's bed. She started to leave and then decided to at least glance at a few things in the local dressmaker's shop, which was next door to the sundry shop. Besides sewing gowns, Mrs. Pippens, the mayor's wife, carried items such as lace and various trimmings and hats and gloves. Ashlyn didn't need anything new but she thought it would be fun to browse.

She approached the shop as two women exited and recognized them as Viscount Martin's daughters, whom she'd met on two separate occasions. While she liked the thoughtful, cheery Lady Edith, her sister puzzled Ashlyn. When they'd been introduced the first time, Lady Eden had been exceedingly quiet and subdued. It was hard to draw a word from her. At the next event, a small dinner hosted by the local clergyman, Lady Eden had been boisterous and giggled throughout the entire meal. She'd seem like almost two different people. Ashlyn didn't envy Lord Martin for having to deal with the mercurial girl.

"Lady Dunwood, good afternoon," Lady Edith said. "It's a pleasant surprise to find you here."

"I came into Gillbrook to pay a few merchants and pick up a few things. Good afternoon, Lady Eden. I hope you are well."

The girl shrugged. Ashlyn thought her rather immature though very pretty.

"I'm getting ready for the Season," Lady Eden said. "Mrs. Pippens had me try on a few gowns."

"And are you also going to London with your sister?" Ashlyn asked Lady Edith.

"I am. Father is hoping this will be the year I find a husband."

"I've already found mine," Lady Eden said slyly.

"Oh, then will you announce your engagement while you're in London?" she asked politely, not really caring one way or the other.

The girl sniffed. "He won't be in London. Papa is making me go. I see no reason why I have to do so when I've got a perfectly good duke here to wed."

Ashlyn felt as if she'd been stabbed. *Gilford was going to wed this creature?* Anger and hurt, mixed with disappointment, filled her.

"Eden, you mustn't say such things," her sister chided.

Ashlyn found her voice and asked, "Oh, is the engagement a secret?"

"Yes." Lady Eden giggled. "From even the duke."

She frowned. "I'm not sure I understand."

Lady Edith shook her head. "My sister seems to have an interest in the new Duke of Gilford. Papa had him to dinner recently and Eden was quite taken with him." She sighed. "I don't think Gilford has any interest in her, though."

Relief swept through Ashlyn. "I see."

"He doesn't," Lady Eden said. "But he will. I'm the prettiest girl in the county. Young and fresh. Not old as you are."

Lady Edith gasped. "Eden! Apologize at once to Lady Dunwood."

"Why should I?" her sister said angrily, her face flushed. "She *is* old. She's already been married and had a child, even if he is dead. She's had her chance. I want mine. I want Gilford. He'll see at the ball that I'm his only choice. My dress is divine. He won't be able to take his eyes off me," she declared.

Ashlyn tried to shrug off the angry words hurled at her and instead pitied Lady Edith for having to put up with her younger sister. She'd heard whispers of the girls' mother being put away for safekeeping and hadn't really understood. Now, she assumed it was because the mother was mad and a danger to herself and others. It seemed Lady Eden had inherited some of that wildness and volatility.

"It's quite all right, Lady Edith," she assured the older sister, who looked mortified at her sister's outburst. "I look forward to seeing you at the ball."

"Don't think he'll look at you," Lady Eden murmured softly, though Ashlyn caught the words and ignored them. She moved to step around the pair when she heard a familiar voice.

"Good afternoon, ladies," said the Duke of Gilford.

CHAPTER TWELVE

REID LEFT THE local inn, where he'd spent longer than he'd planned with the innkeeper, catching up on local gossip. This morning, he'd sent out half a score of footmen and grooms to deliver the ball invitations his secretary and estate manager wrote out all Sunday. Though his butler said they would send to London for flowers and some of the food, there were still items to be ordered in town. Reid thought it would mean something to the village folk if he himself delivered their invitations while he placed those orders. He planned to spend tomorrow the same way, riding across the estate and seeing that every tenant received an invitation to Gillingham by his hand and knew they were expected come Saturday evening.

He emerged from the inn where he'd wanted to stay and have a bite to eat but was afraid if he did he might never escape. It was shortly after one and the day had turned out more pleasant than he'd expected. He'd covered the entire village that morning and would now head home to catch up on his correspondence and look at materials Gray and Burke had both brought regarding new seeds and livestock methods.

Reid took a few steps and then saw directly across the street from him a sight for sore eyes. Ashlyn stood talking with two women. Then he saw who they were and cursed under his breath. He'd wanted to strike Lord Martin and his two daughters from the guest list but his secretary wouldn't hear of it. The man had lectured him a good five minutes on the sensibility of including everyone from the neighborhood. Reid couldn't explain his objections and decided with a ballroom full of people that Lady Eden wouldn't have a chance to catch him in seclusion and bring about a scandal.

The conversation wasn't going well, though, based upon the frantic look on Lady Edith's face and Ashlyn's stiffer than usual posture. Reid crossed the street in a few strides and saw Lady Eden's hate-filled face glaring at Ashlyn.

"Good afternoon, ladies," he said pleasantly.

Ashlyn whirled about, her features tense.

"I thought you were going to wait for me, Lady Dunwood," he said smoothly, taking her hand and slipping it through the crook of his arm and then placing his other hand atop hers.

She caught on immediately. "I didn't mean to keep you waiting, Your Grace. I thought I had time for a last errand at Mrs. Pippens' before we met up."

"Well, we're already here so we might as well go inside." He nodded at the two sisters. "I look forward to seeing you and your father at my ball."

"Thank you for inviting us, Your Grace," Lady Edith said earnestly. "Both Eden and I are looking forward to it."

Lady Eden took a step toward him, her eyes shining brightly. "I look forward to dancing with you, Your Grace."

He clucked his tongue. "As the host—and with my stepmother away visiting her brother—I'm afraid I won't have much time for dancing, my lady. But I'm sure you'll have your choice of partners, thanks to your beauty and grace." Reid glanced to Ashlyn. "Come, my lady," and pulled her toward the dress shop.

They entered and she let out a long breath.

"Saved you, didn't I?" he asked.

"I am grateful for your impeccable timing," she admitted. "Though I'd met the ladies before, this was the first time Lady Eden was quite so . . . well . . . so . . ." Her voice trailed off.

"Spiteful? Vindictive? Rude?"

Ashlyn stifled a smile. "Your assessment is correct."

Mrs. Pippens came toward them and curtseyed. "Your Grace. Lady Dunwood. It's so nice to see you. You've been gone a good while."

The dress shop owner eyed them speculatively and Reid knew by the time he arrived back at Gillingham that she would have spoken with everyone in the village, coupling his name with Ashlyn's.

Perfect.

"It's always a pleasure to see you, as well, Mrs. Pippens. I delivered an invitation to your husband earlier and hope to see you at the ball I'll be hosting come Saturday."

Her eyes shone brightly. "Oh, Your Grace, we will be happy to attend." She glanced to his companion. "Are you going as well, Lady Dunwood?"

"Yes, which is why I came in."

"Are you in need of a new gown?" Mrs. Pippens asked.

"No, I already have something to wear."

"The purple," Reid prompted. "I liked that very much."

Again, he saw Mrs. Pippens file away that bit of information—as well as the blush springing to Ashlyn's cheeks.

"Yes, I will wear it but I thought I might add some lace trimming to the neckline."

He'd thought the neckline quite scrumptious as it was, showing off the upper curves of her breasts. Any lace that covered up her creamy flesh wouldn't do.

"I don't think that's necessary," he said quickly. "The dress is perfect as it is and you will look lovely in it."

"Very well," she murmured. "I'm sorry, Mrs. Pippens, but I won't need anything today after all."

The older woman smiled. "That's quite all right, my lady. I look forward to seeing you on Saturday."

Reid said goodbye and led Ashlyn from the store. He paused once outside and saw the Martin girls were nowhere in sight.

"Thank you again for rescuing me," Ashlyn told him.

"You can thank me by spending a few minutes with me at the inn. I find myself ravenous and thirsty, as well. Delivering invitations works up a powerful thirst."

She laughed and he promised himself he would make her do so each day because he loved the sound so much.

"Come along," he said, heading back to the inn.

They entered and Mr. Carson greeted them. "I see you're back, Your Grace, and this time in good company. Good afternoon, Lady Dunwood."

"Hello, Mr. Carson," she said.

"I'm starving and I'm sure Lady Dunwood is, too. Please bring us two bowls of stew and a loaf of bread. And two large tankards of ale."

"Right away, Your Grace," the innkeeper said.

Reid led her to a table in the corner, greeting a few others along the way. He seated her and then himself.

"I find it interesting you're delivering your own invitations," Ashlyn said. "I would think that would be a task for your servants."

"Oh, I have others out now riding to my various neighbors. I thought the townsfolk would appreciate the personal touch, especially since it's been many years since I saw most of them. I plan to do the same tomorrow and ride to each tenant's cottage so I can personally encourage everyone to attend."

She nodded with approval—and it surprised Reid how badly he wanted it from her.

Mrs. Carson arrived with a tray and set everything on the table for them.

"Anything else you need, just let me know, Your Grace."

"Thank you," he told the innkeeper's wife. "It smells wonderful."

He dug into the savory stew. After a few bites, he said, "This is much better than the camp fare I endured for all those years. And the food at school, as well."

Ashlyn patted her mouth with a napkin. "That's one thing I

insisted upon when I started Dunwood Academy. The food should be fresh. Tasty. Plentiful. I want my students well fed. Mrs. George, my cook, does an excellent job, though I'll admit I never knew how much growing boys ate. It seems they all possess hollow legs which must be filled anew each day."

They spent a pleasant half-hour enjoying their meal. Their conversation assured Reid he'd made a good choice in his decision to make Ashlyn his wife. She was an independent woman, though, and he still hadn't hit upon the best way to approach her regarding their marriage. He wished he could announce their engagement at the upcoming ball and knew that would be impossible. Still, he needed to find ways such as today in order to spend more time with her. Make her comfortable around him. Get her to see that a marriage between them would be beneficial for them both.

She set down her tankard. "Oh, I'm so very full. I hadn't anticipated eating while I was in Gillbrook."

"I'm glad you did and that you shared the meal with me."

Their gazes met and, for a moment, it was just the two of them in the public room. Reid wished he could kiss her. He'd thought of little else for the past two days.

She looked away and picked up her reticule. "I need to be going."

"Of course."

He helped her from her chair and escorted her to the cart she'd driven into the village.

"Thank you again for the meal, Your Grace."

"Reid," he prompted.

She shook her head. "I simply cannot call you that, Your Grace. Your Christian name should be reserved for your family and very close friends. I am neither."

"I think we are friends, Ashlyn. And we could be more," he added.

His words seemed to fluster her and Reid decided he liked a slightly off-balanced Ashlyn. Before she could say anything, he captured her waist and lifted her into the cart.

"I will see you on Saturday. I expect you to dance with me at least twice."

"But you told Lady Eden—"

"Never mind what I told the girl. I have no intentions of dancing with her." He looked into Ashlyn's magnificent amethyst eyes. "I do, however, plan to dance with you. Save the opening dance for me. The supper one, as well."

After a moment's hesitation, she said, "I will."

Reid took her hand and pressed a kiss onto it. "Until then."

ASHLYN BRUSHED HER hair and then wound it into a chignon. She wore the purple dress the Duke of Gilford had admired, still wishing she'd added a bit of lace to it. Once she'd given birth to Gregory, her breasts had remained larger than she liked and she felt this dress displayed too much of them, though most would have thought the gown contained a moderate neckline. Apparently, Gilford was one of those. She should have bought the lace and sewn it onto the gown in spite of him.

She'd done her best during the week to push all thoughts of the handsome duke away every time they popped up. It helped that all of the boys insisted upon extra dancing lessons this week, even forsaking their riding lessons in order to be prepared for tonight's ball. Ashlyn had even drafted Betty and Louise to come dance with the boys, telling Mrs. Clayton that the maids were needed more for their dancing abilities than dusting ones. She believed each boy would be a shining example to Dunwood Academy, both in dance and conversation skills. It helped that this ball wouldn't be as formal as other ones, with people from the village and farmers from Gillingham attending.

Not that she would know what a ball was like. Ashlyn had never been to one herself. Once again, she felt regret in missing her London come-out and all of the activities of that Season. Still, she wouldn't trade a thousand balls for the four years she'd had with her son.

She left her bedchamber and went downstairs. All dozen of her pupils were lined up in their uniforms. They'd all had baths and hummed with energy. Her tutors also showed their excitement. The four men had been startled—and then quite pleased—to have been included in the duke's invitation. Ashlyn had asked them to enjoy themselves while still helping her keep an eye on each boy.

"You look very nice, Lady Dunwood," Harry said. "I'm excited to be going home for a few hours."

"You and Arthur will have to help the other boys, Harry. Make them feel at ease. Show them around a bit."

"We will," he said enthusiastically. "I hope Mrs. Cook has made some of her cakes. Hers are so moist and her frosting is the best."

Mr. Phillips came up. "Lady Dunwood, the ducal carriage has arrived."

Ashlyn had received a note from the duke that stated he would send his carriage for her and some of the boys since the school only had one. Still, it would take a couple of trips to ferry everyone to Gillingham. She debated upon whether she should accompany the first group or remain behind and go with the last and thought Gilford would be displeased if she delayed her departure.

The truth was, she was eager to see him—and that frustrated her. He'd paid special attention to her. He'd kissed her as if there'd be no tomorrow. The awful man had made her fall in love with him without even trying to. Ashlyn should be avoiding him, especially knowing he was ready to take on a duchess. And yet, she was helplessly drawn to him. His strength. His good looks. His wit and charm. She still toyed with the idea of asking him to bed her once. Perhaps she could somehow bring it up tonight.

If she could summon the nerve to do so.

As it was, she already looked forward to dancing with him. Twice. If there was anything Ashlyn loved to do, it was dance. It was her favorite part of the time she spent with her boys, seeing them grow from awkward, gangly children with no sense of rhythm and having two left feet to becoming skilled and smooth in their movements. Tonight, she knew dancing with the Duke of Gilford would be just like something out of a fairy tale. One had only to look at the man and know he could dance.

"Thank you, Mr. Phillips. Boys, gather around," she called and they ceased speaking and formed a circle.

Ashlyn assigned each pupil and tutor to a carriage, with twelve of them going in the first leg and the remaining to join them after a second trip was made.

"Remember, you represent not only Dunwood Academy but yourselves and your families tonight. Be on your best behavior. Be gracious and courteous. Since this is a country ball, there will be a wide range of society in attendance at Gillingham, from noblemen and farmers to shopkeepers and villagers. I expect you to speak with everyone respectfully. You are guests in someone's home tonight, boys. Good manners should always accompany you in your daily lives but they are especially important when you have been invited somewhere. Visitors who display civility and kindness are more likely to be asked back again.

"I also want you to enjoy yourselves. See that you dance often and talk to as many people as you can. And remember when it is time to dine, you are not to gorge yourself with sweets. Place a good variety of foods on your plate and treat sweets as the special treat that they are." She looked out at the eager faces and smiled. "I am already very proud of you and I know the community will be impressed with each and every one of you."

"May we speak to His Grace?" asked Edward. "I'd like to thank him for inviting us tonight."

"There should be a receiving line," she said. "That would be an appropriate time to express your gratitude." She paused. "Is that it? All right, let's depart."

Anticipation filled Ashlyn during the short carriage ride to Gillingham. She alighted and saw other carriages coming up the lane, along with carts from the village. Others walked across the open lawn from their cottages on the grounds. The buzz of conversation and excitement filled the air as she made sure all her pupils and the two tutors that accompanied them got out and joined the line entering the house.

The mass of people went up the stairs and then came to a halt. She spoke to the town doctor and his wife, who were in front of her, all the while making sure her students behaved themselves. As she reached the landing, she heard her name being called from above and spied Lady Weston.

"Come join us," the countess urged.

Ashlyn looked back at her group and Mr. Peterson said, "Go, my lady. Mr. Selleck and I have things in hand and as you can see, the boys are doing well."

"Find me if you need anything," she said and then made her way up the stairs to where Lord and Lady Weston stood.

The countess embraced her. "I'm so happy to see you again. Have you thought any more of coming to see Burke and me?"

"I will try to do so."

"Trying isn't good enough for my Gemma," Lord Weston said. "You must show up, Lady Dunwood. That's all there is to it. Gemma won't rest until you do."

"Perhaps I could visit for a day during the boys' Easter break," she said.

"Wonderful," Lady Weston proclaimed. "I'll tell Charlotte. She'll want to come, as well. We both so enjoyed your company."

"Will Lady Crampton be here tonight?"

"Oh, yes," Lady Weston said. "She and Gray will want to support Reid in this first social event he holds. Those men are like brothers. Even closer than most, I'd daresay."

They moved up the stairs and down the corridor. Ashlyn now saw the Duke of Gilford as he greeted his guests. His formal, black evening wear made him even more handsome than she'd thought possible and her mouth grew dry. She knew she'd only have to say a few words to him but even that seemed overwhelming.

Finally, she reached him. He'd already spoken to Lord and Lady Weston and then turned to her.

"Ashlyn," he said, taking her hands. "I'm so very happy you're here."

"How could I miss the affair everyone has been talking of?" she said lightly.

Gilford squeezed her fingers. "Though tonight's ball is informal with no dance cards to be signed, remember that you've promised me the first dance—and the supper one. We'll dine with my friends."

"I look forward to doing so, Your Grace."

She found Lord and Lady Crampton waiting for them in the ballroom and renewed her acquaintance with the couple and then mingled with others, all the while keeping an eye out for what her students did. They were a bit wide-eyed but looked to be doing well. She noticed Edward speaking with one of the musicians. It didn't surprise her that the boy had gravitated in that direction since he had a fondness and talent for music.

The musicians lifted their instruments and began tuning them. Glancing around, she saw the ballroom was now filled and knew the evening was about to begin.

Suddenly, the Duke of Gilford appeared at her elbow.

"I'm sorry to have rushed you through the line. There were just so many I had to welcome."

"Everyone is pleased you decided to hold this ball," she told him. "And my boys are the most thrilled of all at being included."

He smiled. "Yes, every one of them thanked me as they came through the receiving line. I'm glad you allowed them to attend."

"They've looked forward to it all week. My feet are tired from all of the extra dancing practice we've put in to prepare for tonight."

"Not too tired, I hope, to dance with me."

"Not at all, Your Grace. In fact, I've looked forward to it more than you could know. You see, this is my first ball."

Chapter Thirteen

THE STARTLED LOOK on Gilford's face made Ashlyn wish she hadn't shared something so personal with him.

"How could that be?" He shook his head. "Never mind. It just lets me know there are many things I don't know about you. I'll learn them all in time."

Placing her hand atop his arm, he led her to the center of the ballroom. He clasped one hand and placed the other against the small of her back.

Ashlyn said, "Wait. No one else is out here."

"We'll open the ball. Others will join us after a few bars." The duke nodded to the musicians and they struck up the first tune.

Immediately, he swept her across the floor. Within moments, it was apparent the Duke of Gilford was an accomplished dancer. He moved with confidence and grace and made for a wonderful partner, making her feel as if she were a part of the music.

A part of him.

She beamed at him, caught up in the music and the dance, lost in his warm, chocolate brown eyes. It wasn't until the music stopped and he brought them to a halt that she realized no other couples had joined them. Instant applause broke out and she glanced across the room, seeing nothing but smiling faces.

"Again!" Gilford cried and the musicians began the same song.

This time, other couples flooded the dance floor. The second dance was just as thrilling as the first. Because the floor was so crowded, Gilford pulled her closer. Ashlyn's breasts grazed against the hard wall of his chest. She inhaled the spicy cologne he wore, reminding her of when she sat in his lap and kissed him for what seemed like hours.

The music died away and they retreated from the floor, coming to stand next to the Cramptons and Westons.

"I will see you again for our second dance," he told her.

"But we've already danced twice now, Your Grace. A second time isn't necessary."

His stern look took her aback. "You promised me the supper dance. I'll have it." With that, he bowed.

"What a marvelous couple you make!" Lady Crampton exclaimed. "It was as if you were born to dance with one another."

Ashlyn had thought the same but would never echo the countess' comment. Instead, she looked around for her boys.

"We've already spoken to four of your students," Lord Weston remarked. "All very well-mannered and polite."

"They are so eager to be here tonight," she told them. "We practiced dancing extra hours this week to prepare."

"I would love to dance with some of them," Lady Weston said.

"So would I," agreed Lady Crampton.

"Then come with me," Ashlyn said, leading the two women to a trio of students.

She made the introductions and Drake paired with Lady Crampton, while Edward took Lady Weston to dance. She allowed Arthur to take her to the middle of the floor.

As they danced, she told him, "You must have inherited rhythm and grace from your father, Master Arthur. Your brother, His Grace, also possesses it."

The boy beamed at her compliment. "Thank you, my lady. My brother is the most talented dancer here tonight." He sighed. "I remember how Father loved to dance before he grew too sick to do so."

"I'm sure he's here in spirit tonight."

She was pleased Arthur hadn't corrected her and addressed Gilford as his half-brother. Another piece of the transformation from the incorrigible Arthur Baker to the one before her.

A couple bumped into them and it took the boy a moment to regain his equilibrium. He did, though, and they continued.

"Lady Dunwood, may I thank you?"

"For what, Master Arthur?"

"You've made Harry and I feel welcomed at Dunwood Academy. You've made us feel as though we matter."

"Of course you do," she said fervently.

He shrugged. "We got a little lost in the shuffle while my father was ill. It's nice to be noticed again and feel important once more."

"We're all important in our own way, Master Arthur."

After that, she danced with more of her boys and gave the mayor his promised dance. Several in the crowd made a point to remark to her how well her students represented Dunwood Academy tonight. Each time she heard them praised, it thrilled her.

The only thing that bothered her was catching sight of Lady Eden. The Martin girl had flashed Ashlyn a hateful look. She'd noticed that Lady Eden also turned down every Dunwood male that asked her to dance, be they tutor or student. While the girl's pettiness shouldn't have bothered Ashlyn, it did. She'd told her boys not every woman would accept their invitation to dance. She only hoped her students had proven gracious during the refusal. She doubted Lady Eden had been.

Edward came and asked her to dance and she readily agreed.

"I noticed you sought out Lady Edith early in the evening when she stood alone and asked her to dance."

"Yes, my lady. She's been kind to me when I see her in the village. Before I was your student. No one had partnered with her and I thought I would ask to do so."

Ashlyn smiled. "I'm glad you did. Because of that, others

noticed and she's danced almost every number this evening. It's always important to seek out others who look lonely."

"I wanted to make her feel important. Like you've done for me, my lady. I used to be no one and now I have friends and I have a positive attitude about every day."

"That's a great life lesson to learn, Master Edward."

When the music ended, Edward asked her if she'd like some punch.

"That sounds marvelous. Thank you."

She received the punch and then spent time on the sidelines, talking with some of Gilford's tenants. They seemed to already think a great deal of the duke, which made her like him even more. He had a common touch that drew others in.

If only she hadn't fallen in love with him. She knew no good would ever come of it.

REID SPLIT HIS time between being a good host and mingling among his guests and dancing with one every now and then. No matter what he did, though, he always kept track of where Ashlyn was and who spoke with her. She seemed comfortable conversing with everyone and danced with a variety of people. He contrived this affair tonight to spend time with her but now saw it was good that she also spent time with all of his neighbors. She would soon be his duchess and he liked how she got along with everyone, no matter their age or class.

The only thing which troubled him was seeing how Eden Martin had glared at Ashlyn. He decided it wouldn't hurt to ask the girl and her sister to dance. The large crowd ensured nothing wrong could occur and it would keep the chit from staring at Ashlyn.

He made his way over to the sisters, who stood chatting with Viscount Ransom, a former schoolmate of his from years ago.

"Good evening, ladies. Ransom. I was hoping to dance with the both of you." Reid looked to Lady Edith first.

"I'm afraid Lady Edith is taken for the next dance," the viscount said possessively.

Reid smiled at the older Martin daughter. Ransom would be a perfect match for her. If tonight's ball only resulted in the pair noticing one another, then the effort had been worth it.

"Perhaps later, Lady Edith."

She smiled demurely. "Certainly, Your Grace."

The couple strolled off, leaving him with the younger Martin girl.

"Would you care to dance the next tune with me, Lady Eden?"

Her eyes glittered. "Oh, yes, Your Grace," she said breathlessly.

He offered his arm. "Shall we?"

They moved to the floor and he decided no conversation was necessary. He was merely fulfilling an obligation by dancing with the chit, one he hoped never to repeat.

"Do you think I'm pretty?" she asked suddenly.

If Reid said yes, it would encourage her. If he said no, she might cause a scene and ruin everything.

"I think there's more than outward looks, my lady. It's inside one's heart which is more important."

A pout settled over her face. "You told me before I was pretty. When I was ten. Papa brought us to a garden party the duke gave to see you off to war. You gave me a biscuit and told me I was pretty and that I would break many hearts one day."

Though Reid barely remembered that long ago day, he thought it sounded exactly like something he would say.

"I'm sure you will, my lady. You're off to your London Season after Easter. You will attend parties and routs. Balls and teas. Ride in Hyde Park. Dozens of young, eligible gentlemen will visit you, bringing bouquets. I'm sure you'll find one of them is meant for you."

"I don't care to go to London. Not since you've come back home."

He better nip this in the bud now.

"While you are attractive, Lady Eden, you are very young. And I am old. Thirty. Soon to be thirty-one. When I decide to wed, I will want a more mature woman, one closer to my age."

She sniffed. "Like Lady Dunwood, I suppose."

Not wanting to tip his hand to this girl, he said, "Lady Dunwood is of an appropriate age. So are several others in the neighborhood. Focus on what's ahead of you, Lady Eden. A wonderful Season with many opportunities to meet gentlemen. Who knows? You might even fall in love with one of your many suitors."

"I'm in love with you," she said stubbornly. "I have been for years. We were meant to be together. I want you as my husband."

"No. You aren't in love with me." His firm tone offered no argument. "I paid a brief bit of attention to you many years ago. Because of it, you've idealized me. You don't know who I am, my lady." Reid paused. "You don't want to know the darkness inside of me."

Her mouth trembled and she looked a bit fearful, which he didn't mind in the least. He stopped dancing and led her from the floor, despite the fact that the song hadn't ended yet.

Bowing, he said, "Thank you for the dance," and strode away.

He found Burke and paused next to him.

"Trouble with the lady?" his friend asked.

"She's all of eighteen and claims to be in love with me."

His friend chuckled. "She certainly doesn't know you then. We all do and I guarantee none of us would ever fall in love with you."

Gray joined them. "What went wrong with Eden Martin?"

Reid blew out a breath. "Is everyone here watching my every move?"

Gray shrugged. "It gives me something to do. With all of

Lady Dunwood's students and tutors here, there are men in surplus. I haven't danced as much as usual. Besides, you know I enjoy observing others. I gather the girl's in love with you."

"How did you know?"

"Because she's young and looked smitten as you danced together. I wouldn't do so again, Reid," Gray warned. "I've seen her toss some angry looks Lady Dunwood's way."

"No sense in borrowing trouble," Burke added.

"I didn't even want to invite her," he confided and explained how Eden had wanted to trap him in marriage.

"She's dangerous. You know madness runs in the family," Burke said.

"I do. And I think she's been touched by it. She's a bit irrational at times."

Gray clasped Reid's shoulder. "It's almost the supper dance. Let's go find our ladies and enjoy."

Both Gray and Burke strode off in search of their wives. Reid had lost track of Ashlyn and had to focus in order to find her. When he did, he made straight for her.

"Lady Dunwood, I've come to claim the supper dance."

"Well, I'm good and famished. I thought I had danced overmuch this week with my boys. I'm certainly in need of sustenance soon."

Reid smiled. "I like a woman with an appetite. For many things," he added cryptically and escorted her onto the dance floor.

The lead musician announced it was the supper dance and they would be taking a respite afterward. Quickly, the floor filled, everyone eager to dance before they went into the prepared buffet room.

He curled his fingers around Ashlyn's. "I hope you're enjoying your first ball," he said as the music began.

Her face glowed. "It's been even better than I'd anticipated. I believe I will forever be partial to a country ball versus a more formal one in London, though I doubt I'll ever attend one there."

As they moved in time to the music, he asked, "How is it that you've never been to a ball? So many occur during the Season."

She bit her lip in hesitation and he saw she worried how much to share with him.

"Tell me," he said softly. "Trust me."

Her gaze met his for a long moment. Finally, she said, "I was about to have my come-out when I met my husband at an assembly shortly before Papa and I left for London. I was frequenting them, trying out my dancing skills. We . . . wed rather quickly and then his regiment was called away."

"Leaving you alone. With child."

"Yes," she whispered.

"I'm sure that was a difficult time for you. You must have cared a great deal for him if you wed so soon after meeting."

She remained silent and Reid wondered what he was missing.

"It's in the past," she said. "And I was fortunate enough to have Gregory. He was the light of my life for the four years he walked the earth."

"Where did you live?" He needed to know what she wasn't saying and hoped by asking her other questions he'd be able to fill in the missing pieces.

"With Daniel's family." Her eyes widened and then she cast them downward. "They spent most of the year in London so Gregory and I enjoyed their country estate."

Reid had a better idea now of her past. Whispered promises of love between heated kisses. A rushed marriage. The regiment being called away soon after. Ashlyn left in England with strangers, then abandoned on an estate where she had no one except her young son. Yet she'd turned out to be a strong, resilient woman, one he was growing to care about a great deal.

"I'm sure you loved your husband and am sorry he was lost in the war. Many good men were."

Ashlyn looked at him bleakly. "I was forced to wed Daniel. I never loved him." Tears brimmed in her eyes. "I barely knew him."

CHAPTER FOURTEEN

Ashlyn immediately regretted her confession regarding her marriage. She noticed Gilford maintained his composure with her admission. Then she realized the music had stopped and they were the only pair left in the ballroom. Embarrassment filled her at such carelessness.

He released his hold on her. "Come. Let's go into supper."

"I don't know if I can," she admitted.

The duke gazed at her intently. "I believe you can do anything you put your mind to, Ashlyn. Anything. As my guest—a hungry one at that—I am obligated to feed you. Mrs. Cook has been preparing a feast for days. You must taste her fare."

He took her arm and guided her from the ballroom.

"Your cook is named Mrs. Cook?"

Gilford chuckled. "Yes. She's married to Cook, my head gardener."

She let him take her to the rooms where tables were stacked with food. Her mouth salivated with the sight of it. The lines were long and Gilford took her to where Lady Crampton and Lady Weston sat.

"There you are," Lady Weston said. "We wondered what happened to you."

Ashlyn felt her face grow flush with color.

"We merely avoided the crowd," Gilford said lightly. He seated her and then said, "Do you trust me to bring back a little of everything for you?"

"Of course."

He bowed and left to join his friends, leaving the three ladies to talk.

"Gemma tells me you've promised to come visit her over the school's Easter break," Lady Crampton said. "Please let me also know the days. I would enjoy coming, as well."

"I'll do so, my lady."

She shook her head. "You simply must call me Charlotte. I don't stand much on ceremony."

"And I'm Gemma. We're friends and should address each other as such."

It moved her that these two women had taken to her so quickly. "Then call me Ashlyn."

"Oh, what a lovely name," Charlotte said. "I've never heard another woman with that name before."

"My mother named me. She died when I was young so I never learned why she chose it. Papa didn't know."

Charlotte eyed her with sympathy. "I lost my mother when I was about two."

"I also lost my mother at a very young age," Gemma added. "It seems that is something that will bond us."

They continued chatting until the men arrived. Ashlyn eyed the plates Gilford returned with.

"I don't think I'll be able to eat a third of that," she proclaimed.

He grinned. "I'm like one of your boys. Don't worry. Whatever you can't eat, I'll finish."

They spent a merry hour in conversation. The two earls were witty and charming. She could see why their wives loved them so.

Lord Weston said, "Reid tells us this is your first ball to attend, Lady Dunwood. What has been your favorite part so far?"

"It's hard to say." She thought of how much she'd enjoyed being in Gilford's arms and knew she couldn't admit that aloud.

"The dancing has been divine. The conversation stimulating. My boys have performed beautifully."

"They have," Gemma agreed. "I've danced with six of them and hope I can work in the other half-dozen."

Her husband lifted her hand and kissed it. "Don't forget me."

She smiled. "I never could, my love." Then looking back to Ashlyn, Gemma said, "My favorite part of tonight was watching you and Reid open the ball. You danced as if you'd done so together all your lives. Everyone was enthralled. It was quite romantic."

Ashlyn's cheeks heated and she glanced down and retrieved her cup. She sipped from it.

Gilford said, "Lady Dunwood was meant to dance. No wonder her students do so well. She is the perfect instructor."

Under the table, he captured her hand and squeezed before releasing it.

"Why have you never attended a ball before?" Lord Crampton asked.

This time, she was better prepared and said, "I married rather young. Before I made my come-out. My husband went to war shortly after and I didn't feel right gallivanting about London, dancing until the wee hours of the morning, while he suffered so."

"That is very noble of you," Lord Crampton said. "War is a terrible thing. I hope it ends soon with Bonaparte's defeat."

"Ashlyn has confirmed she will visit us at Westbrook," Gemma said. "She'll look at her schedule for the dates."

Lord Weston said, "So it's Ashlyn now? Then you must call me Burke, especially if you're coming to see us next month."

"And I better be Gray to you then," Lord Crampton added. "I'm actually Danforth Grayson but I was called Gray from the cradle."

It was one thing to address the women by their Christian names but another entirely different matter to call the men so. If she agreed to use Burke and Gray's first names, she would have no excuse to keep calling the duke Gilford.

"I'm glad you brought this up," the duke said, pouncing on the issue. "I've insisted Ashlyn call me Reid and she refuses to."

"Why not?" Charlotte asked, clearly confused.

"First, Gilford is a duke. There is a certain level of respect that must come when one addresses a person of His Grace's rank." Even to her own ears, Ashlyn sounded like the headmistress she was, giving the group a lecture. "Furthermore, His Grace has placed his brothers in my care. That requires a certain degree of formality on my part, not familiarity."

"Hogwash," the duke said. "When we are around others and the situation warrants it, I have no problem being His Grace. Any other time, I expect you to call me Reid. I won't tolerate any more nonsense. The matter is settled."

His authority cemented his opinion. Ashlyn felt her argument wither and then crumble.

"On a lighter note," he added, "my half-brothers are behaving admirably."

"I wish you would merely call them your brothers," she said. "I've never seen the need to distinguish siblings simply because one has a different mother or father than another. Besides, Arthur has referred to you as his brother just tonight."

"Truly?" He smiled and told the others, "I've called Ashlyn a miracle worker. Who would have thought she could take two hellions and turn them into young gentlemen in a few short weeks?"

They chatted for a few minutes and then she noticed others making their way back to the ballroom.

"Would you care to stroll a bit?" the duke asked.

Ashlyn didn't trust herself to be alone with him now. She was feeling vulnerable, especially after what she'd told him about her marriage to Daniel.

"No, I believe I will visit the retiring room."

"We'll join you," Charlotte said and the three made their way there.

Once they returned to the ballroom, she danced with several others—and noted that Reid danced with no one.

Reid. She liked the name. His name. Whether she'd be brave enough to use it or not was another matter. Of course, she'd been considering asking him to bed her. She supposed it would be wise if that ever did occur to call him Reid instead of Your Grace if they found themselves beneath the covers.

The dancing only lasted for an hour after supper ended and she supposed country balls ended sooner than those in town. She'd heard most would return to their homes tonight but a few, such as Charlotte and Gray, would stay overnight since they had a longer way to travel.

The last song ended and she began rounding up her students. William and Jeremy asked if they could see her out. She allowed each boy to take one of her arms and guide her down the staircase. They only had another six steps to go when she felt someone step on the back of her gown. Since her foot was already in mid-air, she quickly released her hold on the two boys, not wanting them to fall. Instead, she was the one who tumbled and hit the marble floor, crying out as she landed wrong on her ankle.

Both boys scrambled to her side, along with Lord Martin.

"I'm terribly sorry, Lady Dunwood. I must have stepped on the hem of your gown. How very clumsy of me. I sincerely apologize."

Over the viscount's shoulder, she saw Lady Eden smirking.

And knew exactly who'd caused her fall.

Suddenly, Reid arrived and scooped her up in his strong arms. "Summon the doctor, Martin. He should still be outside."

"Of course, Your Grace." The viscount hurried away.

Reid gazed at her in concern. "What's hurt?"

"My left ankle."

The duke looked at the two boys who stood nearby. "Your headmistress will need to remain overnight at Gillingham. Perhaps longer. Tell your tutors so they'll be aware and watch out for you."

With that, he carried her up the stairs in his arms, as if she weighed next to nothing. He took her to a bedchamber and set her down gently before turning her gown up a few inches. Already, her ankle had begun to swell. Reid eased off her slipper and then reached up her leg and rolled her stocking down before carefully removing it. The unexpected, sensual brush of his fingers in a place where no man had touched her before caused a frisson of desire to ripple through her.

Their gazes met, the air charged between them.

Ashlyn wondered if he would kiss her.

REID WANTED NOTHING more than to kiss Ashlyn but knew the doctor would step foot into the chamber at any moment. He tamped down his desire and glanced back at her ankle. The uninjured right one was slender and trim. The left sitting next to it was already swollen and discolored.

He'd been at the top of the stairs and had seen Eden Martin lunge forward. He hadn't understood what she did until he saw Ashlyn stumble and fall. Reid wondered if she knew—or suspected—what had truly happened.

"Do you know why you fell?" he asked as he perched on the bed next to her.

She looked away. "Lord Martin apologized to me for stepping on my gown and throwing me off-balance." She paused, licking her lips nervously, and then added, "But I think his daughter did it. On purpose."

"She did. From where I stood, I saw exactly what occurred."

Ashlyn frowned. "Why would she do something like that? I barely know her."

"She's jealous of you," he said. "I witnessed her giving you ugly looks all evening long."

Puzzlement filled her face. "What on earth would she have to be jealous of regarding me?"

"Lady Eden informed me this evening that she's in love with me and wishes for us to wed."

"What?" she cried.

Reid shook his head. "Surely you know I would never wish to wed an immature girl straight from the schoolroom." He sighed. "She knows you and I are friends. She sees you as a threat to getting what she wants. Me."

"That's absurd."

He shrugged. "Absurd or not, she set out to hurt you—and did. I will see to her."

"What will you—"

"Where is my patient?" a voice boomed.

Reid turned and saw the doctor enter the room, closely followed by Viscount Martin, a worried look on his face.

He stood. "Lady Dunwood's ankle is swollen from her fall."

The physician clucked his tongue as he came toward the bed. "Here. Let me see. We'll hope it's a sprain instead of a break."

Lord Martin said, "I hope it's not serious, my lady. Again, I regret the incident. My deepest apologies."

Reid gave the viscount his stoniest look. "Come with me."

He swept past the man and then waited at the door, ushering Martin out and then closing the door.

"Why did you take the blame for Lady Dunwood's fall when it was your daughter that caused it?" he demanded.

Martin's jaw dropped. Quickly, he recovered and said, "No, it was I who stepped—"

"It was not," Reid interrupted. "I saw what happened. Lady Eden acted deliberately. With malice."

The viscount shook his head. "She acts before she thinks sometimes, Your Grace. She's a bit immature."

"Lady Dunwood could have been injured far worse. She might have broken a bone. Hit her head. Don't excuse what your daughter did by calling her impulsive, Martin. She acted in a reprehensible manner. Earlier this evening, she told me she was in love with me and demanded we wed. I told her that would never happen. Lady Eden tried to hurt Lady Dunwood because she is jealous of her."

Martin paled.

"It's not the first time I've witnessed her act irrationally. When I left your home after dinner recently, she threatened to go to you and pretend I'd somehow compromised her in order for you to force a marriage between us." Reid paused. "It's time you did something about her, Martin. As you did your wife."

Anguish filled the viscount's face. "Eden is a good girl, Your Grace. She just has a few fanciful notions. I can rid her of those. I understand why you wouldn't want to wed the girl."

"It's more than that. She needs help beyond what you can give her."

The viscount's shoulders sagged in defeat. "You want me to put her away as I did her mother."

Reid knew how difficult it must be for the man and said, "I think you need to have her examined by professionals who might better understand her condition. Take their advice. If not, you're going to be ostracized by Polite Society. I can no longer have Lady Eden in my home. Others will feel the same. You don't want that to affect Lady Edith's chances at happiness. I saw her with Viscount Ransom earlier this evening. The two make a lovely pair. I'll encourage him regarding his interest in Lady Edith."

He'd been at school with Ransom, who was half a dozen years younger, and had saved him from a ring of vicious bullies. Ransom had idolized Reid after that. A word in his ear and the viscount would earnestly pursue Edith Martin.

"All right," Martin said dejectedly.

"Are your daughters still here?"

"Yes. I sent them to the carriage while I fetched the doctor."

"Then I will speak to them now."

Reid accompanied the viscount outside. His and the doctor's

carriage were the only ones remaining by this time. Reid opened the door and climbed inside, shutting it behind him. Lady Edith appeared shocked. Lady Eden looked like a cat who'd licked all the cream from an unattended pitcher.

Turning his attention to the older daughter, he said, "I hope you enjoyed the ball tonight, my lady. I noticed Viscount Ransom paid particular interest in you. We were at school together and I think very highly of him. You couldn't do better than Ransom."

She blushed. "He's very kind."

"I hope you will give him every consideration."

Then he wheeled to face Lady Eden. "What you did to Lady Dunwood tonight was shameful. Your actions were deplorable. You need to take ownership of what you did and pen an apology to Lady Dunwood the moment you reach home. Have the note delivered here since she is injured and will need to remain a few days in order to recover."

The girl shook her head furiously. "I won't. I did nothing wrong. It was my father who caused her to stumble."

His gaze locked on hers as he evenly said, "I saw what unfolded, my lady. You aren't blameless in the matter. You caused the fall of one of my guests. Because of your wretched behavior, you will no longer be invited to Gillingham."

"But we're going to be—"

"We will never wed. Never," he said emphatically. "You must accept that."

Her eyes grew wild. "No! You think I'm pretty. You're going to marry me, Your Grace. You'll see."

He knew any further discussion would be hopeless. He'd never convince her.

Opening the door, he climbed out without a goodbye and said to Lord Martin, "Bring in help for your daughter—or I will see that it is done."

Lord Martin nodded brusquely and entered the carriage. A footman closed it.

Reid watched the vehicle leave and then strode back to the

house. Though he would never have wished harm to come to Ashlyn, the fact remained that she had been hurt—and her injury would keep her at Gillingham for the foreseeable future.

He intended to press his suit with her and hope for the best. Especially now that he knew how unhappy she'd been in her marriage.

Chapter Fifteen

Ashlyn watched as Mrs. Paul, the housekeeper at Gillingham, set down a breakfast tray. The woman had helped Ashlyn out of her gown and corset last night and she'd slept in her chemise. Fortunately, the bedclothes had been ample and she hadn't taken a chill. The housekeeper had also seen Ashlyn had a cold compress for the swelling and brought extra pillows to keep her injured ankle elevated.

"Thank you, Mrs. Paul."

"A footman will bring up your trunk soon, my lady."

She frowned. "What trunk? I don't understand."

"His Grace had me go early this morning to Dunwood Academy. Your Mrs. Clayton helped me pack a few things for you. Once you've eaten, I'll have hot water sent up and help you to dress for the day. I know you're supposed to rest but you may have visitors drop by to see how you are."

Ashlyn appreciated Reid's thoughtfulness. She hadn't even had time to worry about clothing. Her thoughts had been focused on missing time with her boys. "I would appreciate your help. By any chance, did you happen to bring my dressing gown? I'm a bit chilled."

A footman appeared, a small trunk on his shoulder, and Mrs. Paul had him place it in the corner. She opened it and withdrew the dressing gown, bringing it to Ashlyn and helping her shrug into it. As Ashlyn ate her breakfast, Mrs. Paul unpacked. It alarmed her when she saw so many gowns come from the trunk.

"How long did you and Mrs. Clayton think I was staying at Gillingham?" she asked carefully.

"His Grace told us to pack enough for a week. He didn't know how long the doctor wants you off your feet and wanted to make sure you had all you needed with the one trip."

The doctor had told her last night to stay off her feet today and tomorrow. He would return sometime Monday afternoon to see how she fared. Ashlyn didn't mind missing Sunday at Dunwood Academy but, tomorrow, classes would resume and she hated being away from her pupils for even a single day.

"I doubt I'll be here beyond tomorrow, Mrs. Paul."

The housekeeper closed the empty trunk. "I'll see to your hot water now, my lady."

As she left, Gray and Charlotte peeked inside and Ashlyn waved them in.

Charlotte came and took her hands. "How are you, Ashlyn? Is there any pain?"

"It throbbed a good deal last night but the doctor gave me a sleeping powder and I fell asleep soon after he left." She glanced down at the ankle perched on a pillow. "He said to keep it elevated and stay off it two days. He'll be back tomorrow to check on me. I'm certain I can go home then."

"Gray and I were about to leave but if you'd like, I'll stay and keep you company."

Her husband cleared his throat. "I'm sure Ashlyn will have all the company she needs, Charlotte."

A look passed between the couple, one Ashlyn wasn't privy to.

"You're right, Gray. We should get home to the children. You do still plan to come to Gemma's, though?" Charlotte asked hopefully.

"I see no reason not to do so. The boys will be on holiday for two weeks at Easter. I can easily slip away to Westbrook for a day or two next month."

"Write to me when you've decided the dates." Charlotte kissed her cheek. "I hope all goes well while you're at Gillingham."

"Goodbye, Ashlyn," Gray said. "I wish you a speedy recovery."

Mrs. Paul returned with the hot water and helped Ashlyn ready herself for the day.

"Thank you for all of your help, Mrs. Paul. I know you have much to attend to now that the ball is over and the overnight guests are departing."

"I'll be back to check on you, my lady," the housekeeper promised. "Would you like the door open or closed?"

"Open, please."

Ashlyn didn't remember the last time she wasn't doing something. She always had an endless list of tasks to accomplish at Dunwood Academy that kept her busy. Between running a school and household, she had little free time. She closed her eyes and savored the peace and quiet, hoping she wouldn't grow bored over the next two days.

A knock sounded at the open door. She opened her eyes and saw Reid standing there, wearing a coat of hunter green and fawn breeches, looking impossibly handsome, although the man could be dressed in rags and she would still find him attractive.

"May I come in?"

"Of course."

Her heart pounded more quickly as it did every time he came near. He paused at her bedside and glanced at her ankle and then asked, "How are you feeling today?"

"Much better. The throbbing has subsided to a dull ache. It's still a bit tender. I must thank you for sending for my clothes."

"It was the least I could do. I also included a letter that informed your housekeeper of what the doctor said and asked that she share it with your staff."

"I should return tomorrow, I would think, or the day after at the latest."

"Don't rush things, Ashlyn," he said. "The first week after an injury such as this you'll need to protect your ankle to avoid further damage. You're welcome to stay at Gillingham as long as necessary."

"I don't want to impose."

He gave her a crooked smile. "You aren't. In fact, I'll enjoy the company."

"I don't expect you to entertain me," she protested. "I know how busy you must be, running such a large property."

Reid took her hand and butterflies exploded inside her belly. "I have others who help me. Besides, I would rather be with you."

Warmth spread through her as he continued to gaze at her. She was tired of fighting her attraction to him. Being at Gillingham might afford her the one chance she sought to couple with him. She tried to think of a way to ask him to do so without seeming brazen but her thoughts became muddled the more he looked upon her.

Finally, he said, "I know you're to rest but no one says it has to be in a bed. I'm afraid you'll become bored easily with all that you normally do. If you'd like, you can lie on a settee downstairs. I can bring you books. You could write letters. Whatever you wish."

What she wished is for him to kiss her.

Instead, she said, "That would be lovely."

Reid leaned over and scooped her from the bed. Her arms went around his neck and, for a moment, her cheek grazed his freshly-shaved one. How she longed to nuzzle it.

He carried her downstairs. "The library or the drawing room?"

"Either will suit me."

"The drawing room gets more sun in the morning. We'll go there."

He laid her upon a settee and retrieved pillows, slipping them under her ankle.

"The doctor said to keep it elevated and bandaged. Your wrapping seems to have come a bit loose. May I have your permission to fix it?" he asked.

Ashlyn nodded and he unwound the cloth. She saw the dark bruise and shuddered, thinking she was lucky to have only a sprained ankle. It could have been much worse.

He touched it gingerly. "It looks bad."

"It's a little sensitive. I'm just grateful it's not broken. I can't imagine being laid up for weeks."

As he began rewrapping it, she asked, "Did you speak with Lady Eden?"

He didn't answer, concentrating on what he was doing. Once he finished and propped her foot up, he said, "I did." He withdrew a folded sheet from inside his coat. "This came for you from her."

She took it reluctantly and opened it, reading the contents. She looked up. "It's an apology. She admits she caused the fall and says she is sorry for the inconvenience she caused me. I'm stunned. You called me a miracle worker but you are the one who seems to have done the impossible."

"May I?"

He held his hand out and she passed the note to him. She watched him read it, noticing the flicker of displeasure that crossed his face.

"I'm not happy with the wording," he said. "Being sorry for an inconvenience isn't good enough. She should say she was sorry for causing you harm." He folded the page again and set it on a nearby table.

"It's fine, Reid," she told him. "She's taking responsibility. That's all that matters."

He grinned. "I like that you're finally calling me Reid."

Ashlyn shrugged. "What can I say? You're a very persuasive man."

"Do you play chess?"

"I haven't for a long time but I used to play every night with

Papa. Why?"

"Let's play now."

He brought over a small table and placed it beside her before retrieving a chess set. He dragged a chair close in order to be opposite her.

"Don't think I'll let you win simply because you're a woman. And out of practice," he warned.

"Is that a challenge?" she retorted.

His eyes gleamed. "I do believe it is."

They played for an hour, each studying the board carefully before making a move. In the end, Reid won.

"How long has it been since you played?" he asked.

"Eight years. Maybe nine."

"I barely claimed victory. I think if we played again, you would beat me."

"Perhaps we can have a rematch tomorrow before I return to Dunwood Academy."

"If you return. We must see what the doctor says. I would enjoy another game with you, Ashlyn. I believe we are well matched."

His voice had dropped and a shiver along her spine made her tingle.

"Would you care to read?"

"Yes. Bring me anything. I have little time to read for pleasure."

He retreated to the shelves and she admired how he filled out his finely-tailored clothes.

And wondered what he looked like underneath them.

She shook her head. These insane notions came to her at the most inappropriate times, surprising her to no end.

He returned with two books in hand. "You have a choice. A novel or a Shakespeare play."

"Leave them both. I may try one and switch to the other."

He returned to the shelves and selected a volume for himself, coming back and taking a nearby seat.

"Are you going to read?" she asked.

"I'm going to try. I won't make any promises."

Ashlyn thought that an odd thing to say. She opened the novel and began reading but, after a few pages, glanced up and saw Reid staring at her.

"What?"

"Nothing," he said, going back to his book.

Several times after that, she felt his eyes upon her but refused to stop and engage him in conversation.

He had luncheon brought in to them and it was an intimate affair with only the two of them present. Afterward, she grew sleepy.

"You look ready to drop off at any moment," he told her. "Let me return you to your room."

He lifted her from the settee and her arms went around him again. This time, she placed her cheek against his chest and could feel his beating heart.

She napped for a few hours and then lay awake, idle thoughts drifting like clouds through her mind. Mrs. Paul checked on her twice and then Reid himself brought a large tray to the bedchamber.

"I knew you couldn't come to dinner so I brought dinner—and me—to you."

A footman rolled in a cart, which included more food, along with wine and two glasses. Once the servant left, Reid poured each of them a glass and then opened the covered dishes.

"Mrs. Cook is a marvelous cook," she exclaimed when the meal ended. "The food at the ball was magnificent and this dinner is just as good if not better."

He began covering dishes again and lifted a tray. Disappointment filled her, knowing he was already leaving, which was ridiculous. He wasn't a nursemaid. He was a duke. Reid had better things to do than sit with an invalid.

She thought it odd that he didn't tell her goodnight as he opened the door. Then he set the tray outside the door and returned for the cart, rolling it from the room and then closing the door. Her pulse pounded wildly as he walked back toward her. He knelt beside the bed, his large hands taking hers.

"If I don't kiss you, Ashlyn, I may go mad."

Knowing it was now or never, she replied, "I want more than your kiss, Reid. I want you."

CHAPTER SIXTEEN

REID STILLED AT Ashlyn's bold declaration.

She wanted him . . .

A slow smile spread across his face as he gazed at her. Her lips trembled and he saw that if he didn't act quickly, regret at what she'd spoken might set in.

He closed the distance between them and sat next to her on the bed. His hands cupped her face.

"You are so very beautiful, Ashlyn," he said softly. "The most beautiful woman I know. And a good part of that is the inner beauty that glows from within."

His mouth moved to hers and touched it gently, pressing the softest of kisses upon it. He couldn't believe how fortunate he was for this magnificent woman to have come into his life. Coming home from war and finding he was the new Duke of Gilford changed many things for him. Seeing how happy Gray and Burke were in their marriages had brought about the desire to find a wife himself.

And now the most desirable woman he'd ever met wanted him.

He increased the pressure of the kiss, tamping down the urge to gobble her up. Then he eased his lips away, sliding them along her cheek and down to her jaw. He nibbled his way along it and then returned to her delectable mouth. His tongue slowly outlined the shape of it and her palms moved to his chest. She opened for him and he slipped his tongue into the honeyed depths.

They kissed for endless minutes. He didn't rush for he knew they would have all night.

Until they didn't.

A knock sounded at the door and Reid broke the kiss, springing off the bed and standing tall, his hands behind his back as he called out, "Come."

The ever efficient Mrs. Paul bustled in. If she were surprised to seeing him standing alone in a lady's bedchamber, she didn't show it. Ashlyn, however, looked dazed and blinked several times, trying to regain her composure.

"I've just come to help Lady Dunwood undress," she said, bringing all kinds of wonderful images to Reid's mind. He wanted to usher his housekeeper out and perform the job himself.

Instead, he praised her. "You're such a good help, Mrs. Paul. I find that I, too, am tired and will retire for the evening." Looking to Ashlyn, he said, "I'm glad you are feeling much better. I'm sure Mrs. Paul can see to all your needs and that you won't require any more help the rest of the night."

He only hoped she understood his message.

"Thank you again for your hospitality," she said sweetly. "I'm sure once Mrs. Paul has me ready for bed, I will take the sleeping draught the doctor left me. I used it last night and slept like the dead."

"Then goodnight to you both," he said and left, returning to his own chamber.

He didn't have to ring for his valet. Anderson was already there.

"I find I'm tired," he proclaimed and yawned for good measure as he sat.

His former batman removed Reid's boot and said, "The servants have mentioned how nice it is to have Lady Dunwood here."

"Oh, have they?"

Reid had quickly learned that anything the household wanted

their duke to know was funneled through his valet. No one, save for Bellows, his butler, came to him directly for anything. Instead, the others told Anderson their concerns, knowing the valet would pass along the tidbits in everyday conversation as he readied the duke.

"Yes, she's quite a favorite," Anderson continued as the other boot came off. "She visited a few times before your father became so ill. She was also gracious at the ball and danced with a groom and two footmen, as well as a few farmers. She's highly thought of by all, Your Grace."

He refrained from laughing and said, "She's more than a favorite of mine, Anderson."

The valet paused. "Is that so, Your Grace?"

Nodding, Reid said, "I intend to make her my duchess."

A smile broke out on Anderson's plain face. "Now that's very good news, indeed, Your Grace."

"She doesn't know so yet. You'll need to keep it to yourself."

"Of course."

He knew, though, that Anderson would leave here and return to the servants' hall, where he would announce the duke's intentions. It wouldn't hurt to have an entire household of servants on his side. Convincing Ashlyn to marry him might take all of them—and more.

Once Reid had on his dressing gown, he dismissed the servant, saying, "I won't need anything else from you the rest of the night."

"Very good, Your Grace."

What he would need is Ashlyn in his bed. Soon.

He waited an hour, wanting the household to settle down. Anderson already had the bed turned back. Reid left the candles burning and made his way down the corridor to the guestroom Ashlyn stayed in. He didn't bother to knock but merely opened the door and slipped inside.

She waited on the bed, wide awake, wearing a pale blue dressing gown. Mrs. Paul had plaited her hair into a single braid.

The first thing he would do is unloose it.

ASHLYN HOPED SHE'D understood what Reid meant.

That he'd be back.

That's why she'd specifically told Mrs. Paul she would be ingesting the sleeping draught. She didn't want the housekeeper to check on her again this evening. If she did, the woman would find the Duke of Gilford in Ashlyn's bed.

At least, she prayed that was the case.

Though she'd told him she wanted him, she still had a thousand questions as to what that meant. When she'd coupled with Daniel, they had kissed briefly. Nothing like she and Reid had engaged in. She'd kept still on the bed as her groom raised the hem of her night rail to her waist, thankful of the darkness surrounding them. He'd straddled her, pushing her legs apart, and she'd felt his member pressing against her. Suddenly, he'd jammed it inside her, tearing her in two. He'd moved on top of her and in her and then cried out hoarsely as tears slid from her eyes into her hair.

Ashlyn hadn't experienced the feelings for Daniel that she did for Reid. Even knowing it would end in excruciating pain, she wanted him to come to her bed. This time, she didn't want to lie still. She wanted to touch him. Taste him. Fan the desire she felt for him.

She kept watch on the door and, finally, it opened. Reid crept in, closing it behind him. He wore a dressing gown of dark maroon and no slippers. The sight of his bare feet made her smile.

"Feeling sleepy?" he asked as he paused next to the bed.

"Not in the least," she said cheerily.

"Good. I trust the wonderful Mrs. Paul won't show up any time before morning."

"I doubt it."

He lifted her gently and carried her across the room.

"Where are we going?" she asked, confused.

"I want you in *my* bed, Ashlyn. It's where you belong." His voice, low and rough, heightened her anticipation.

Reid had her open the door and then close it behind them. She found her hand against his chest. The bare skin glowed with heat. She couldn't wait to see it. To see all of him. She'd never seen Daniel and wanted tonight to be as different from her wedding night as possible. After all, this would be her lone time with Reid—and final time with any man.

His bedchamber door was already open and they entered. He nudged the door shut with his foot and then threw the lock. That action caused her to giggle.

"You find something humorous, Lady Dunwood?" he asked with a straight face.

"No, Your Grace. Dukes are said to be humorless creatures. I'm sure I would never laugh in the presence of one."

As he carried her to a massive bed, he said, "You may laugh some tonight. I hope you do. More importantly, I hope you cry out my name dozens of times as I pleasure you."

She grew hot at the words. "Pleasure me?" The concept seemed foreign to her. Little if anything Daniel had done that night brought her pleasure.

"Yes," Reid said, placing her upright on the bed. "My every thought will be to give you the night of your life."

He sat beside her, lacing their fingers together. "I want to bring you happiness, Ashlyn. I want to fulfill every need within you." He paused. "From what you told me earlier, you wed a man not of your choosing. I'm sure that affected—"

"It's true I was made to marry Daniel," she interrupted. "Tonight is not about him. I only want it to be you and me. No ghost between us."

Reid raised their joined hands and kissed hers tenderly. The simple gesture moved her beyond words.

"Then tell me what you want."

She bit her lip, not used to anyone asking her that. Not sure if she should actually say the words aloud. Deciding if she only had one night, though, it would be the night of her choosing.

"I'd like you to undress before you douse the candles," she said, fulfilling her wish to see him that way.

A wicked gleam entered his eyes. "There'll be no darkness tonight. Just as you wish to see me, I want to see every inch of you."

"You mean . . . . when we . . ."

"Yes. I plan to touch you. Hold you. Kiss you. See you. When you come, Ashlyn—and you'll come many times—I want to see the look in your eyes."

She hadn't a clue what he meant. He must have seen her confusion.

"Have you never reached orgasm?"

She swallowed. "I don't know. I'm not sure what that is."

He chuckled. "Oh, if you had, you'd know exactly what I meant."

Suddenly, she felt very unsure of herself. This man was a man of the world with a vast amount of experience. She looked away.

His fingers took her chin and turned her back. "I'm sorry. I didn't mean to tease you."

She took a deep breath and let it out slowly. "This may not be a good idea, Reid."

"You and me?"

Ashlyn nodded.

"Oh, it's the best idea in the world," he assured her. "Tell me when your husband went to war. I know we said we wouldn't mention him but I sense you're unsure. Apprehensive. How long were you together?"

She closed her eyes, not wanting to see his reaction. "One night," she whispered.

His fingers tightened on hers. "And how many times did you make love?" he asked gently.

"Once."

"I see." He hesitated a moment and then said, "The first time between a couple—especially ones lacking in experience—can be awkward. Even uncomfortable."

He kissed her brow, his lips warm and firm. The kisses trailed to the bridge of her nose and down it, to the very tip. Ashlyn relaxed and opened her eyes.

Reid kissed her hand again and released it, rising to his feet. He untied his dressing gown and parted it, dropping it to the floor.

Ashlyn's mouth watered as her eyes feasted on him. The powerful arms and legs. The broad shoulders which seemed even wider now. The muscular chest, covered in a matting of dark hair that trailed down to his flat belly and beyond.

It was the beyond that had her worried.

Already his member swelled. Knowing where it was supposed to go—and remembering how much pain Daniel had caused her—she doubted her body could take it in.

"I've changed my mind," she said quickly and stood, gripping the bedpost for support since she didn't want to put weight on her injured ankle.

"Am I that hideous?" he asked.

"You're beautiful," she told him. "Too beautiful for me. And . . . too much for me."

"I see." Reid came toward her slowly, placing his hands on her shoulders. "Since you only coupled with your husband the one time, you may not know that it is only painful for a woman the first time."

Surprised filled her. "Is that true?"

He nodded. "Yes. The first time can be very uncomfortable for a woman. That won't be the case now. Despite your reservations, we will fit together like a hand in a well-tailored glove." He gently squeezed her shoulders. "But I won't force you to do anything you don't want to do, Ashlyn. Why don't we just kiss? I know you enjoy that."

She did want to kiss him. Desperately. And touch that muscular chest. Just a little bit.

"That's all we'll do?"

"We'll kiss and I'll pleasure you some."

She shook her head. "I just don't know what that means," she said in frustration. "I'm petite. Nothing about you is."

"Are you worried we won't fit together?"

"Yes," she said miserably.

"We don't have to do that. As I said, let's just kiss a while. I'll touch you some."

"Can I touch you?"

Reid smiled. "That would be delightful. I can already guess that being touched by you is going to become my favorite thing in the world."

"Don't get used to it," she warned. She knew she should be honest with him and tell him this was the only time they would be together like this. If she even let it get to that point. Something made her hold back, though. If Reid knew the truth, he might not agree to this night together.

"We'll start with kissing and see where things go."

"All right," Ashlyn said. "You may kiss me."

"Wherever I like?"

She supposed he meant her neck as well as her lips. She'd liked that before and wouldn't mind that at all.

"Wherever you like," she agreed.

"Then let's get you ready," he said and reached for the sash of her dressing gown, pulling on where she'd knotted it.

Quickly, she covered his hand. "Wait. I thought we were going to kiss."

"We are. You said wherever I liked." He gave her a wolfish grin. "I want to see you, too, Ashlyn. And there are many places I'm interested in kissing you."

Chapter Seventeen

Reid's words caused her body to flame. She wondered where he might kiss her. Her elbows? Above her bosom? Her belly?

"All right," she said shakily and dropped her hand. She still held tightly to the bedpost with the other.

He worked the knot loose and pushed the dressing gown from her shoulders, forcing her to release her grasp.

"Don't worry. I'll keep your injured ankle in mind," he promised. "No harm will come to it."

Maybe he would kiss her ankle.

The dressing gown slid down her arms and was removed with ease. He draped it across the nearest chair and returned to her. Ashlyn felt vulnerable in only her night rail. Even her husband hadn't seen her undressed. She couldn't understand why she was allowing this man to do so.

Reid lifted the hem of the night rail and raised it slowly, bringing it over her head. He placed it on top of her dressing gown and then faced her. His eyes skimmed up and down, approval shining in them. He came and took her hands.

"You are more lovely than any summer day ever was."

"Are you quoting Shakespeare to me?"

"In a way. I have nothing else to compare you to, Ashlyn. You are perfection."

His hands released hers and went to her waist. As he held her, his thumbs skimmed up and down, brushing her belly, lighting a fire within it.

"I'm going to kiss you now. Hold you. Touch you. Whisper to you. Any time you wish me to stop, say the word."

Her hands went to his chest and she stroked it, loving the feel of the sleek muscles.

"Don't distract me." Reid pulled her hands from him and picked her up. He went to the bed and sat, keeping Ashlyn in his lap. He took a pillow and placed it under her ankle.

"Now we're ready."

His mouth sought hers and she opened eagerly, wanting what they'd started earlier in the evening to continue. Their tongues mated wildly, each warring for dominance. Each kiss thrilled her, heating her blood and skin. His hands began stroking her body and it responded to him, her nipples tightening and her belly coiling and her core thumping. Whether he liked or not, she touched him, too, her fingers gliding along his perfect chest, playing with the hair on it, tugging softly. His hands moved up and down her back in long, deep strokes, the same as his tongue, and then moved to the curve of her hip and along her thigh. Ashlyn shivered, trying to memorize the feel of each stroke against her skin.

His hand gripped her thigh, kneading it. Then he shifted her slightly and his fingers trailed along her inner thigh. The apex at her legs pulsed wildly as they came closer to it. He was going to touch her there. She knew it.

And wanted him to, wanton woman that she'd become.

He toyed with the curls there a moment and then slid his thumb along the seam of her sex, almost causing her to jump from his lap.

"Easy," he said against her lips and then moved his to her neck. His teeth grazed her throat and her core tightened in response.

Reid continued to run his thumb back and forth, driving her to distraction. Then to her shock, he pushed it inside her.

Ashlyn gasped.

"Oh, my."

He pulled it out and disappointment filled her. She shouldn't have said anything. Maybe he didn't mean to do that. Daniel had certainly never attempted anything close to it.

Then he pushed a finger inside her and began stroking her. She groaned. Another one joined it and began working some type of magic. She whimpered. Called his name.

"Yes, love. Say it again."

"Reid!" she cried as she squirmed against him. "Reid!" she said insistently. "What on earth are you doing?"

"What will make you happy. Very happy, I hope."

Happy didn't begin to describe what she was feeling.

As his fingers caressed her, something began building inside her. Something violent and terrible and wonderful. Something that pushed her to the brink. She dug her fingers into his bare shoulders, not caring that she scratched him. Her breathing became rapid and shallow. She tingled from her head to her toes.

He moved until he brushed against something and she made a strangled noise.

"There it is," he said soothingly.

Ashlyn didn't know how he could sound so calm when she was about to explode.

"What?" she demanded, panting.

"Your pearl. The nub that will complete everything."

She didn't know about any pearl but was certainly glad he did. Whatever he'd found seemed the source of the burning need within her. She felt as if she were about to cross a bridge to an unknown place. One from which she could never return—and didn't care. Instead, she eagerly raced across it.

He had her writhing now, whimpering in need. She began clenching, holding fast to his fingers as he drove her over the edge. The explosion burst within her and Ashlyn cried out his name as she moved and bucked and strained. Sensations unlike any she'd ever known poured through her. She no longer saw or heard. Only felt a wild abandon and beauty.

Reid pushed her higher and higher and she reached a peak, going over it into an abyss of pleasure. Gradually, it subsided and Ashlyn felt as weak as a newborn kitten, mewling as the tremors ended, leaving her spent. Somehow, Reid manipulated her from his lap and let her stretch out on the bed, gathering her in his arms, her face buried against his neck. She felt incredibly safe, knowing a peace that went beyond space and time. His lips brushed against the top of her head. Her limbs were lethargic. If she'd needed to move, it would have been impossible.

He kissed her temple and said, "The French call it *la petite mort*. The little death. We English aren't quite so poetic."

"That was orgasm?" she asked.

"Yes."

"It was incredible." She looked up. "For me. I'm afraid nothing happened for you."

He smiled. "Oh, it did. I was able to watch your face. The emotions flitting across it. Your eyes glazed. I heard your cries of satisfaction. Watching you brought me as much pleasure as I hope I gave you."

"Can I make you feel the same?" she asked, having no clue how to achieve it.

He kissed her. "Always thinking of others."

Reid started to kiss her again and Ashlyn placed her fingertips against his lips. "No. Tell me. I want you to feel the same."

He opened his lips and captured her fingers, sucking on them. Ashlyn felt her eyes widen as the pull caused her core to start throbbing again. It seems no matter what he did or where he touched her, Reid made her come alive.

His teeth teased her fingers and she strained against him. Her breasts seemed to swell. With her other hand, she ran her fingers through his hair, loving the texture and thickness of it. Finally, she freed herself from him.

"How can I pleasure you?"

Those chocolate eyes seemed to melt. "In many, many ways.

Kissing would be the start. Our coming together as one would be the finish."

She swallowed, trying to hide her distaste.

"It hurt before, didn't it?"

"Yes," she said dully. "I never wanted to do it again."

"It doesn't hurt after that first time."

"Really? Daniel told me the same but I didn't believe him."

"If you want, I can show you."

She couldn't lie to him. "I'm afraid," she admitted.

"Have you liked what we've done so far?"

"Yes."

"Then you would like it, too."

"How can you be sure?"

His eyes filled with mischief. "Because I know how to make you like it."

She batted at him playfully. "You can be awfully arrogant, you know."

"I do. I was born and bred to be so. Raised from the cradle to be an arrogant duke," he teased. Then his features softened. "I promise you that you will enjoy it, Ashlyn. Give me a chance. If you don't, I'll stop. Trust me."

She looked at him. She did trust him. Moreover, she loved him. It was something she could never, ever tell him. She would have to carry the secret to her grave.

"I do," she said solemnly. "I believe you."

"Then it starts with a kiss," he whispered and captured her mouth with his.

They kissed slowly. Leisurely. As if they had all the time in the world. Reid kept his promise and kissed her everywhere. Her breasts. Behind her knees. Across her belly. Her skin heated. His was already like a furnace. His fingers touched her lovingly. He caressed every part of her. When his fingers teased her fold and then slipped inside, she welcomed them. He brought her to orgasm again, one even longer and more intense than the first one.

Ashlyn still trembled from it when his member pressed against her. She tensed, squeezing her eyes shut.

"Relax, sweetheart. You're dripping for me. With need. With desire. I have what you want. Remember—trust me."

She opened her eyes and saw he told the truth. It caused her to do as he asked and as his mouth took hers, he pushed inside her. At first, his size and the pressure worried her but he withdrew and thrust back into her, causing the most delightful sensation.

"Oh, yes," she urged him on as he repeated the action. This time, she met him. Her arms went around him, her hands running up and down his sleek back. She felt very possessive of him, wanting to take him in. He continued to move within her and they began a dance not unlike the waltz. There was a rhythm, a cadence, a music only they could hear as they joined as one.

Another orgasm overwhelmed her as he pushed into her and she came undone in his arms. He entered a final time and then withdrew quickly, making a strangled sound as something warm touched her belly. Ashlyn glanced down and saw he'd spilled his seed outside her body. No baby was made this night.

Only powerful, lasting memories.

Reid rose from the bed and returned with a cloth. He wiped her belly clean and then returned with a wet one, smoothing it across her and drying her with another. He blew out all but one candle and climbed into bed, gathering her in his arms and wrapping his legs about her, too.

"Why did you leave one candle burning?"

"To watch you sleep."

"Reid!"

"Hush. Close your eyes, Ashlyn. I've worn you out. You need to get some rest."

She wanted to protest but was too tired to do so.

Sometime later, she awoke to him kissing her fingers. She giggled as he worked his way up her hand and then arm. He made love to her again, slowly, sweetly, tenderly. He fell asleep first that time and she watched him slumber, moved by this man. When she awakened again, nestled in his arms, she couldn't help herself and begin pressing soft kisses against his chest. She knew he woke but said nothing so she licked his nipples as he'd done hers.

"Ashlyn!" he cried hoarsely.

She looked up innocently. "Yes, Reid?"

He grinned. "You are very wicked."

"It's the company I keep," she said airily.

"Oh, is it?" he growled and then hovered over her, covering her in kisses and then taking her swiftly.

Each time, he was careful and withdrew. It comforted her to know there would be no child but she realized it left him unfulfilled.

Ashlyn snuggled against him and he said, "No. I need to take you back to your bed. Dawn is near."

He threw on his dressing gown and then reclaimed her night rail and slipped it over her head. The dressing gown came next.

Reid shook his head. "I haven't a clue how to rebraid your hair."

He'd undone it after she'd awakened the first time, wanting to run his fingers through her hair.

"I'll tell Mrs. Paul that it was a little tight and causing a headache. She'll believe me."

He kissed her. "She'll always believe you. Especially over me."

She frowned. "That's an odd remark to make."

"Well, it's natural that the two of you will be spending time together."

Exasperation filled her. "Reid, I will be leaving later today or tomorrow. I'm sure the doctor—"

"Ashlyn, I don't want you to go."

She looked at him longingly. "I can't stay, Reid. You know that." She bit her lip. "Besides, you've told me you already have a lady in mind to be your duchess. Tonight was our only night to be together."

He cupped her face. "Ashlyn, *you* are the lady I referred to."

"Me?"

"Of course. It's been you. Always you." Reid frowned. "You actually think I would make love to you all night when I planned to wed another?" He stepped away but she still sensed the angry waves emanating from him.

He came back and took her elbows. "You came to my bed thinking that. Why? Why would you do that? It seems totally out of character for you."

She stared into the face she'd grown to love. "Because I wanted to know what it would be like. There's been a fierce attraction between us. I've told you—I had one night with a man which was a nightmare. That's all I knew. Between us, though, I sensed it could be so much more. I needed to make love with you, Reid."

Tears filled her eyes. "I've been so alone for so many years. I know it was selfish."

"You are the least selfish person I know." He kissed her tenderly. "You put everyone before you. It's an endearing quality." He kissed her again, longer and with more passion. "Besides, it doesn't matter. There is no other woman. There's only you. I want to marry you, Ashlyn. I want you to be my duchess. I want you to be the mother of our children. My companion for life."

For a moment, Ashlyn wanted that life with him. She realized, though, that Reid needed a woman who would take care of him and the children he wanted. Who would love him as much as he deserved to be loved.

She could never be that woman. Once she'd been a mother and wife. She'd given her entire existence to her child. When she lost Gregory, she'd shut the door on ever giving over to those feelings again. It wouldn't be fair for him to tie himself to her when her heart would be forever closed. Even though she knew she loved Reid, she couldn't risk the sorrow and heartbreaking loss that came with acknowledging that love.

She wished he hadn't said these things. It would make it so much harder to refuse him—but she must. For his own good. For the future and family he would build with another woman.

"Say something, darling. Do you want the banns read? Should I ride to London for a special license? I'll do whatever you wish."

"I wish to go to my room," she said quietly.

He enfolded her in his arms. "I'm sorry if you feel I'm rushing you. I know this is a lot to take in."

Reid picked her up and carried her back to her bedchamber. He placed her on the bed and wiped away the tears that cascaded down her cheeks.

"Forgive me, sweetheart. Take all the time to decide what you want."

Ashlyn steeled herself. There was no sense delaying the inevitable. "I don't need any more time, Your Grace. I don't ever plan to marry you or anyone else."

Chapter Eighteen

Reid's jaw dropped. Surely, he'd heard her wrong.

"Ashlyn, I think I misunderstood you."

She winced as if he'd slapped her and looked as if she'd burst into tears again. Then he watched a change come over her, as if she dug deep within her. Her chin rose a notch and a steely resolve entered those bewitching eyes.

"You didn't, Your Grace. I don't wish to marry you."

Her words took him aback. "But . . . I'm a duke."

"I know that, Your Grace, else I wouldn't address you so. I simply don't want to be your duchess. You'll have to find someone else to take on that task."

He was speechless. Then he realized she must want words from him, as well as actions.

"I'm not Burke or Gray. I can't offer you words of love, Ashlyn. I do care for you a great deal, though. In fact, I admire you greatly. I respect what you've done at Dunwood Academy. If you're worried about being allowed to keep it, I have no objections."

She crossed her arms. "Oh. So you have no objections. You'll *allow* me to keep it."

"Of course," he said, wanting to placate her. "I know the school means a great deal to you. Naturally, you'll need someone to run it for you. You wouldn't be able to remain its headmistress."

Anger sparked in her eyes. "My school means *everything* to me, as do my boys. I built it from nothing. It is my *life*. I'm not going to marry a man who tells me what I can or cannot do with my school or my life. I've been on my own far too long."

"I like that about you, Ashlyn. Your independence. Your spirit."

"How nice. Well, I plan to keep both. I will leave Gillingham today once I've seen the doctor."

"You will not," Reid roared, his patience at an end.

"I won't be bullied into marrying you, Your Grace. I know you aren't told no very often but this is one instance where it applies. I *will* leave once I see the doctor."

"I forbid it." Even to his ears, he knew how pompous he sounded and yet he refused to retract the words.

"So I'm to be a prisoner now?" she challenged. "Held against my will?"

"No. Of course not." He tried to calm himself. He was losing her—and he didn't understand why. "You'll do as the doctor says."

"Or as *you* say? Don't think to waylay him before he sees me," Ashlyn warned.

It was exactly what Reid had planned to do. She was far too clever for her own good.

"I will leave today," she said firmly. "Even if I must crawl back the entire way."

He couldn't persuade her of anything in her current mood. Without a word, Reid left the bedchamber and returned to his own. Collapsing on the bed, the first thing that hit him was the subtle scent of her fragrance on the pillowcase. He turned into it, inhaling deeply.

What had just happened?

He'd spent the best night of his life with Ashlyn. They were well matched in every way imaginable.

Especially in bed.

He couldn't fathom why she didn't want to wed him. She

wasn't some merry widow who bedded every man who asked her. In fact, *she* was the one who had made it known to him of her desire. Why would she want only one night when he offered her a lifetime and wealth and privilege?

Had he bullied her?

Reid associated that behavior with boys at school being harsh toward one another, a larger boy exercising his power over a lesser, weaker one. Guilt flooded him. He'd arrogantly told her he was a duke. She had fired back at him for that. All his life, Reid had been a leader. He told others what to do—and they followed without question. Yet here, he couldn't get one petite spitfire to do his bidding and do what was best for them both.

He knew Dunwood Academy meant a great deal to her but he'd underestimated the depth of those feelings. Her entire identity—even self-worth—was wrapped into the school. He'd not understood that before and it had cost him. He tried to look at things from her perspective. She'd been a young girl who'd been forced to wed a man who was practically a stranger. Obviously, only her father could have exercised such power over her. Ashlyn had been left alone and raised a child in isolation, with little society about her. With the deaths of her husband and child, she'd risen from the ashes of grief and reinvented herself. Starting an academy from scratch must have been exceedingly challenging. She'd done so and seen it grow successful in a short amount of time. He could understand how hard it would be to give it up.

He wasn't asking for that. Yet he realized he'd told her exactly what *he* wanted her to do with her creation. Ordered her was more the truth. No wonder she was resentful. And hurt. He'd have to alter his approach. What worried him was the little time he had left. Reid feared once Ashlyn left Gillingham, she might never return. He'd lose his chance at lasting happiness with the woman he loved.

Wait . . .

No, he didn't love. He didn't know where that notion came

from. He was comfortable in her company. Enjoyed conversing with her. Respected her intelligence. Admitted how much he physically desired her.

But love? No, that was impossible.

Maybe he should just let her go if she was so determined to oppose the match. His happiness and the future of Gillingham didn't depend upon Ashlyn. He was a bloody duke. In the prime of his life. He could attend the upcoming London Season and have his pick of any woman present.

But none of them would be Ashlyn.

Bloody hell. He might actually be in love with her, after all.

He rose and paced the room, his thoughts jumbling. People fell in and out of love all the time. He hadn't even known he was in love with her until now. It shouldn't be that hard to forget her.

Reid collapsed into a chair. It didn't matter what lies he told himself. The truth would always spring to the surface.

He was in love with Ashlyn. And she had rejected him.

It didn't mean it had to remain that way, though. He was a soldier. Used to going into battle. He now found himself in the battle of his life. He must do whatever it took to win Ashlyn.

And her love.

MRS. PAUL BROUGHT in a breakfast tray and set it down. The thought of food made Ashlyn nauseous but she didn't want anyone to know how miserable she was.

The man she loved had proposed marriage and she'd rejected him. It brought a modicum of relief to know there'd been no other woman that Reid had considered for his duchess. Despite the proposal, he'd behaved like a pompous ass. He'd become overbearing, telling her what she could and couldn't do with Dunwood Academy. She'd already been forced into one marriage. She wouldn't make the same mistake twice. Reid tried to bend her to his will. Ashlyn couldn't allow that. She'd built a worthy school of impeccable reputation. She couldn't throw it all away.

Even for a man she loved.

Ashlyn hadn't known she could still have such love in her heart. She thought all those feelings had died with Gregory. Instead, all her emotions had been directed toward her pupils. There were so many misfits that she'd seen make strides. Countless other boys needed her help. She refused to walk away and abandon them because she had feelings for a man who wished her to walk away from everything important to her.

Practically speaking, Reid was a duke. A wealthy, powerful man of privilege. He would have his choice of women. Besides, he'd admitted he didn't love her. He deserved to find a woman he did. His friends had found such women. Reid deserved nothing less. He would find the right wife for him. She knew it in her heart.

"Would you care for a bath this morning, my lady?" Mrs. Paul asked, laying out a dress for Ashlyn to wear today.

She'd forgotten the housekeeper was there.

"Yes, please. The doctor is expected sometime this afternoon so a morning bath is preferable."

"I'll see to your hot water now."

After Mrs. Paul left, Ashlyn toyed with her food, getting down a few bites. She allowed the housekeeper, with the help of a maid, to bathe and dress her. She asked for one of them to pack for her. Mrs. Paul said that she would do so and dismissed the maid after they'd helped Ashlyn to a chair.

As the housekeeper folded Ashlyn's gowns and returned them to the trunk, she said, "Although I'm sorry you injured your ankle, my lady, it was delightful having you here. I look forward to your return soon."

"What return?"

Mrs. Paul demurred. "I'm sorry if I spoke out of turn. I was referring to . . . your . . . understanding with His Grace."

"There is no understanding with His Grace," she said firmly. "Much as I've enjoyed your company, Mrs. Paul, I'm afraid this is the last time we'll meet."

"But . . . I thought . . ."

"I'm sure you are misinformed, Mrs. Paul."

The housekeeper nodded. "Perhaps I am, my lady."

The doctor appeared just after two. His demeanor seemed false and his voice too bright and cheery. She knew Reid had ambushed him.

The physician set aside a cane he'd brought. He knelt and inspected her ankle, rotating it some.

"Any pain?" he asked.

"None. It's just a bit tender."

He rose. "I think you can try walking on it some for the rest of today. Just a few short distances, here and there. Tomorrow, you can be up and about more, especially if you use the cane. By the day after, you can resume your normal schedule but keep to the cane for a few more days. After that, you should be right as rain, my lady."

Testing him, she said, "This could all be accomplished at Dunwood Academy, could it not?"

A pained expression crossed his face. "I believe it would be in your best interest to remain here for the rest of the week."

"I believe being at home is in my best interest. I know Gilford spoke to you. He's being ridiculous. Simply because I had a minor injury in his home doesn't mean he needs to take such responsibility for me. Don't you think it would be better for me to be in my usual surroundings? Sleeping in my own bed?" Ashlyn gave him her best headmistress look and saw him wither.

"You are my patient. I should recommend what's best for you," he agreed, though it was obvious he wasn't happy to do so.

"Will you drive me home now, Doctor?"

He nodded.

"I appreciate your kindness to me. You have been the consummate professional."

"His Grace will need to be notified. He's . . . waiting in the corridor."

She smiled. "Then by all means, have His Grace come in to hear the good news."

The doctor went to summon the duke. Reid strode across the room and gazed at her intently but said nothing.

"The doctor and I agree that I will heal just fine at Dunwood Academy," Ashlyn began.

Reid whirled to the other man. The physician's eyes were already downcast in order to avoid the scathing glance from the duke.

"This is your final word?" he demanded.

"Yes," the doctor said, not daring to lift his head. "I'm to take Lady Dunwood home now."

Reid looked back to her. "You'll not ride in a pony cart. I'll have my carriage brought around. Let me see you out, Doctor."

The men left the room and she breathed a sigh of relief. She thought Reid might have put up more of an argument and was relieved he hadn't.

A footman appeared and placed her trunk on his shoulder and slipped the cane over his forearm. Then Reid appeared. Without a word, he lifted her from where she sat and carried her downstairs. Ashlyn longed to throw her arms about his neck and kiss him one more time. It was a good thing she'd discovered how strong-willed she was the last few years because she drew on that to refrain from doing so.

A footman opened the carriage door and Reid place her onto the plush seat. He took the one opposite her. She should have suspected he would see her home. The door closed and the vehicle launched into motion.

Neither of them spoke. She looked everywhere except at him. At least he wasn't sitting beside her. She didn't know if her willpower would have extended to a carriage ride where he was within reach.

They'd almost reached Dunwood Academy when he leaned

forward and took her hands. It forced her to meet his gaze.

"I was wrong before. I didn't mean to dictate to you in such an oppressive manner. I also discovered something I hadn't known before."

Ashlyn licked her lips nervously. "What?" she asked.

"I'm in love with you, Ashlyn."

She jerked her hands from his and slapped him. Her hand stung from the blow and she saw the red mark that sprang to his face.

"You're an arrogant, insufferable man. You can't stand the thought of anyone—much less a woman—saying no to you. Because of that, you're willing to say whatever you think I want to hear. I'm appalled at the lengths you're willing to go to in order to put me under your thumb. You don't love me, Gilford. You couldn't love anyone but yourself. Get it through your bloody thick skull. I will never wed you. Never."

The door opened and she saw the footman standing there, the cane the doctor had brought in the servant's hands. Ashlyn pushed herself from the seat and reached for the man's hand. She clasped it tightly and kept from wincing as she moved down the handful of stairs. Taking the cane from the servant, she turned back to face the man glaring at her.

"Thank you for your gracious hospitality, Your Grace," she said sweetly and wheeled around. Using the cane, she hobbled inside Dunwood Academy and collapsed onto the nearest chair.

Chapter Nineteen

Ashlyn rode to church in the carriage, three of her tutors sharing the compartment. Mr. Peterson, the fourth, drove the cart which carried all of the boys in its bed.

A week had passed since the country ball at Gillingham. She'd resumed most of her normal duties, aided by the cane which helped her get around with more ease. Yesterday was the first day she hadn't used it but she'd brought it along today since she'd be walking some outdoors on uneven ground.

The vehicle slowed and Mr. Butler got out first and helped lower her to the ground. When she turned, she spied Viscount Ransom, who never missed a Sunday service. What surprised her was that he stood with Lord Martin and Lady Edith, whom she'd never seen at church. Then Ashlyn remembered seeing the viscount dance with Lady Edith and decided a romance must be blossoming between the two.

Ransom waved her over. "Good morning, Lady Dunwood. How are you this fine day?"

The day was overcast and gloomy, with rain threatening. Of course, Ransom was only seeing what he wanted to see through the eyes of love. Ashlyn bit back a smile.

"Good morning, my lord. Lord Martin. Lady Edith."

The young woman looked at her anxiously. Her father avoided all eye contact.

"How do you fare, Lady Dunwood?" the young woman

asked. "I see you're using a cane."

"My ankle is much better. Thank you for asking. I did receive Lady Eden's card." She glanced around. "Is she here so I may thank her for sending it?"

Lord Martin quickly said, "My daughter has gone to stay with relatives in the north. She will be there for some time."

Reid had said he would take care of the girl. Ashlyn wondered if Eden Martin had been permanently banished from the Gillbrook area or if her exile was merely temporary.

"Then I suppose she will miss the upcoming Season. Will you attend it, Lady Edith?"

"Oh, yes, Lady Dunwood. Will you?"

She shook her head. "No, I've my school to run."

"Do you never take time for yourself, my lady?" the viscount asked.

"Well, my pupils have their Easter break coming up soon. All the students and staff will be gone on holiday for two weeks, beginning the Monday before Easter. I will indulge in long walks and afternoon naps, I suppose."

She would also go to visit the Westons but didn't care to share her plans.

"Is that who I think it is?" Lord Ransom asked.

She turned and her stomach lurched.

The Gilford ducal carriage was pulling into the yard. A buzz of voices erupted.

"I wonder why Gilford is coming here when he has his own church to attend?" pondered Lord Ransom.

Ashlyn knew. It was because of her.

Moments later, the Duke of Gilford exited his carriage and made straight for their group, greeting all of them with good cheer. She was thankful he didn't pay her more attention than the others.

"Are you ready for your upcoming Season, Lady Edith?" he asked.

She smiled. "Yes, Your Grace. Very much so." She glanced to

Lord Ransom and back.

"I hope you will save many dances for my friend here," Reid continued, smiling at Lord Ransom.

Ashlyn hadn't known them to be friends since Ransom seemed several years younger and Reid had been away for a decade at war.

Lady Edith blushed prettily. "Oh, I plan to, Your Grace."

She believed the couple would announce their engagement before the end of the Season. Ashlyn decided if so, she would tell young Edward that it was in part because of the kindness he'd shown by dancing with Lady Edith. It had brought her to the attention of the viscount.

"I believe the good reverend is ready to begin," Lord Martin said.

She saw everyone had made their way into the church and looked about to see that her boys had settled down and acted with decorum as they filed in.

"My lady?" Reid offered her his arm.

She didn't want to seem churlish, so she took it. The solid feel of it made her long for things she could never have.

As they went into the church, she asked, "Why are you here today?"

"Because you are."

He seated her and took the spot next to her. Too close for her liking. Reid removed the cane from her hand and rested it against the pew.

"How is your ankle?" he asked quietly.

"Better. I won't need the cane by tomorrow."

Throughout the service, Ashlyn's attention wandered. She couldn't help it. Reid's entire right side nestled against her left. The cologne he always wore wafted about her. His rich baritone drew her in with each verse of every hymn. Images of their night together flooded her mind, causing her color to rise. She wished she had a fan to cool herself.

The congregation stood for a last song and prayer before they were dismissed. Since they were at the front, most present filed out before her row. Reid handed her the cane but took her hand and tucked it possessively into the crook of his arm.

Once they emerged from the church, groups of people stood chatting. Her boys ran around, playing some form of tag with other children. When Arthur and Harry caught sight of their brother, they broke away from the fun and came toward them.

"Good morning, boys," Reid said.

They both greeted him and Harry asked, "What are you doing here?"

He winked conspiratorially. "I thought I would come check on you. And arrange a time for your mother to come visit this week. She returned home yesterday and is anxious to see you." Reid turned to Ashlyn. "Do you have a time that's convenient for Her Grace to stop by the academy?"

She knew any visit would include the duke.

"Tomorrow would be acceptable," she replied evenly.

"Could you and Mama come for tea, Reid?" Arthur asked eagerly and then glanced to her. "If that's all right, my lady?"

"Tea can be a rather boisterous affair with a dozen lads and their tutors," she said. "I could have you and your mother served in the small parlor. That would be more conducive for conversation."

"Could you come ride with us first, Reid?" Harry pleaded. "Monday's a riding day. We do so before tea."

"I don't see why not. That is, if Lady Dunwood wouldn't mind entertaining your mother."

"I'd be happy to show Her Grace around the school while you ride with your brothers," she said. "For now, though, it's time we left."

"You'll ride home with me," Reid said.

Her brows arched.

"Would you care to ride with me, Lady Dunwood?" he amended, his tone tempered.

"Oh, can we come along, too?" Harry asked.

"Yes, that would be excellent," Arthur seconded.

Ashlyn knew it would be good for them to spend time with their brother.

"Yes, you may."

"Race you!" Arthur cried and the two boys ran for the ducal carriage.

"Will you come?" Reid asked softly.

"Yes."

She didn't see the harm and told herself it would be good to observe the interaction between the three brothers.

Reid escorted her to the coach and assisted her inside. The boys already sat together, leaving her to sit beside Reid.

Ashlyn didn't speak during the ride to Dunwood Academy, letting the conversation flow between the brothers. The boys told Reid about various classes and their friends. Harry was concerned about a horse who'd pulled up lame. Arthur shared a difficult equation that he and Edward had solved together. As they pulled up to the school, Reid gave her a smile. The boys scrambled out, leaving them alone.

"They are happy," he said. "Thanks to you."

"I'm a small part of things. They have managed to make themselves happy by participating and finding new friends."

He took her hand and lifted it to his lips, his eyes never leaving hers. He pressed a kiss onto her fingers.

"Until tomorrow."

ASHLYN WAS WORKING in her study when Mrs. Clayton announced Her Grace, the Dowager Duchess of Gilford, had arrived.

"I've placed Her Grace in the small parlor where you requested tea be sent after the boys' ride," the housekeeper said.

"Thank you, Mrs. Clayton."

She went and greeted their guest and asked, "Would you care for a tour of Dunwood Academy, Your Grace?"

"I would like that very much."

Ashlyn showed her the boys' bedchambers first and then the various study rooms and classrooms. She introduced the dowager duchess to Mr. Butler and Mr. Peterson, telling her that Mr. Selleck was chaperoning the boys on their ride, along with Mr. Jarrett, their head groom.

"The only one missing is Mr. Phillips," she said. "He went into the village shortly before you arrived."

"What does he teach?"

"Music and drawing. Both Master Arthur and Master Harry have taken up the pianoforte. Mr. Phillips also assists me in teaching dancing and comportments."

"His Grace told me of the country ball he held while I was away. He said your pupils were impeccably behaved and a credit to Dunwood Academy."

By now, they'd returned to the parlor and Ashlyn indicated for the dowager duchess to sit.

"I was very pleased with His Grace inviting our pupils, as well as how they accounted for themselves."

The older woman gazed steadily at Ashlyn. "He's also told me how my boys now conduct themselves." She sighed. "I knew at the time I was neglecting Arthur and Harry in favor of their father. I told myself I only had a limited amount of time with my husband and that I would have my sons forever. I'm afraid I almost lost them."

"They are the same boys you've always known," Ashlyn assured. "They lost their way for a bit but they are back now. I find them eager and interested in many subjects. Arthur is quieter and more disciplined, while Harry is gregarious and tries very hard."

"I'm relieved to hear this. His Grace told me the same but it is good hearing this from a woman."

The door opened and Reid and the two boys came in, all of

them in high spirits.

"Don't worry, Lady Dunwood," Arthur said. "We washed up before we came to tea."

"I am relieved to hear that."

The boys greeted their mother affectionately with hugs and kisses. It was very different from the goodbyes they'd given her when they'd first been dropped off at the school.

They spent a pleasant teatime, though Ashlyn avoided meeting Reid's gaze and she never directly spoke to him.

"Could we take Mama to the stables?" Harry asked. "We muck them, you know," he said proudly.

"You . . . what?" their mother asked, looking bewildered.

"It's a part of learning responsibility, Mama," Arthur said with pride. "We also feed and curry the horses."

"You must come meet the horses, Mama," Harry insisted. "They're nice to pet."

"All right," she agreed and rose. "We'll be back shortly," she said, taking her children's hands.

Leaving Ashlyn alone with Reid.

The door closed and she steeled herself for an onslaught—but none came. Instead, he politely spoke of things they'd seen on the afternoon ride and asked about several of the boys he'd met. She wondered what game he played. Perhaps he thought by asking about her pupils it would endear him to her.

"I haven't changed my mind," she blurted out.

A shadow crossed Reid's face. "I didn't think you would so soon. I intend to prove myself to you, Ashlyn. To make myself worthy of you."

She sighed. "There's no future for us, Your Grace. It would be wrong if I allowed you to think so. What you should do is get yourself to London for the Season and find a suitable bride on the Marriage Mart."

Determination sprang into his eyes. "I will persevere, Ashlyn. No matter how long it takes. I will see that you understand how much I love you. Need you. How I want to—"

The door swung open and the trio returned.

"Mama fed two of the horses their apple," Harry proclaimed. "She wasn't afraid at all. I told her she'd like them."

Ashlyn rose and Reid did the same.

"I'm so glad you were able to visit, Your Grace," she told the boys' mother. "Feel free to stay as long as you wish but I have business to attend to." She glanced back to Reid and curtseyed. "Your Grace."

She escaped the room, worried that Reid might eventually wear down her resolve.

"Don't give up your hard won freedom for him," she told herself as she returned to her study, trying to get her emotions under control.

Minutes later, she watched out the window as the ducal carriage pulled away.

Chapter Twenty

ASHLYN WATCHED AS various pairs of boys descended the stairs ferrying trunks. Drake and Peter were the last down, bearing hers.

"Place it next to the door," she instructed them and then went outside, where a flurry of carriages made their way up the drive.

Her students and staff were all leaving this morning. The boys would be returning to their homes, except for Edward, who'd been invited by Arthur to visit at Gillingham for a few days. Her tutors had departed an hour earlier to catch the mail coach for the Lake District, which the four men would tour together during the holiday. Mrs. Clayton and Mrs. George were off to London, where they planned to stay with Mrs. Clayton's sister and take in the city's sights. Betty and Louise had left minutes before and would be visiting their families.

She spotted the Gilford carriage among the others and saw Reid hugging Harry. Quickly, she looked away. Samuel's father came toward her and they conversed briefly. By the time Samuel joined them and they ascended inside their coach, the duke's carriage traveled down the lane. It passed another carriage and when it arrived, Burke jumped out and waved.

Mr. Jarrett came toward her. "Everything will be in good hands, my lady. I'll care for all of the animals."

"I'll see you in two days, Mr. Jarrett."

"Is your trunk in the hallway?"

"Yes."

"I'll fetch it for you."

Burke stepped toward her. "It's a fine day to be going on holiday." He kissed her hand.

"You didn't have to come," she gently chided.

"Oh, I did. Gemma was afraid you'd find something last minute that would require you to stay here. I was charged to bring you back to Westbrook, being my charming self and talking you into doing so if necessary."

Ashlyn laughed. "Aren't you always charming?"

"These days? I try to do everything to please my wife and her growing belly."

She saw Jarrett pass her trunk to one of the Weston footmen. By now, the last vehicle had pulled away.

"I suppose I'm ready," she said.

Burke saw her inside the carriage and they spoke of local affairs until they arrived at Westbrook. She was shown into a sunny parlor, where Charlotte and Gemma waited.

Charlotte rose and kissed Ashlyn's cheeks. "It's so good to see you."

Gemma, who was stretched out on a settee, said, "I would rise but I find getting up is starting to be more difficult and not worth the effort."

Ashlyn went and kissed her hostess. "I remember those days."

"I've told her to wait until she no longer can see her feet. My belly swelled so much that it blocked them from view," Charlotte declared.

"It's best when that occurs," Ashlyn said. "By then, your poor ankles are so swollen you don't want to see them. And slippers? Forget wearing them. They no longer fit." She took a seat.

"I don't need to hear that," Gemma complained. She indicted her slippers, resting on the floor. "Already, I'm tired of them. My back is starting to ache. And I have the most awful heartburn."

"That's right," Ashlyn said. "I'd forgotten about that."

Gemma rang for tea and they talked for several hours. Charlotte entertained them with a few stories about her young son, warning Gemma of what lay ahead.

"There are times I want to kill him. Instead, I smother him in kisses, knowing the day will come when he won't let me do so." Charlotte looked at Ashlyn. "Did you feel the same about your son?"

She chuckled. "Gregory was the most curious child ever born. He was always into everything, wanting to know how things worked and where things came from."

Charlotte took Ashlyn's hand. "I know you must miss him a great deal. Have you thought about having another child?"

Both Charlotte and Gemma looked at her expectantly. She might have known she wouldn't be able to avoid the topic of Reid during her visit to Westbrook.

"I won't wed again so birthing another child is out of the question," she said plainly.

"What about Reid?" Gemma asked. "We know he cares for you a great deal. We hoped the feeling would be mutual."

Ashlyn burst into tears.

Charlotte wrapped her arms about Ashlyn and she cried for some minutes. When she stopped, she apologized.

"I didn't know I had so many tears in me."

"Have you quarreled with Reid?" Gemma asked.

"I hesitate to say anything. You are his friends."

"We are also your friends, Ashlyn," Gemma quietly reminded.

She decided to be frank. "Reid asked me to marry him. He said he didn't love me but that he cared a great deal for me and thought we would suit."

"Love can grow," Charlotte said encouragingly.

"I already love him," Ashlyn admitted. "For a brief moment, I thought that would be enough. I believed Reid would treat me with courtesy and respect and that it could be a successful marriage. Then before I could answer him, he began telling me what I could and couldn't do with Dunwood Academy."

"Oh, no," Gemma moaned.

"Oh, yes," Ashlyn assured her. "I was pushed into marrying my first husband and that turned out to be a disastrous union. I wasn't about to be bullied into wedding a second one—especially when he believes being a duke gives him *carte blanche* to do and say whatever he chooses."

"Gray says that Reid has always been a leader with strong opinions. That what he said was always accepted by all as others followed him. He's certainly not used to someone standing up to him," Charlotte said. "But I don't think he was malicious."

"No. He merely informed me of the wealth and privilege that would come if I agreed to the match. Then he tried to take my school away from me. He wanted someone else to run it." She paused. "I built Dunwood Academy from nothing. To have it ripped from my grasp is not something I'll ever agree to."

Ashlyn placed her cup down in its saucer. "Then after rejecting his offer, he came to me the next day and said he loved me—as if he told me what he thought I wanted to hear would change my mind."

"The next day?" Gemma mused. "Perhaps that gave Reid time to think things over. Knowing you'd turned him down. Realizing what a life without you would be like. He might have figured out that he couldn't be without you. That he *did* love you."

That prospect hadn't occurred to Ashlyn in the heat of the moment. In fact, she recalled he'd apologized for dictating to her and then told her he loved her.

Had she misjudged him?

Burke sailed into the room. "I've been sent to summon you ladies to dinner," he said.

"Oh, do we need to change first?" Ashlyn asked.

"No," Gemma said. "It's just the four of us." She smiled at her husband. "For a former spy who used to be so observant, he's merely a clueless earl now when it comes to women's fashions."

He laughed. "I notice nothing about other women ever since I've become a married man. You could wear the same gown three days in a row, Ashlyn, and I would never know." His eyes twinkled. "But if Gemma changed her slippers or necklace, I would be the first to comment." He took his wife's hand and kissed it lovingly before placing her slippers on her feet and helping her rise.

The four went to a small dining room and dined on roasted lamb and asparagus. Ashlyn was quiet during the meal, pondering Gemma's words.

"Would you care for a sherry?" Gemma asked. "We ladies could return to my sitting room."

"That would be lovely," Charlotte said and Ashlyn agreed.

They'd talked for a good hour when Burke entered the room again, a solemn look on his face.

"Ashlyn, Reid is here to see you."

Panic filled her. She wasn't ready to confront him yet. She still had too much to think about.

Before she could answer, Gemma said, "Ashlyn is feeling a bit vulnerable now, darling. Perhaps in a day or two Reid could come back and they could speak then."

"No," Burke said, his attention on Ashlyn. "You don't want to refuse. He's here about Dunwood Academy."

She quickly stood. "What? What's wrong?"

Reid strode into the room and came to stand before her. He took her hands and studied her for a moment.

"Ashlyn, something has happened that you must be made aware of."

"What?" she asked. She tried to pull her hands from his but his fingers tightened about hers.

"Dunwood Academy burned to the ground today," he said. "I'm so sorry."

She tried to speak but only a strangled noise emerged. Then the room swayed and a black fog engulfed her.

REID CAUGHT ASHLYN and sat in the nearest chair. He'd known the news would upset her. Everything she'd worked for had literally gone up in flames.

Charlotte touched his shoulder. "Reid, you need to put Ashlyn down."

His arms tightened possessively about her.

"She's very fragile now," Charlotte continued. "Waking up in your arms in front of her friends would make things awkward for her."

"I only want to protect her," he said fiercely. "I love her."

"I'm glad you do but Charlotte is right," Gemma said.

If they'd been alone, he would have kept Ashlyn in his lap. He knew these women were wise, though, and decided to listen to their advice. Reid rose and placed Ashlyn on the nearest settee.

"May I at least hold her hand?" he pleaded.

"Of course," Gemma said. "Burke, place a few pillows behind Ashlyn's head."

Her husband complied and asked, "Should we send for smelling salts?"

"No!" Gemma and Charlotte answered in unison and Charlotte added, "When you've had such a great upset, the last thing you want is to be jolted awake by something so foul-smelling. Give her time. She'll come around and it will be far gentler and kinder, done in her own time."

Reid knelt by Ashlyn's side, waiting for her to arouse herself. The group sat silently. Then she began to stir, her eyelashes fluttering. His pulse quickened.

Ashlyn opened her eyes and he was lost in the pools of amethyst.

She glanced about the room and then her gaze focused on him.

"What . . . you told me. It's true?"

"Yes." Reid wanted to tell her he had a good idea of who caused the fire but refused to make any accusation without proof.

"I don't see how it could have happened," she said, her brow creased as she tried to make sense of his news. "I went through the entire house myself before everyone left. No fires were going. The last to be put out were the cook fires and Mrs. George saw to dousing them after preparing breakfast. I don't see how a fire could have started, much less one that would burn a complete structure of that size."

Before he could reply, panic lit her face. "Mr. Jarrett! The animals!" she cried and struggled to rise.

Reid said, "Stay," firmly but softly and she complied. "They are fine. The stables and pens are far enough away from the house and suffered no damage. Jarrett was out exercising one of the horses. When he returned, he saw the fire." He paused. "It was deliberately set, Ashlyn. As Jarrett approached, he saw flames in every window. All the curtains had been set ablaze. I was out helping repair a fence when I saw the billowing clouds of smoke. Many of my tenants rushed with me to help but by the time we reached the property, it was already too late."

Tears slid down her cheeks. "I can't imagine anyone doing something so horrible. What about my boys? My poor boys. Some of them will be fine but others still need time for us to bolster their confidence. They aren't ready to go to another school yet." She shuddered. "And my tutors. The staff. They will have nowhere to go. It's all gone."

She wiped away tears. "I will be ruined," she said softly. "I don't have the funds to give to Mr. Thorn to rebuild Thornhill. It's why I rented a property in the first place."

She began weeping profusely and Reid felt his heart ripped from his chest. Suddenly, he knew what to do. A way to help Ashlyn—and himself. A way to let her see they could share the best of their worlds.

Tenderly, he cupped her cheeks. "I'm not here just to bring bad news, Ashlyn, but good. You know how large Gillingham is.

Hundreds of rooms, many of which we never use. I'm offering you the entire south wing. We can open it. It has enough rooms to house your classrooms. Your students. Your staff."

His thumbs stroked her damp cheeks. "Let me do this for you. Please."

Emotions flitted rapidly across her face. He held his breath, hoping she wouldn't let pride get in her way and refuse him.

A sense of calm descended over her and Ashlyn met his gaze.

"I accept."

Chapter Twenty-One

Ashlyn strolled the gardens at Gillingham, taking a few minutes for herself after an incredibly hectic two weeks.

Reid had been a godsend. His offer to house Dunwood Academy within Gillingham's walls was too good to pass up.

At least for now.

He'd helped her every step of the way. They'd met with the local magistrate regarding the fire. The officer of the court told them he would begin an immediate investigation into the matter, even sharing that on rare occasions there were people who received an unnatural thrill from lighting fires and watching them burn and that this could be the case in this instance. She'd never heard of such behavior before but it was the only thing that explained what had happened at her school. She was eternally grateful that the blaze had been set only after everyone was gone from the house and that no one was injured or killed.

Reid was the one who wrote to Lord Thorn and explained about Thornhill's destruction. A reply had come from Lord Thorn's solicitor, telling them the elderly owner was in poor health and they would have to postpone meeting with Ashlyn and deciding what she was responsible for. Since Lord Thorn rarely used his country property and she still had two more years on the lease, the matter could be resolved at a later date.

Reid had taken Ashlyn to London, where they'd gone to several bookstores in order to replace some of the volumes lost in the fire. He'd also offered the boys and their tutors the use of his library, as well. He'd walked the entire south wing with her and helped her decide which rooms would be turned into classrooms and study areas, as well as assigned the various bedchambers to pupils and tutors. Mrs. George and Mrs. Clayton, as well as Betty and Louise, would be given rooms near the other Gillingham servants. Ashlyn had sat with Mrs. Paul, the Gillingham housekeeper, and Mrs. Cook, the cook, and worked out a schedule regarding meals and where those would take place for her students and staff.

Her four servants had come back early to help prepare the new school, thanks to Reid's messengers tracking them down. Her tutors would arrive this afternoon from their Lake District tour. Mr. Jarrett awaited the men and would bring them to Gillingham. Her groom had been allowed to bring all of their horses and other animals to Gillingham in order for the boys to continue being responsible for the care of the animals.

Each of her pupils' families had been contacted and informed of Dunwood Academy's move to Gillingham. No mention of the fire was made. Reid had been adamant that Ashlyn keep that quiet, telling her it might impede the investigation. Instead, she informed the parents of the move to larger quarters, where the students would have the same quality of education in a similar setting, all under the auspices of the Duke of Gilford. Naturally, every reply was favorable, citing the duke's patronage of Dunwood Academy as a positive sign. Her boys would arrive tomorrow and the next term would start the following day.

The only thing Ashlyn had to do now was speak to Reid about her living arrangements. She couldn't stay at Gillingham and needed to find other quarters for herself. If she didn't, she might find herself tapping on his door and making herself cozy in his bed. When she'd come to Gillingham from the Westons, Ashlyn had worried about being in such close contact with Reid. He'd proven to be a perfect gentlemen, never discussing anything too personal with her nor even sitting too close to her, much less attempting a kiss. She'd grown from being relieved to anxious to downright frustrated by his behavior. How ironic that she'd been the one to tell him they had no future and yet all she could think about was him.

Ashlyn had thought long and hard on what Gemma had said and wanted to bring up the subject to Reid—but didn't know how. It wasn't as if over tea she could simply drop into the conversation of how he'd decided that he'd fallen in love with her. Even if he did love her, her first and only loyalty lay with her boys and her school. Reid was a duke, one of the elite of England. He would never consider wedding a woman who earned her living. He needed a hostess. Someone to manage his household for him. She didn't fit the bill in that regard, not with devoting so much time to other matters.

She turned the corner, where she planned to sit in the gazebo, and found it already occupied—by Reid.

"Good afternoon," he said pleasantly, giving her a smile.

"I'm sorry. I don't mean to bother you."

"No, please. Come and sit. I'd enjoy your company."

Reluctantly, she joined him.

"I come here sometimes to think," he said. "Or not." He took a deep breath and expelled it. "Sometimes, things get so busy that it's nice to escape here and merely sit. Not think about anything at all. It's a true luxury."

"I know my having Dunwood Academy here has caused much activity and the boys aren't even here yet. You've been so helpful, though I know you've put things aside to ensure the school will be up and running when everyone returns."

"It's my pleasure to offer space to Dunwood Academy. The south wing sat empty as it is. It's nice to see it put to such good use."

"I do have one thing to speak to you about," she began, hesitant to bring up the subject.

A teasing light came into his eyes. "And here I thought we'd taken care of everything. What's on your endless list of things to do that hasn't been done yet, Ashlyn?"

"I am going to need a place to stay."

He frowned. "Is there something wrong with the bedchamber you were given?"

"No, nothing at all. It is light and airy and beautifully decorated."

"Then why the need for a different place?"

She couldn't tell him the truth. How desperately she longed to be in his bed. How it would be impossible for her to be so close to him and keep herself out of his bed. Instead, she told him the version Polite Society would understand.

"I don't feel it's appropriate for me to stay at Gillingham."

"I'm perplexed. It's your school. You should be with your students as you were previously. Why would you live away from them?"

"It's just that . . . well . . . although I am a widow, it doesn't seem proper for me to reside under your roof. You are an eligible bachelor. Society would frown on these arrangements. I don't want any of my students' parents to think unseemly of me. I have a reputation to maintain. It must remain spotless if I am to continue to attract pupils to Dunwood Academy." She paused. "It would also be difficult for you to convince a woman you wish to be your wife that nothing untoward has occurred between us with me residing at Gillingham."

"You don't think the fact that we are living in entirely different wings of an enormous house makes a difference? This isn't London, you know." He suppressed a smile. "Not to mention the fact that the only woman I'm trying to persuade to marry me is you."

Ashlyn's cheeks heated. "I've talked to you about that, Your Grace."

"Quit *Your Gracing* me," he said, his annoyance clear.

"Your Grace," she said with deliberateness, "I have told you we have no future. Beyond Dunwood Academy temporarily existing within the walls of your country house. Once I'm able to locate a new property to rent, I will see my school relocated."

"Ashlyn," he said slowly and edged toward her. "There's no need to move your school. There's plenty of room for it here. Always."

He laced his fingers through hers and her heart skipped a beat.

"Just as there's room here for you, as well. In my heart. In my life. I was a fool to try and run roughshod over you. You are an intelligent, capable woman who established an entire school from nothing. Dunwood Academy is as a child to you. You gave it life. You nurture it. You guide it as it grows. I would expect nothing less than for you to continue to be involved in its day-to-day running."

Reid lifted their joined hands and kissed her fingers. "Nothing would change regarding this—even if you were my wife."

Her eyes filled with tears as hope sprang within her. Hope that they might truly be together. "Do you mean that?"

He smiled gently at her. "I do. My life is nothing without you in it. I need my own headmistress to keep me in line, probably more so than some of your wayward boys." He hesitated and then said, "I love you, Ashlyn. I didn't realize it until I chased you away. I hurt you. Deeply. I understand that now." He kissed her fingers again. "I plan to spend the rest of my life making it up to you. If you'll let me."

She saw Reid's eyes full of hope, his soul laid bare to her. "You truly would let me stay fully involved in my school?"

"I would insist upon it."

"Even to the detriment of managing your household."

He shrugged. "That's what servants are for. Mrs. Paul and Mr. Bellows already do an excellent job of keeping this place running. I want you to do whatever's important to you. If that's running Dunwood Academy, so be it. If you eat with your students, then so will I. If you ride with them, I'll accompany you. If you want me to muck stalls as they do, I'm happy to do so. I'll do anything to be with you, love. Anything."

"The Duke of Gilford would muck stalls?" she asked, her smile growing.

"If his duchess demanded he do so."

She smiled at him shyly. "I wouldn't have to eat every meal with the boys. I could compromise and choose only breakfast. That is helpful because it starts their day off right."

"Then we'll both eat breakfast with them. I want my day to begin on the right foot, too."

"Are you sure, Reid?" she asked earnestly. "I wouldn't be a conventional duchess. I might never wish to do the London Season."

"I would be grateful if you didn't." His teeth grazed her knuckles, causing a shiver to run along her spine. "The Season is vastly overrated."

"Do you want children?" she asked.

"Of course. Our boys will attend Dunwood Academy, naturally, a school with one of the finest reputations in England. And our girls?" His face lit with mischief. "Why, we might need to start a school for females, as well, in the east wing." Reid sighed. "I just want to be with you, Ashlyn, and with any children we're blessed to have. It's all I ask."

"You never asked me if I love you," she said softly.

"You do," he said, a bit of swagger in his voice. "I'm positive of it. We're a love match, Ashlyn. It merely took me longer to discover that."

"I do love you, you arrogant man." She laughed. "More than I should."

He cradled her face in his large hands. "We'll love each other more than others think wise. It won't make a bit of difference to us because we'll love one another more with every tomorrow. Our love will grow until it bursts from Gillingham."

Ashlyn smiled. "I think that's a wonderful thing. I love you, Reid. So very, very much."

"I love you, my darling."

He kissed her. The kiss was achingly tender. Beautiful. Sweet.

One she would remember the rest of her lifetime because it spoke of the promises between them.

He broke it and moved from the bench they sat on to one knee.

Grinning, Reid said, "I want this to be official. I don't want you telling our children that their papa never asked their mama to wed him. That he was an arrogant duke who told her they would marry and never gave her a chance to refuse him." A worried look crossed his face. "Unless you are going to refuse me again."

Ashlyn smiled. "Why don't you ask me and find out, Your Grace?"

"Ah, you're a sneaky one, Lady Dunwood. Very well." He cleared his throat and took her hands in his. "Ashlyn, I—"

"Yes," she interrupted, laughing. "Yes."

"No," he said sternly. "You can't answer a question that hasn't been asked. Now, behave before I pinch your bottom."

"You promise?"

"Oh, for the love of God, you're killing me, Woman."

Reid cleared his throat again, arching his eyebrows in a very ducal manner. She sat demurely and watched him.

"I shall begin again. Ashlyn, my love, you are beyond what I dreamed of wanting in a woman. You're sophisticated. Charming. Brilliant. Compassionate." He lowered his voice. "Passionate."

She smiled.

"You are more than a perfect partner for me. And that's what we'll be, my love. Partners. Equals in all that we do. You will give me wise counsel and I shall take it because you'll always know what's best for the both of us. I will be the best husband and father I can be and I promise that I will always satisfy you in bed."

She blushed.

"Ashlyn, Lady Dunwood, would you do me the greatest honor of accepting my marriage proposal and being my wife?"

She squeezed his fingers. "I can think of nothing more that I would rather do than spend the rest of my days—and nights—

with you."

He rose and brought her to her feet. "We're going to be incredibly happy, love. Happier than Gray and Charlotte. Happier than Burke and Gemma."

"I don't know. They all seem very much in love. The four of them are always flirting and touching. Kissing in public."

Reid's smile was like the sun in its brilliance. "Then I suppose we better start practicing all of those things so we'll be better than them at all of it."

His arms went around her. His eyes shone with love.

"Are you always this competitive?" she teased.

"I strive to be the best at everything I do. That will now include making you sigh my name. Making you come several times a night. Giving you—"

Ashlyn placed two fingers over his lips to silence him. "Quit telling me what you're going to do and just start doing it, Your Grace."

"With pleasure."

Reid sat and placed her in his lap and kissed her until teatime.

Chapter Twenty-Two

A very naked Ashlyn sprawled across Reid's chest, her cheek nestled against his beating heart. He slid his hand down her bare back, beyond her waist, until he squeezed the sweet curve of her rounded buttock.

"I still don't understand why you have to go to the cottage," he complained.

She raised her head, giving him her best headmistress look. "Because of this," she said and lowered her head again. "If I reside inside Gillingham, I will be tempted to come to your bed on a regular basis."

"So it's my large bed that tempts you and not me?" he teased.

Her low, throaty chuckle rumbled against his chest.

"I cannot be seen skulking about from your bedchamber to mine. It would be even worse if you were seen leaving mine. What would my boys think?"

"That I'm a very lucky man?"

Ashlyn punched him in the shoulder.

"Well, I am. Because you said yes to me. Every day is a blessed one now."

"I'm still going to the cottage," she told him.

Reid cursed under his breath.

"It will only be for two months. Actually, a week less than that. That's when the summer holidays begin."

They'd decided sometime during their long night of lovemaking that they would wed as soon as the current school session ended.

"We know when," he said. "But what kind of wedding do you want? I know you have been married before and want this ceremony to be different from the last."

"That wedding was rushed." She propped her chin on his chest. "My stepmother demanded it happen quickly." Ashlyn placed her cheek against him again.

She'd never told him exactly what had brought about such a quick marriage and Reid decided he would never ask. It surprised him when she began speaking of it.

"I was close to my father," she said. "Mama died when I was very young. I spent every waking hour with Papa. When he remarried many years later, my stepmother was jealous of our close relationship."

He remained silent, merely stroking her back in comfort.

"I danced with Daniel at the assembly rooms that night. We went out for some air since the rooms were heated and the dance had been lively." Ashlyn paused. "He asked me for a kiss. He'd never had one before and knew he would soon go off to war. Our kiss was brief. Chaste. But my stepmother had followed us outside. She caused an uproar, demanding that I'd been compromised and we must wed immediately. Papa knew I didn't want to marry a stranger but he listened to her in order to keep the peace in his household. You know the rest."

Reid's fingers found her hair and combed through the long, golden tresses.

"The wedding was in our drawing room. Only a handful attended. Daniel didn't have the money for the special license my stepmother demanded so Papa rode to London and paid for it himself."

She raised her head again and propped her hands under her chin.

"You were the one who wrote to me of Daniel's death."

"What?"

"He was under your command. Daniel Clarke. I kept the letter telling me he died not on the battlefield in glory but wasting away from dysentery."

Reid vaguely remembered a young, timid officer of that name and certainly didn't remember writing to Ashlyn in regard to her husband's death.

"Unfortunately, I had to write far too many of those letters over the years in my decade of service to the crown," he told her. "I do recall your husband but I didn't know him very well. I'm sorry."

"I'm not," she said boldly. "Marrying Daniel and then being left on my own taught me about myself. Especially after his death. I didn't know how strong I was and what I could accomplish. Besides, my path finally brought me to you." She sighed. "I don't have the letter now. It was lost in the blaze, along with most everything I owned. I only had a handful of dresses with me when I went to visit Gemma."

He hadn't realized that. "Then you'll need a full wardrobe, especially now that you're to be a duchess."

"Oh, the Gillbrook seamstress can make me a few things."

"A few," he said grudgingly. "I'll send to London, though. You'll need many things, include wedding finery."

"Even though I don't want to do a Season?"

"Even then," he told her. "You might have a hand in the planning but you will always be my hostess when we entertain. You'll need the appropriate clothes to do so."

"I suppose."

"Back to our wedding. Would it be acceptable to have the banns read soon and then marry here at Gillingham's chapel?" he asked.

"I like the thought of marrying in our chapel. When will you have the banns read?"

"We have ninety days after the third reading to wed. If you wish, we can start this Sunday," he suggested. "No. Wait. I have a better idea. How about we announce our news at a ball?"

She frowned. "It's a lovely idea but I'm not sure anyone would come. The Season is just underway in London and most of your neighbors have gone to town."

"We're not that far from London," he pointed out. "We could hold a country ball in ten days." He chuckled. "That would give my staff almost double the time I gave them to prepare for the last ball. Whoever comes, comes. And all of Gillingham's tenants will be invited as before. Your boys, too."

Her eyes lit with excitement. "Oh, that would be lovely, Reid. They enjoyed the last ball so much. I did, too."

"That settles it. We'll announce our engagement that Saturday and start the banns at the following morning's service."

She planted a sweet kiss on his chest. "With that, I must return to my room." Ashlyn pushed herself from the bed and began slipping her night rail over her head.

Reid followed, putting on his dressing gown as she did the same.

"I'll walk you back to your room."

"You will not," she said sternly, the headmistress coming out in her tone. "You will instead give me a thorough kiss here, behind closed doors, and then I'll be gone."

He did as told, always eager to follow any direction she gave him, especially if kissing was involved. Reid poured every bit of himself into the kiss, all his longing and love, wanting Ashlyn to feel how much he treasured her.

She broke the kiss. "I'm glad we shared this night. It will have to last us for the next two months."

"No sneaking into your cottage?" he asked hopefully.

Ashlyn's brows arched in answer.

"Kissing only," she said and slipped from the room.

ASHLYN JOINED REID at breakfast a short time later, sitting to his right. They were alone in the small breakfast room since the dowager duchess preferred keeping to her room for the meal.

"Bellows told me that your cottage has been prepared. Mrs. Paul oversaw the airing and cleaning. Your things are being moved there now."

What Reid didn't mention to Ashlyn was that he had arranged for an armed footman to watch over the cottage each night. He didn't want her to worry needlessly. She would still be guaranteed privacy and he would have peace of mind, knowing his own man guarded Ashlyn.

Once they'd eaten, he walked her the half-mile to her temporary quarters since it was such a beautiful spring day. They entered and he saw how small it was.

"Are you certain you wish to live here?"

"Yes. First of all, most of my waking hours will be spent at Gillingham, either in my study or with my students. I'll also eat meals there. The cottage is for sleeping." She eyed him. "Sleeping. Period. Besides, I've never been on my own like this. I'm actually looking forward to the peace."

"Bellows said that getting hot water to you might be a problem. Maids will bring fresh water each morning and evening and clean every day while you're gone but you might want to retain your former bedchamber to use for bathing."

"That's a good idea. I could also use it when dressing for our engagement ball."

He saw the idea of the ball had been a good one as she looked around the cottage. He noticed Mrs. Paul had taken the time to have fresh flowers brought in and a few other homey touches. Whether Ashlyn knew it or not, he'd decided he would pay her a few midnight visits over the weeks ahead. Having already sampled her sweetness, kisses alone wouldn't hold him until their wedding. Reid looked forward to slipping into her bed and surprising her, knowing his servant on duty outside the cottage would turn a blind eye to Reid's comings and goings.

"We should return," she said. "The boys will be arriving

soon."

He escorted her back, saying, "I will be waiting to walk you to Gillingham every morning and back at night."

"That isn't necessary, Reid."

He grinned. "It might not be necessary to you, Lady Dunwood, but spending time alone with you twice a day as we stroll to and from your cottage is more than an obligation to me. They will be my favorite times of each day."

Her eyes sparked with mischief. "You think so?"

"I know so. Especially because I will need to see you inside safely."

"And kiss me, I suppose."

He tried to look innocent. "The idea hadn't occurred to me. I'm glad it did you. You seem to possess some very wicked thoughts when it comes to me and my body, Lady Dunwood."

"You're impossible, Your Grace."

"And I plan to stay that way—in order to have your steady hand ride roughshod over me."

She gave him a haughty look. "I can be a tyrant, you know."

Reid smiled. "Oh, but you are *my* Lady Tyrant. No one else's. That makes all the difference."

They arrived back at the house and Ashlyn went to check on the buffet Mrs. Cook and Mrs. George had laid out. She'd told him that she expected a good majority of the parents to accompany their boys back to school, even though the Season had already begun.

"They won't want to miss seeing Gillingham and the possibility of meeting you," she'd explained to Reid.

Her words proved true. He waited with her and greeted every carriage that pulled up the lane. Arthur, Harry, and Edward took it upon themselves to lead impromptu tours of the south wing, showing each boy where his new bedchamber was and which rooms had been designated for classrooms. The Dunwood tutors were also on hand, answering questions about each boy. Parents were then funneled into the room where the buffet was laid out.

Reid made sure to invite each of them to the upcoming ball, noting that it was a celebration of many things, including the start of a long relationship he intended to have with Dunwood Academy. He'd pulled Bellows aside and informed him of the ball's date. His butler had received the news without a blink, merely thanking Reid for telling him and saying he had much to attend to.

The final pupil arrived and the last of the parents left, each promising to return for the ball.

"That went well," he told Ashlyn.

"Everyone is happy that Dunwood Academy is now associated with the powerful Duke of Gilford," she said. "It will only add to the prestige of my little school."

"They'll be even more impressed when they learn a duchess will be running it."

After dinner, Reid walked Ashlyn back to her cottage and, once inside, gave her a very thorough kiss. He didn't plan to visit her tonight, knowing she'd had little sleep the night before and that tomorrow would be the first day in the school's new rooms.

Besides, he had other things to attend to. He'd spent the last two weeks helping Ashlyn prepare for tomorrow's opening. Now, though, he would begin in earnest to learn who had caused the fire at Thornhill.

Reid knew exactly where to start.

Chapter Twenty-Three

REID BREAKFASTED WITH the boys for the first time, learning of the delightful *penny for your thoughts* that they participated in each morning. He saw how the practice would instill confidence and empathy in young men—and that one day his own sons would sit at this table and learn these lessons from their mother and fellow students.

He'd never been fixated on having children. The idea of sons and daughters had seemed far in his future when he soldiered on the Continent. Staying alive to fight another day dominated his existence. Now that he was back at Gillingham—and the duke—it was natural his thoughts would turn to children, especially because he needed to provide an heir for the title and estate. This time next year, Ashlyn might even carry his child. It was enough to boggle his mind.

The boys transferred their dishes from the table to bins on a cart and then filed out to head to class. Reid took a moment to give his fiancée a long kiss in this private moment.

"I've much to attend to today," he told her when he finally broke it. "I doubt I'll see you until dinnertime."

"I'm sure that's how every day will be unless you can find time to join us at tea."

"I'll try most days but for now I'm off." He gave her a swift kiss and then left, heading directly to the stables.

He hadn't told her he would travel to London today. Reid

figured he could go and be back and she would never know.

In the stables, he had Thunder saddled and he rode northwest toward the great city. It was close to noon when he arrived at the Gilford townhome, which he hadn't seen in over a decade. He admonished the groom to give Thunder a thorough rubdown and as many oats as the horse wanted and had another horse saddled to ride to his destination.

Viscount Martin's.

He arrived and rapped on the door, which a butler promptly opened.

"I'm here to see Lord Martin," Reid said, pushing his way past the man.

Jarred by the rude behavior, the butler said stiffly, "If you will give me your calling card, my lord, I shall see if Lord Martin is receiving."

Though Reid had been home close to two months, he hadn't bothered having cards made up while in the country. He gave the servant his haughtiest look and said, "It's Your Grace. The Duke of Gilford."

The butler's jaw dropped and then he quickly regained his composure. "If you'll come with me, Your Grace."

He led Reid up a wide staircase and down a corridor before pausing in front of an elaborately carved door.

"Please, Your Grace, let me at least announce you. I don't care to lose my position."

Reid didn't want the man's job to be in jeopardy simply because he was angry at Martin. "Very well."

The servant opened the door and announced him, then stepped aside. Reid strode into the room, which had several people inside, including Viscount Ransom. They all rose.

"Your Grace!" Lady Edith said, surprise evident in her voice. "How lovely to see you."

He moved toward her and she curtseyed. Ransom stood on her right and they shook hands. Lord Martin reluctantly offered his and Reid took it. The viscount introduced the other two men present, a baron and an earl, and Reid got the impression they were waiting on Eden Martin.

He was offered a seat and after taking it asked, "How are you enjoying this current Season, my lady?"

Lady Edith blushed. "Very much, Your Grace. In fact, Viscount Martin is escorting me to a garden party this afternoon. My sister will also accompany us, along with these two gentlemen."

Reid turned to his friend. "Have you offered for Lady Edith yet?"

Ransom sputtered, "What?"

"You should do it soon, Ransom," he calmly said. "Lady Edith is quite the catch. I've learned not to waste time where matters of the heart are concerned."

The young woman had turned beet red, while Ransom's mouth twisted this way and that. Finally, he found his voice and said, "I know exactly how special Lady Edith is, Gilford."

"Then do something about it," Reid prompted his friend.

"Why . . . why . . . I believe I will," Ransom proclaimed.

The two other visitors watched in shock, while Lord Martin looked bemused.

Ransom turned to Lady Edith and said, "From the moment I saw you dancing with that young boy at the Gillingham ball, I knew you were the one for me. You were smiling and looked so beautiful. You treated Master Edward with kindness and I see you treat others equally as well. You are sweet-natured, Lady Edith, and I can be myself when I'm with you. There's no pretense between us." He swallowed. "I love you."

The young viscount pushed from the settee and dropped to a knee. Taking her hands, he said, "Make me the happiest of men and say you'll be my wife."

Tears of happiness cascaded down her cheeks. "Yes. Of course, yes."

Ransom pulled them both to their feet and the couple gazed at each other in love. Then he glanced to her father.

"Lord Martin, might I have your permission to wed your

daughter?"

"Yes," the viscount said, his voice shaking. "You make Edith happy. That's what matters most."

Reid grinned. "I hope to be invited to the wedding."

The couple turned to him, both beaming, and Lady Edith said, "Yours will be the first invitation issued, Your Grace."

"Would you care to walk in the gardens before we leave?" Ransom asked his new fiancée.

"I would."

They left and Reid said, "If I could have a few minutes alone with Viscount Martin, gentlemen?"

The baron and earl rose. Both nodded and vacated the room.

"Thank you," Lord Martin said. "I can't believe you just did what you did, Gilford, but to know Edith is cared for brings me great relief."

"I'm here to discuss your other daughter. Did you do as I asked? Have the right doctors brought in to see her?"

The viscount nodded warily. "I did have two doctors examine her. One merely thought her lacking in maturity and good judgment. The other felt there was a deeper problem to address, especially her obsession with you. Eden was confined for a week to her rooms, where she spent many hours speaking with this physician. When he wasn't present, a nurse watched over her. She seemed to calm considerably and quit mentioning you altogether. The doctor was pleased with the progress she made and gave me permission to bring her to London. She will continue to see this doctor once a week during the Season. The nurse is still here, acting more as a lady's maid to Eden and making sure she remains tranquil."

"I think Lady Eden started the fire at Dunwood Academy."

The man's faced turned ashen. "What fire?" he asked, his voice a whisper.

"Fire was set to Thornhill. Fortunately, the students and staff had left earlier that day for their Easter holidays. The groom was the only one on the property. When he returned from a ride, he saw fire in every window. The structure burned to the ground." He paused. "It was deliberately set."

All color now drained from Lord Martin's face. "You think . . . Eden . . . did this."

"I do. No one hates Lady Dunwood more than your daughter."

"What day did this happen?"

Reid told him. "What day did you travel to London?" he countered.

"The same," Martin said dully. "We left mid-afternoon. Eden seemed anxious to leave. I thought it was because she was excited for her come-out." He shook his head and then Reid watched as determination filled the viscount. "No, it can't be. You're wrong, Your Grace. My girl wouldn't have gone there and done such a thing. I refuse to believe it. Where is your proof? Your witnesses?"

He had neither but Reid wanted to confront Eden Martin, nonetheless, and see her reaction to his accusation.

"I demand to see Lady Eden," he told the viscount, knowing it would be well within the man's rights to refuse. He prepared himself for that, knowing Martin would want to protect his younger daughter.

"Your Grace! What a wonderful surprise. I didn't know you'd be coming to London, much less to visit us."

Reid turned and saw the object of their conversation float into the room, trailed by her two suitors. She looked very young and pretty, wearing a pale pink gown with pink ribbons running through her hair. She curtseyed to him.

"I was telling your father that Dunwood Academy burned recently," he said.

"Is that so? How awful. I hope no one was injured." Her face remained a mask, void of emotion, but a glint in her eyes told Reid all he needed to know.

"No one was inside at the time," he said brusquely and then searched her features. "You wouldn't know anything about it, would you, my lady?"

"Me?" she asked guilelessly. "Why, I've been in London. This is certainly news to me. I'm sure it is to Papa, too." She turned toward him, looking innocent and vulnerable.

"Yes, Eden. I told His Grace we were in London when this happened."

That's not what Lord Martin had said earlier but Reid didn't call him out. Instead, he looked to the other two men.

"Shouldn't you be leaving with Lady Eden for the garden party?"

"Yes," they replied in unison.

"I will see you later, Papa." Eden kissed his cheek. "And I hope to see more of you, Your Grace. You know we consider you family."

She curtseyed again and sauntered from the room, the two gentlemen trailing her wordlessly.

After the door closed, Reid said, "She did it. You know she did."

"I know nothing of the sort, Your Grace," the viscount said stubbornly. "I insist you stop this slander against my child. You'll ruin her reputation if you persist."

"Just as she ruined Thornhill? What if Lady Dunwood or her students had been inside, Martin?"

He shook his head. "You're mistaken. Eden is not like her mother."

"Don't bring her back to Gillbrook," Reid warned.

"Eden won't need to return there. She's going to make a brilliant match this Season."

Reid knew in his heart that Eden had lit the fire that destroyed Dunwood Academy but without evidence or eyewitness testimony, she would never be charged.

"I will cease my accusations," he promised Lord Martin. "At the same time, you need to keep a careful eye on your daughter. I fear she's capable of terrible things."

For a moment, he saw fear in the viscount's eyes that Martin also believed the same.

With a curt "Good day" Reid left and made a quick stop in Doctors' Commons before he returned to his London residence. He met with a few servants, informing them he would be coming to town in late June with his new duchess.

"Make sure everything is immaculate," he instructed.

Ashlyn had never visited London and he wanted to show her the city. He'd take her to the opera and theater. Museums. Parks. He intended to find the best modiste and have her create an entire wardrobe for his bride.

As he rode back to Gillingham, he regretted not being able to get a confession from Eden Martin, though. As long as Lord Martin kept his daughter away from Ashlyn, that was all that mattered. He prayed the girl would make a match with some gentleman that lived in the far north and that they'd never see her again.

Reid arrived back home and left Thunder in the stables. He had time to bathe the dust of the road away and changed into fresh clothes before going downstairs to dinner. Dalinda greeted him.

"I haven't seen you all day," she said.

"I was out and about," he said vaguely.

"I haven't told you, but I think it was very kind of you to house Dunwood Academy here at Gillingham. Selfishly, it will allow me to see Arthur and Harry more often. Lady Dunwood has done the impossible and brought my boys back to me. They are as sweet as they were before."

"She has a way with people," he agreed.

"And with you?" Dalinda asked.

"Why do you say that?"

She laughed. "Oh, Reid, you should see the way you look at her. If you haven't kissed her yet, you certainly need to do so."

"We're going to be married," he said. "I'm holding a ball a week from this Saturday. I'll announce our engagement that night. Until then, pretend that you don't know."

Ashlyn entered the dining room. "Good evening."

"The same to you, Lady Dunwood," Dalinda said. "How was the first day in your new classrooms?"

Reid seated them both as Ashlyn told of the classes she'd observed while soup was served. He watched her speak animatedly and fell in love with her anew. He suspected this would happen to him on a regular basis as the years passed.

Once dinner ended, he offered to walk her back to her cottage. He asked about various boys in order to keep her from asking about his day. They reached the door and he opened it. A lamp had been lit and he assumed Mrs. Paul had seen to that.

Reid wrapped his arms about her. "I'm glad it was a good first day for Dunwood Academy in its new surroundings."

She placed her palms against his cheeks. "The boys have taken to it well." She tugged on him, bringing his face down to hers and kissing him sweetly.

"I should leave you. I'm sure you're tired," he said.

Ashlyn walked him to the door and they kissed again. Reid left and returned to his study, where he spent an hour going over some figures his estate manager wanted him to review. Then he decided it was time to pay another visit to his fiancée.

He slipped from the house and walked the half-mile to her cottage, testing the door and finding it unlocked. Normally, he would admonish her for it but she was safe on Gillingham grounds. Besides, it made it much easier to make his way to her bed.

Reid crept from the front room to the back one, which served as a bedroom. She'd left a window open and a soft breeze drifted in. Moonlight poured through it, making it easy to see her. In sleep, Ashlyn looked younger and softer, not the resolute headmistress who took on the world every day.

Quickly, he shed his clothes and slipped under the bedclothes, an arm going about her. His lips touched her hair and he inhaled the faint fragrance that clung to it. She stirred and he kissed her neck.

Suddenly, she stiffened and drew breath for a scream.

"It's only me, love. I couldn't keep away."

Ashlyn turned. "You gave me a fright, Reid."

"You should use the bar on the door. Or not," he murmured as he nuzzled her neck.

"Oh . . ."

"Oh, is right," he agreed.

He made love to her tenderly, pulling out at the last moment. He couldn't wait for the day he could pump his seed into her and see their child grow in her belly. Ashlyn was the most nurturing woman he knew and would make for the best mother.

"You can't stay," she said, her voice trailing off as she fell asleep.

"I can . . . for a while," he told her.

Reid allowed himself an hour to enjoy the feel of her nestled in his arms and then eased from the bed. He planned to come back every night.

If she'd let him.

Chapter Twenty-Four

Ashlyn finished her correspondence and left her study. She returned to the main wing of Gillingham and gave the letters to a footman to be posted. Several servants traipsed past her, large pots of flowers in hand, and she followed them up the stairs to the ballroom. Mr. Bellows supervised the decorating, along with Mrs. Paul, and the two servants stood viewing things with a critical eye.

"Everything looks wonderful, Mr. Bellows," she praised. "You and Mrs. Paul have done an outstanding job. His Grace will be so pleased."

"Thank you, my lady. The servants and tenants are eager for another ball to be held in such a short space of time, especially since they are invited once again."

"My pupils are equally ready to dance tonight. Are there many guests in attendance?"

Ashlyn had left all the details up to Reid and his staff, rather liking the idea that she would be surprised along with all of the guests.

"There will be a large turnout, my lady. Every parent of a Dunwood Academy student responded they would come. Almost all of His Grace's neighbors will also attend, as will his tenants."

"Will Lord Martin and his daughter come?" she asked, remembering how strongly Reid felt about Lady Eden's behavior at the last ball. With the girl visiting relatives in the north, though, she hoped the pair would come without worry.

Bellows replied carefully, "The Martins were not invited although Viscount Ransom asked and will bring his fiancée."

Ashlyn had been delighted to hear the couple was engaged and was glad that Lady Edith would attend tonight's festivities. She liked the young woman and hated to think her sister's actions would reflect poorly upon the family.

"I see." She excused herself and went downstairs, knowing their friends were due soon. Ashlyn had requested Charlotte and Gemma come early so they could spend several hours together before the ball began. Both the Cramptons and Westons would be staying the night, the only guests who would do so. She looked forward to her time with her friends before the festivities began.

Reid appeared and said, "I saw carriages from my window in the study. Let's go greet our first guests." He slipped an arm about her waist and led her out the front door.

Four carriages appeared in the lane, the first two traveling at the usual pace, while the third and fourth seemed to crawl along.

The first arrived and Gray jumped out, helping Charlotte and their three children from the vehicle.

Gray kissed her cheek and Charlotte did the same, their young son squirming in her arms. She set the boy down and he toddled off, soon chased by his nursery governess, who emerged from the second carriage, which carried the Crampton servants.

The two girls came and curtseyed to Ashlyn.

"Thank you for allowing us to come to your ball, Lady Dunwood," Lady Harriet said.

"We can't wait to dance!" squealed Lady Jane.

"I thought you would enjoy coming since my students will also be in attendance and are your same ages," Ashlyn said.

Gray looked at the girls with mock sternness. "Remember, I'll have my eyes on you all night long."

"Oh, Gray, don't worry," she assured him. "My boys will be beautifully behaved."

He chuckled. "It's not your boys I'm worried about, Ashlyn. It's my mischievous girls influencing them."

Charlotte placed her hands on the girls' shoulders. "They will be perfect, Gray. You have nothing to worry about." Then she leaned down and softly said, "You two better be good or he'll lock you up until you're thirty."

By now, the other two carriages had arrived. Gemma poked her head out the window and waved merrily as Burke opened the door and exited the vehicle. He lifted Gemma down with great care. Ashlyn saw in the three weeks since she'd seen her friend that Gemma's belly had popped.

They all greeted the couple. Gemma patted her belly. "It seemed to happen overnight. I only hope there's one inside me and not two."

"When are you due?" Reid asked.

"The end of June or the first week in July. In the worst of the summer heat," she said. "Burke already has to rub my feet every night and place cold compresses upon my brow. I'm sure I'll think of other things he must do to make it up to me."

Servants were toting bags inside and the nanny and governess whisked the children away.

Ashlyn said, "The first thing you need to know is that Reid and I are engaged."

All four beamed with delight and offered congratulations to them.

"We planned to wed once the spring term at Dunwood Academy ended and the boys left for their summer holiday," she continued. "Now, I don't think that's a wise idea."

Reid said sternly, "No delays, Ashlyn."

"Oh, no, I wasn't thinking about a delay. I thought we might need to move the wedding up."

In response, he kissed her soundly as their friends chuckled.

"I don't mind you changing your mind but may I ask why—and when?" Reid asked.

"Just look at Gemma," Ashlyn said. "In another six weeks she won't feel like walking ten feet, much less riding from Westbrook to here in order to sit through a ceremony."

"Burke made the horses walk the entire way here," Gemma said. "It took forever to drive the three miles but he didn't want me jostled about."

Ashlyn looked at Reid. "It's only ten o'clock. If you rode to London now, you could purchase a special license. We could announce our engagement tonight and then wed tomorrow. Or perhaps Monday."

Reid withdrew something from his coat pocket and handed it to her. "Open it."

She did. "It's . . . a special license for us to wed," she said, astounded. "Dated earlier this week."

He laughed. "I know we planned for the banns to be read starting tomorrow but I had business in London and thought it would be wise to have this just in case. It's good for ninety days. We could still marry in the chapel at Gillingham but now we don't have to wait."

Ashlyn smiled. "You never cease to amaze me."

"Like headmistresses, army officers like to be prepared for any circumstances. Tomorrow will be taken up with Sunday services." Reid took her hand and kissed it. "Would you care to marry me Monday morning, Lady Dunwood?"

"I most certainly would, Your Grace." She turned to their friends. "If you're willing to stay until then for the ceremony."

Gray laughed. "Charlotte always brings extra clothes wherever we go. She'll have something to wear for a wedding, I'm sure."

"I don't," Gemma complained. "But we're so close that I can send someone back to Westbrook for a gown. Or a sack. That would be nice and roomy."

Burke cradled her cheek. "You would look lovely in a sack, my dear."

"Fortunately, if I wear one, no one will be looking at me," Gemma quipped. "All eyes will be on the beautiful bride."

"The very person who has nothing to wear to her own wedding," Ashlyn informed them. "I already had the Gillbrook seamstress make me a gown for tonight's ball. Perhaps I should wear it."

"I like that idea," Reid said. He took back the special license and returned it to his pocket. "We can use flowers from the ball to decorate the church. I'll need to arrange with our good reverend a time for the ceremony to take place." He looked to his friends. "Care to walk down to the church with me?"

"Of course," Gray said and the three men set off.

"I suppose I'll need to tell Mr. Bellows and Mrs. Paul of our sudden plans. And Mrs. Cook. Poor thing. She's been cooking along with Mrs. George for days to prepare tonight's feast. Now she'll have a wedding breakfast to supply."

Charlotte and Gemma linked arms with Ashlyn. Charlotte said, "They'll all be happy to do so because they'll be getting a wonderful mistress in return."

They went into the house and Ashlyn asked for tea to be brought to the drawing room with eight cups and asked the footman to have Lady Gilford join them. The tea arrived when Dalinda did and Ashlyn then rang for the various servants she needed. After they arrived, she invited them to sit and poured tea for them all. Mr. Bellows and Mrs. Paul looked uncomfortable doing so but Mrs. Cook and Mrs. George eagerly took a place.

"I know how very hard you've all worked in order for tonight's ball to be a success," Ashlyn said. "I'm afraid I have more to ask of you, though." She paused. "His Grace and I plan to announce our engagement tonight."

They offered immediate congratulations, telling Ashlyn how happy they were to have her as the new duchess. She could tell by Dalinda's face that the dowager duchess had already guessed at the news.

"We wish to wed on Monday in the Gillingham chapel. His Grace has purchased a special license. I know you're exhausted but—"

"Don't you worry about a thing, my lady," Mrs. Cook interrupted. "Mrs. George and I will give you a lovely wedding breakfast. It will be our pleasure."

"And Mr. Bellows and I will see the church decorated properly," Mrs. Paul added.

"Hopefully, we can use some of the flowers from tonight's event," Ashlyn suggested.

"It will be taken care of," Mr. Bellows assured her and then added, "the staff at Gillingham will be delighted with this news, Lady Dunwood."

"How many will attend the breakfast?" Mrs. George asked.

Ashlyn said, "The Dowager Duchess of Gilford and her sons. Lord and Lady Crampton with their children and Lord and Lady Weston, of course. Possibly Viscount Ransom and Lady Edith Martin."

Dalinda spoke up. "I believe it would mean a great deal if your boys and their tutors were invited." She gave Ashlyn a warm smile.

"That's a wonderful idea. Yes, we must include the boys and their tutors." She thought a moment. "Other than those guests, I believe that should do it. If you will keep the news to yourselves for now, I'd appreciate it. I'd rather all of tonight's ball guests leave without being obligated to invite them to the wedding. We prefer a more intimate affair."

"Nothing will be mentioned until the last guest has left, my lady," Bellows guaranteed.

"Thank you, Mr. Bellows. Thank you all," Ashlyn said. She lifted her teacup and turned to the two cooks. "Let's talk about the wedding breakfast."

ASHLYN WAS EXCITED for her second ball in such a short time. After all of the guests arrived, Reid led her to the center of the floor and then laced his fingers through hers. She heard the murmurs flow through the room at such an intimate gesture in public.

Reid addressed the room. "We are here tonight, in part, to celebrate my permanent association with Dunwood Academy and its being situated within Gillingham. What I really want to share, however, is that Lady Dunwood has agreed to become my wife."

Applause broke out as he lifted their joined hands and kissed hers. For a moment, as her gaze met his, Ashlyn felt as if it were only the two of them in the room.

"I love you," Reid said and kissed her hand again. Then he called out, "Please join my fiancée and me in this first dance."

The musicians struck up a tune and Reid swept her across the dance floor.

"I thought you were going to make the announcement at supper."

He grinned sheepishly. "I thought so, too. Then I saw how lovely you looked and pride rose within me, knowing you will soon be my duchess. I couldn't help myself." A devilish glint came into his eyes. "Besides, this way, I can dance every number with you without fear of gossip. No one can blame me for being besotted with my fiancée."

"That would be extremely bad manners, Your Grace. You can't neglect your guests that way."

He sighed. "You're right, as always, though everyone here will want to dance with the duchess-to-be."

The music ended and Reid escorted her from the floor. Ashlyn found herself surrounded by well-wishers and danced every time the music struck up. She made a point to alternate partners between gentry, tenants, and her pupils.

Finally, supper came and she joined Reid at a table with the Cramptons and Westons. She was happy to find Viscount Ransom and Lady Edith also at their table.

"I must offer you congratulations on your engagement," Ashlyn said.

"The same to you, Lady Dunwood," Ransom said.

"We are very happy for you," Lady Edith added. "The duke looks so pleased."

As the men left the table to fill plates for everyone, Ashlyn asked, "When is your wedding going to be held?"

"Ransom wants us to wait until September. He wants me to enjoy the full season and still have plenty of time to plan for the ceremony."

"That is thoughtful of him," Ashlyn said. "It will also give your sister more than ample time to return from her visit to your relatives in the north."

The younger woman's cheeks reddened. "Eden is in London, my lady. She is making her come-out this Season as planned."

Ashlyn wondered if Reid knew this. "I see."

"Once again, I am very sorry about what Eden did to you," Lady Edith said.

"You had nothing to do with the incident," she assured the young woman." Besides, it's already forgotten." Wanting to change the subject, she asked, "Where will your wedding take place?"

"At the Gillbrook church. Ransom hopes His Grace will agree to stand with him. They were at school together. Ransom was several years younger and His Grace put a halt to some vicious bullying that had been going on. Ransom worshipped His Grace after that and still thinks highly of him."

Ashlyn smiled, thinking of Reid standing up to a group of bullies so that younger boys might feel safe. She hoped their sons would also have such strength of character.

It surprised her that the thought of children brought no heartache. For a long time after losing Gregory, it had pained her to think of children. She'd never intended to have a child again but Reid had changed all of that. Now, Ashlyn couldn't wait to give him sons and daughters.

After supper ended, she made sure to dance with the few remaining students she hadn't partnered with earlier. Each boy expressed his delight at her upcoming marriage.

Ashlyn joined Reid, who stood with Gray, Charlotte, and their two girls.

"I hope you have enjoyed your first country ball," she told Harriet and Jane.

"We have, my lady," Harriet said, her eyes shining. "Jane and I have decided we should be allowed to attend every ball."

"I believe that's called a come-out," Gray said. "Which you will make when you turn eighteen. Tonight's ball was an exception." He smoothed both girls' hair. "I don't want you growing up too fast, you know."

Dalinda approached, her hands on the backs of her sons, guiding the boys toward them. Both Harry and Arthur looked shyly at Harriet and Jane and then their gaze shifted to their shoes.

Dalinda leaned down and murmured something in Harry's ear and he nodded. Glancing up, he asked, "Lady Harriet, would you like to dance the next number?"

"And will you dance with me, Lady Jane?" Arthur quickly interjected.

The girls glanced to each other and giggled. Harriet answered for them both, saying, "We would be honored to dance with you."

Harry offered Harriet his arm and Arthur did the same to Jane. Both boys led their new dance partners onto the floor as the adults looked on with smiles.

"I believe my sons may have a crush on your daughters," Dalinda told Gray and Charlotte.

"Don't they look sweet together?" Ashlyn said, slipping her hand through Reid's arm.

As they watched the children dance, her gaze swept across the room, watching all her pupils dancing. She spied Edward, who partnered with the head groom's daughter.

"Do you see Edward?" she asked Reid. "He looks so happy. As if he hadn't a care in the world."

"Edward is a special boy," her fiancé agreed. "He has made great strides under your care. Perhaps with his mathematical skills, he will one day become our steward—or even our banker."

She smiled. "That would be lovely."

When the ball came to a close, Reid had Ashlyn stand with him as they said goodbye to the departing guests. Gemma and Burke had excused themselves after supper. She'd looked very tired after being on her feet for several hours. They said goodnight to Charlotte and Gray and then Reid looked at her.

"Am I to walk you back to your cottage now—or will you stay with me tonight?"

A shiver of anticipation rippled through her.

"I came and dressed for the ball here," she said. "I had thought about sleeping in that bedchamber tonight."

His hands encircled her waist and he pulled her close.

"If you're staying under my roof, then you'll be sleeping in my bed. *Our* bed. And this time when I make love to you, Ashlyn, I will complete the act with you."

Chapter Twenty-Five

REID LED ASHLYN to his bedchamber, glad the corridor was empty. He hadn't known if she would say yes to his request and was grateful she'd agreed to spend what was left of the night with him.

He pushed open the door and then swept her into his arms and entered, shoving the door closed with his foot. He carried her to a chair and sat with her in his lap, not wanting to rush things. They kissed for a long time, his blood heating, his desire for her as strong as ever.

Reid nuzzled her neck and gave her tiny love bites, enjoying the pleased murmurs that came from her.

"I meant what I said earlier. Once we're wed, you may use the bedchamber intended for the duchess—but only to store your clothes. Or possibly dress there." Reid kissed her. "I want you in my bed every night, Ashlyn. I want my arms about you. Our bare skin touching. There's to be none of this going to visit you and then returning alone to a cold, empty bed. We will be together every night."

She stroked his cheek. "Won't the servants find that odd?"

"I don't care what they think. I'm the duke—and I want my duchess in my bed."

"To pleasure you every night, Your Grace?" she asked saucily.

"Yes," he growled and then added, "and so I may pleasure you in return."

Reid kissed her again hungrily. His hand cupped her breast and she sighed.

"Enough talk—and enough with clothes," he proclaimed, standing up and setting her on her feet. "Since you've no lady's maid, I suppose I shall I have to attend to you."

She slid a finger slowly down his chest. "I think that's a marvelous idea. Even if you are a duke and are used to others waiting upon you."

He wrapped his arms around her. "I haven't been a duke for very long. Don't forget I was away on the Continent for many years."

She chuckled. "You may not have been a duke all that long but you've certainly taken to it. You're incredibly bossy. And you certainly don't take no for an answer."

"Sounds like a headmistress I know," he said huskily and kissed her, long and deep, finally breaking the kiss. "Let's get you naked as you should be."

He carefully unbuttoned and unfurled everything having to do with the gown and then removed the layers underneath it.

"You do that with ease. I'd say you've played lady's maid to more than me, Your Grace."

He gave her a solemn look. "His Grace has only undressed you, Lady Dunwood. Lieutenant-Colonel Baker might have had a hand helping other women, though."

Ashlyn kissed him. "I'm only interested in His Grace. Now and from this moment forward."

He liked that about her. Not caring that either of them held on to their pasts. Only that they had now—and their futures together.

Reid bent and removed her stockings and slippers, leaving her with nothing on. His eyes roamed the pale, smooth flesh as his hands settled on her hips.

"This is how I like you best. How only I see you. Touch you. Taste you."

Ashlyn looked over his shoulder and around the room. "I

don't see any valet here, Your Grace. I suppose I can return the favor."

He kissed the tip of her perfect nose. "I wish you would, my lady."

She took her time getting him from his clothes. Unbuttoning each button leisurely. Untying his cravat and sliding it from him. Reid wanted to set her aside and shuck off his clothes but then he saw that she moved deliberately, peeling away each layer with precision, building anticipation within him.

When at last they stood face to face, bare as the day they'd been born, he said, "I cannot wait to be inside you. To come inside you. I figure since we're little more than a day away from our wedding that it's safe to spill my seed within you."

Ashlyn wrapped her arms about his waist. "Do you want a boy or a girl first?"

He cradled her face in his palms. "It doesn't matter. I assume we'll have plenty of both. I know I should say a boy so an heir is confirmed but all I see is a little girl with blond locks as her mother, twisting me about her little finger, making me dance to her tune."

"Speaking of dancing . . . shall we go to bed?"

"Ah, my favorite type of dance to engage in. No wonder we are so well suited, Lady Dunwood. We favor the same kind of dancing."

Reid scooped her into his arms and tossed her onto the bed, jumping next to her. Ashlyn giggled as he began touching her. But soon, the giggles turned to sighs and then whimpers. His fingers glided along her satin skin. His mouth feasted upon her breasts. Then he moved his lips down her belly and beyond, reaching the tuft of curls.

Her fingers pushed into his hair, forcing his head up. "What are you doing?"

"Making you mine," he growled.

He removed her fingers from his hair and pushed them onto the bed next to her hips, gently holding her wrists in place.

"Reid," she said, squirming.

"You've trusted me before, Ashlyn. Trust me now."

"All right," she agreed and stilled.

He released her wrists and reached for her ankles, pulling on them until her feet rested flat, her knees bent. He captured her wrists again lightly.

And ran his tongue along the seam of her sex.

"Reid!" she squealed. "That's . . . sinful."

"Then sinning never felt so good," he replied—and did it again.

Within minutes, Ashlyn writhed on the bed as his tongue explored her. Her little gasps became big ones. Then moans. Then groans. Then she called his name several times as she orgasmed.

He worked his way back up her luscious body, taking his time until their lips met again. When they did, he placed his cock in position and then pushed inside her. Ashlyn called out something which was lost in their kiss and then he pumped into her with a mix of reverence and enthusiasm. For the first time, Reid came inside her and they clung to one another. He collapsed atop her and, conscious of his weight, quickly rolled to his back, bringing her with him.

He caught sight of the dazed look on her face, her eyes glazed in the aftermath of their lovemaking. He cupped her nape and pushed her head to his chest. She nestled her cheek against it, her breathing still as erratic as his. Together, they fell back to earth.

"I hope we made a baby," she mumbled and then he heard her soft snores.

Kissing the top of her head, he said, "I hope so, too."

Reid didn't sleep. He couldn't. He didn't want to miss a moment of Ashlyn being in his arms. He supposed the newness of his love for her would pass but he couldn't imagine a day—or night—when he wouldn't crave this woman.

He let her sleep another hour and then awakened her.

"Time to return to your temporary bedchamber, Lady Dunwood."

She looked at him sleepily. "Must I, Your Grace?"

"I think it wise. Then you can breakfast with our friends and we can go to church together. I'd like to confirm everything regarding tomorrow's ceremony with the clergyman after this morning's service."

Reid tossed back the bedclothes and shrugged into his dressing gown. He helped Ashlyn into her layers of clothing and then walked with her to her bedchamber.

"Dalinda is still using the bedchamber designated for the Duchess of Gilford. I'll see that the servants move her things sometime today."

"There's no rush, Reid. I don't want her to feel awkward about it."

He kissed her. "She'll understand. I'll speak to her about it."

He returned to his room and rang for Anderson. The valet appeared, jovial as ever.

"Good morning, Your Grace. Felicitations to you upon your engagement. Lady Dunwood is quite popular with the staff."

"Thank you, Anderson. I find she's very popular with me, as well. Could you bring hot water? I'll dress afterward."

"Certainly, Your Grace."

His valet returned a short time later and once Reid was ready, he went downstairs. Both Gray and Burke were already present in the small breakfast room, their plates piled high.

"You look exhilarated," Burke said. "I assume I know what you and Ashlyn were up to after the ball."

He couldn't keep the smile from his face. "We're almost married. And we're in love."

"It doesn't get old, my friend," Gray shared. "Just when I don't think I can love Charlotte any more than I do, my wonderful Miss Nott goes and does something or says something, and I find myself giddy with joy and bursting with love anew for her."

Reid laughed as he filled a plate. "I'm glad I'm not the only one making a fool of myself."

"The only fools are those who never admit love exists," Burke declared. "We three are better men for doing so—and for wedding women even better than us."

"Ashlyn does seem to get along well with Gemma and Charlotte," he said. "That's convenient."

"Ashlyn could get along with a boulder sitting in a field," Gemma declared as she entered the breakfast room. "I'm so glad you love her, Reid. She is immensely loveable."

"She is," he agreed pleasantly. "Every inch of her is loveable." He grinned. "I know from experience."

Gemma swatted him as she passed and took a seat. "Watch your tongue, Your Grace. Be glad you're among friends."

"I wouldn't speak of her this way to anyone else," he said. "I'm merely reeling with love."

Ashlyn and Charlotte came in several minutes later, followed by Dalinda, and the group had a lively conversation before they left for church.

As they waited for the carriage, Reid drew Dalinda aside.

"Since Ashlyn and I are marrying tomorrow, I was hoping you wouldn't mind vacating the suite of rooms you now use."

"I am one step ahead of you, Reid," Dalinda said. "I spoke to Mrs. Paul about it yesterday once Ashlyn informed us of your engagement. It will be taken care of today once everything having to do with the ball has been undone."

"That was very thoughtful of you, Dalinda."

She smiled. "I'm glad to see you this way, Reid. Your father would also have been happy that you've found love." A shadow crossed her face. "I think it will be good for me to have new rooms. The old ones have too many memories in them."

"I know you miss him."

"I do. Rather, I miss the man I married and had for ten years. Once he became ill, he was very different. I suppose that helped me in the end, letting him go. He was a stranger by then."

"I'm sorry."

"Don't be," Dalinda assured him. "I still have Arthur and

Harry. They are the best parts of him."

"You know you're still young. Barely older than I am. Perhaps you'll wed again someday."

"It's possible. Who knows what lies in the future?"

After the Sunday service, Reid produced the special license and he and Ashlyn confirmed all of the details with Reverend Jackson. They set the time for ten o'clock the following morning.

The rest of the day was spent with their friends, though Gemma disappeared for an afternoon nap. Gray and Charlotte's children joined them as they played lawn croquet and Jane turned up the surprise winner. They had an early dinner and then Ashlyn insisted on returning to her cottage. Reid walked her back, reluctant to leave her even for a few hours.

"I think it best if we spend our wedding eve apart," she told him. "I've sent everything for tomorrow's ceremony ahead to Gillingham. Mrs. Paul told me it will all be laid out and ready for me. I'll come to the house early to bathe and dress."

"I'll come get you."

"No, it's bad luck for the groom to see his bride before the ceremony. The first time you see me tomorrow will be when I come down the aisle. Gray already offered to escort me to Gillingham tomorrow morning."

"He better not take his time," Reid grumbled. "I don't want to wait any longer than necessary."

They reached the cottage and he said, "Since I won't see you until tomorrow, I suppose I should give this to you now." He pulled something sparkling from his pocket and opened his palm.

Ashlyn saw a diamond bracelet resting there. "Oh, Reid, it's beautiful."

He slipped it onto her wrist and she admired it.

"I'll certainly wear this tomorrow. I've never owned anything so fine."

"Until you received this." He reached into a different pocket and extracted a matching necklace.

Her eyes widened. "It's incredible."

He placed the necklace around her neck and fastened the clasp. She touched it with her fingers, in awe of the piece.

"As Duchess of Gilford, you will have access to many jewels—but know this, Ashlyn—you are the most valuable jewel of all."

Reid kissed her tenderly and Ashlyn felt treasured in that moment. She was marrying a good man and knew he would always keep her safe.

He broke the kiss and opened the cottage door.

"This is as far as you go, Your Grace," she told him. "I will see you in the chapel tomorrow morning."

Reid gave her a soft, sweet kiss. "Until tomorrow, Lady Dunwood."

She sighed. "I do love you."

"I love you more," he replied. He kissed her again and then said, "Goodnight, my lady. You realize when I say that this time tomorrow, I will be speaking to Lady Gilford, my wife." His eyes twinkled at her. "I like the sound of that. Goodnight, Your Grace," he tried out. "Yes, that sounds right."

Ashlyn laughed softly. "It most certainly does."

With that, she closed the door.

Reid whistled the entire way back to Gillingham.

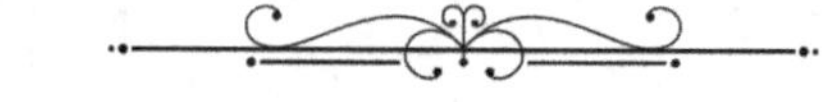

Chapter Twenty-Six

Ashlyn leaned against the door, smiling to herself, fingering the new necklace she wore.

This time tomorrow, she would be Her Grace, the Duchess of Gilford.

The title she could do without but what she could never be without was Reid. He had made such a difference in her life. She would have a second chance at marriage. At having children. And it was her first and only time to fall in love. Her circumstances almost overwhelmed her.

She thought back to his idea of opening a girls' school, a companion to the boys, and decided she liked that quite a bit. She still wanted to keep Dunwood Academy small, servicing no more than a dozen or so boys. Having an equal number of girls would nicely balance things. It would be good for the genders to mix in a few activities, such as riding and dancing lessons. Perhaps music, as well. The thought of her own sons and daughters attending Dunwood Academy made her swell with pride. Ashlyn would look into the matter over the summer break, knowing that Reid would give her good counsel. The idea of them working together in creating a new school made her very happy.

As did the idea of them having children. She placed a hand on her belly, wondering if even now Reid's child might be growing inside her. She hoped she was still fertile. It had taken only one coupling between her and Daniel to produce Gregory. Possibly by this time next year, she and Reid would already have the first of what she hoped would be many offspring.

Ashlyn picked up the lamp to light her way into the other room, grateful that Mrs. Paul always made sure this small gesture was taken care of. She looked forward to getting to know the housekeeper and all of Reid's servants better.

She took a few steps and froze, her mind not quite understanding what lay before her as a disheveled Eden Martin stepped from the darkened bedchamber. She was covered in dust from the road and the hem of her gown and one sleeve were torn. Half her hair had fallen from its elaborate coil, giving her a lopsided appearance. Her eyes darted about like a wild animal that had been cornered.

But what frightened Ashlyn most was the pistol in Eden's hand—aimed directly at Ashlyn.

Drawing from wells of strength she hoped wouldn't disappear, she calmly said, "I'm surprised to see you here, Lady Eden."

The younger woman looked perplexed, as if Ashlyn spoke to her in some foreign tongue. Ashlyn wanted to run. To scream. To hide. Any of those might get her killed. Instead, she held her ground and tried to look upon the intruder benignly, not wanting Eden to feel threatened.

"He doesn't love you," Eden said, her voice breathy. "I heard him tell you that. But he loves me. And I love him. I have ever since I was a girl." She paused, her eyes glassy. "I decided then I would marry him. That I would become the Duchess of Gilford one day."

Ashlyn swallowed, unsure what to say. She decided to try to distract Eden.

"Your sister tells me you've made a brilliant come-out. That you have gentlemen calling on you left and right. She says you are the most popular girl making her debut this Season."

Eden nodded. "I have many men interested in me."

"I'm sure you do," she encouraged. "Handsome men. Men with lofty titles and vast amounts of wealth. You'll have your pick of whomever you choose to wed, Eden."

"No!" the girl said, stamping her foot. "I want Gilford. No one else." She paused. "He called you Ashlyn. It's a pretty name."

The compliment caught her off-guard. "Thank you, Eden. I like your name, as well."

"My name means *delight*. Eden was a paradise. That is what Gilford and I will live in. Paradise. Just as Adam and Eve did."

Ashlyn refrained from mentioning that Adam and Eve were thrust from paradise because they'd disobeyed God.

"Edith told me you were going to wed Gilford. I'm here to prevent that mistake," the young woman continued, nervously swaying from side to side, the gun wavering in all directions. "Gilford will marry me instead. He thinks he wants you but he doesn't. He doesn't know me. He thinks I'm some silly little schoolgirl. He doesn't understand how much I love him. I will do anything to be with him. *Anything*."

Ashlyn's mind raced, whirling with a thousand thoughts, none of them forming into a way to help her escape this creature.

"Perhaps we should go see His Grace," she suggested, hoping that if they left the cottage, she might have a chance to escape the range of Eden's pistol. She doubted the girl had ever fired a weapon. The likelihood of her missing, especially a moving target, was what Ashlyn clung to.

"No. I'll go."

She gripped the lamp she held. "Then I'll stay here and wait for you."

Eden quit moving and raised the gun, pointing it at Ashlyn. "No. I don't want you here. If you're here, you'd be a reminder to Gilford. I want you gone. Forever."

"Then I'll leave, Eden," she quickly said. "Tell me where you want me to go."

An evil smile lit the girl's face. "I want you to join your dead husband and dead son, Ashlyn."

AS REID APPROACHED the house, he saw a carriage racing up the lane and went to see who might be calling at Gillingham at such a late hour. It startled him to see Ransom fling open the door and bound out. He handed Lady Edith down as Reid reached them.

"We went home to London today," Lady Edith said, her agitation obvious as she wrung her hands together. "I told Papa of your engagement to Lady Dunwood. Eden overheard me. She became like a wild woman, Your Grace. She screamed obscenities. Shattered vases. Stormed from the room. Papa sent for the doctor but when he arrived, we couldn't find her anywhere. He sent servants out but they came home without her."

"We believe she may have come to Gillingham," Ransom continued, wrapping his arm protectively around his fiancée. "A groom reported a horse missing from the stables."

"Warn my servants," Reid cried and took off, running back toward Ashlyn's cottage. Fear gave him a burst of energy as he raced across the lawn.

Who knew what actions Eden Martin was capable of, especially with her demented mind? He had to reach Ashlyn in time. He couldn't live his life without her. It had taken him almost thirty years to find someone to love. Someone he could trust. The woman he wanted to birth his children. The only one he wanted in his bed and by his side, now and forever.

The cottage appeared and Reid saw a faint light still glowed within. He didn't know if that was a good sign or bad as he burst through the door.

He went cold as he caught sight of Eden Martin facing his direction, the pistol in her hands pointed at Ashlyn. Quickly, he leaped in front of Ashlyn, knowing his frame would block any bullet Eden attempted to fire.

"Move, Gilford. She can't be part of our lives," demanded Eden.

At that moment, he knew the young woman had slipped into madness. Reid needed to get Ashlyn safely from the cottage. To do so, he needed to feed the monster within Eden.

"I don't want Ashlyn in our lives, Eden," he said soothingly. "I just want her to be gone. Seeing you makes me realize that. You came all this way—because you love me."

A brilliant smile lit Eden's face. "I do, Gilford. I truly do," she said earnestly.

"Any woman who would do so must love me a great deal," he continued. "Ashlyn certainly wouldn't ride hours in order to make such a declaration." Reid held out his arms, palms up. "I've been blind, Eden. A fool. You've been before me all along. I only now see how much you care for me." He paused, hating the words he uttered but hoping it would convince the girl to put the firearm aside. "I can deny it no longer. I care for you, as well."

Her smile twisted her features from malevolent to almost girlish. "You do? You care for me? Do you love me, Gilford?"

Reid nodded. "I do, Eden. I suppose we were always meant to be, from that day at the garden party. I had to go a world away and fight our enemy before I could return home and find your sweet love waiting for me."

She lowered the gun, adoration plain on her face. "Oh, I love you, Gilford. So very, very, much." Then she frowned. "But Ashlyn is in our way."

"She is nothing to me," he proclaimed. "My eyes have been opened. I only see you, Eden. Only you." He looked over his shoulder and saw Ashlyn's wide eyes. "You may go, Lady Dunwood. I have no further need of you. We are no longer engaged." He implored her with his eyes to leave.

"You never truly cared for me," she said, playing along. "You always cared for Eden. I thought I would be good for you but I see now how mistaken I was." Her voice broke on the last word.

"Go," Reid ordered, taking the lamp from her. It would allow Ashlyn to slip away in darkness and he would still have light to see Eden and hopefully disarm her quickly. He turned away from the woman he loved, pinning his gaze on the crazed one in front of him. The gun still remained lowered to her side. He prayed Ashlyn would be able to get out safely before Eden changed her mind.

"No," Eden said harshly. "She will not give up so easily on you. She's only pretending to, Gilford. She will always be there, trying to win you back."

"But I will be faithful to you, Eden. Only you. You are the one I love."

"Move, I say." Eden raised the gun again.

"No, Eden. I cannot let you kill Lady Dunwood. She is too well known. The authorities would investigate. They would take you away from me. I won't allow that to happen." He glanced over his shoulder. "Go!" he hissed at Ashlyn and she took a few steps back.

As Reid turned, Eden rushed toward him, trying to push him aside to get to Ashlyn. She knocked the lamp he held from his hands and it crashed to the floor as the gun discharged. Searing pain flashed along his outer thigh and he swallowed the shout that threatened to erupt. Flames leaped up, catching the hem of Eden's gown on fire. She screamed and Reid flung himself at her, knocking her to the ground, away from the spilled oil and fire. He pushed to his feet to strip off his coat as Ashlyn grabbed her shawl from a peg near the door and ran to Eden, throwing it atop her lower legs, smothering the flames.

"We've got to get out!" he cried, bending to lift Eden into his arms and hoping his leg would hold up as blood dribbled down his limb.

Reid and Ashlyn circled around the growing fire and hurried through the open door. Eden wailed as they moved away from the cottage. He saw Gray and Burke headed toward them. Ransom and Bellows weren't far behind.

The four men reached them and Reid said, "We'll need a doctor for Lady Eden. Her legs suffered some burns."

He raised the edge of her charred gown slightly, thankful to see very little damage to her flesh. "You're going to be fine, my lady," he assured her. "The doctor will merely be a precaution."

"I'll take care of that, Your Grace," Bellows said and wheeled, retreating in the opposite direction.

"We can help you carry Lady Eden back to Gillingham," Gray said.

"I don't want to go to Gillingham!" Eden shouted. "Put me down."

Reid lowered her feet to the ground and released her. She grabbed his arm to steady herself and said angrily, "You don't love me. You love her. You lied to me, Gilford."

"I do love Ashlyn," he admitted. "But I care what happens to you, Lady Eden. You need help. Not just with your legs but your mind."

Her eyes narrowed. "You think I'm mad. Like Mama."

When Reid didn't answer, she began sobbing. She released his arm and stumbled away. He started to go after her but Burke held him back.

"Let her be, Reid. She needs a few moments," his friend advised.

Reid reached for Ashlyn and pulled her into his arms. "I almost lost you. She would have shot you dead."

She gazed up at him, tears filling her eyes. "You came. You saved me. That's all that matters."

He kissed her, a life-affirming kiss. They had been through much this night and he prayed the nightmares wouldn't linger.

"Stop her!" Gray shouted and Reid broke the kiss, watching Gray take off as Eden Martin ran toward the burning cottage.

In horror, he saw her plunge into the abode and slam the door shut. Gray wrapped his hand around his coattails and tried to open the door.

"She's barred the door!" he shouted.

"Get away, Gray!" Reid yelled as Burke ran to Gray and pulled him away from the structure and back to them.

By now, the entire cottage burned, the flames lighting the night sky.

"She didn't want to live if she couldn't have you," Ashlyn said, slipping her hand around his. "Her mind was twisted. She couldn't understand reality. The madness had taken hold of her too deeply."

Several tenants joined them as they silently watched the cottage burn. None of them mentioned to the newcomers about Eden being inside. The roof collapsed and Reid knew there was no way Eden could have survived. In his mind, he understood he bore no guilt—but his heart would always carry the burden of the young girl who thought she was meant to wed a duke.

"Let's go home," he said wearily and sucked in a loud breath as Ashlyn bumped against his leg.

"Reid? What's wrong?" she asked, glancing down. Then she gasped. "You're bleeding."

"The gun went off when Eden rushed forward," he explained. Shaking his head, he added, "To think I served in His Majesty's Army for ten years without a scrape. It took returning home to England to get shot. At least the bullet merely grazed me. It's nothing serious," he assured her.

"Burke, Gray, get on both sides of him," Ashlyn ordered, turning full headmistress. "Have him keep all his weight off the injured leg. I'll go ahead and have water boiled and the doctor sent for."

"It's merely a flesh wound, my love," Reid reassured her.

"Flesh wound or not, infection—and fever—can set in." She cradled his face in her hands. "I've waited my entire life for you, Reid, and I refuse to lose you now."

Ashlyn took off, her skirts held high as she raced back toward Gillingham.

"She has quite the trim ankles," Burke said slyly as he draped one of Reid's arms across his shoulders.

"Very trim, indeed," noted Gray, doing the same with Reid's other arm.

"Quit ogling my future wife's ankles and get me back to Gillingham," he growled. "And if I didn't know you were teasing me and had wives you adore, I would be spilling some of your blood now."

His friends laughed and teased Reid all the way home.

EPILOGUE

Two weeks later . . .

ASHLYN AWOKE IN the bedchamber designated for the Duchess of Gilford. She'd stayed in the rooms ever since the night of the fire.

Today was her wedding day. The day she and Reid would become one. They would put the tragic events behind them and commit to one another for the rest of time.

It saddened her to think of Eden Martin. How the girl's madness had been inherited from her mother. How it had grown over the years, more than anyone could have suspected, until it led to her perishing in fire.

Once Reid's leg had been tended to and the doctor had assured her that no harm would beset Reid since the bullet had truly just grazed him, she and Reid had accompanied Lady Edith and Viscount Ransom back to London in order to break the news to Lord Martin regarding his daughter's tragic death. He turned old before their eyes, sobbing that he'd let down his younger daughter. After he'd finally calmed, he begged them to keep silent regarding the circumstances of Eden's death, not wanting her actions to color the reputation of Edith or Ransom. Ashlyn and Reid agreed to do so.

Lord Martin decided he would put out that his daughter impulsively decided to elope to Gretna Green and that he'd given chase. He would refuse to name the young gentleman involved in the affair and let it be known that Eden was being punished by having to remain in the north with distant relatives and miss the rest of her first Season. The story would allow Edith to continue to accept social invitations and wed Ransom quietly in the autumn, where only a handful of guests would attend. By then, Lord Martin would say Eden was ill and had to miss her sister's wedding since traveling so far would be out of the question. The viscount intended Eden to pass on sometime shortly afterward. By the start of the next Season, few would remember the girl and those who asked would be told of her untimely death.

Martin had also begged Ashlyn's forgiveness, telling her he hadn't realized how his daughter's infatuation with Gilford had taken hold of her very soul. Having known the loss of a child herself, she had accepted his apology, though she knew it would take Reid longer to come around.

A knock sounded at the door and Mrs. Paul entered, bearing a tray with tea and toast. As Ashlyn ate, an army of servants entered with buckets of hot water. Soon, she was bathed, perfumed, and dressed in a gown created in haste by a famous London modiste, who'd also provided Ashlyn with a few other gowns. The local Gillbrook seamstress also made up a few more dresses since she'd lost everything in the cottage fire. Reid promised once they went to spend time in London during her students' summer holidays, she'd complete her wardrobe.

Charlotte and Gemma arrived and Charlotte styled Ashlyn's hair for her, while Gemma made sure the diamond necklace and bracelet Reid had presented as a wedding gift were placed around Ashlyn's neck and on her wrist.

"You look lovely," Charlotte said wistfully.

"You're the most beautiful bride I've ever seen," Gemma added.

She took their hands. "I value your friendship and look forward to many years together."

A loud rap sounded at the door and Charlotte answered it.

Ashlyn saw Gray and Burke standing in the hallway.

"It's time to leave for the church," Gray said.

He took his wife's and Gemma's arms while Burke offered Ashlyn his and they went down to the waiting carriage for the short trip to the chapel.

"Gray and I would like to escort you to Reid," Burke said. "Would that be acceptable?"

Tears formed in her eyes. "That would be perfect," she told him.

When they arrived at the chapel, Ashlyn saw Arthur and Harry waiting outside. Both boys wore new clothes from head to toe and, for a moment, she glimpsed the men they would one day become.

Gray and Burke handed the women down and the boys came toward them.

"Lady Dunwood, Harry and I would like the honor of escorting you down the aisle if you'd allow us to do so."

Before she could reply and tell them she'd already committed to Burke and Gray, Burke said, "We were just talking about that in the carriage ride over. I think it's a splendid idea, don't you, Gray?"

"Yes," Gray said with enthusiasm. "Keeping it in the family."

Ashlyn gave them both a grateful smile. Looking at her soon-to-be brothers-in-law, she said, "I would be proud to have you assume the task."

"Then we better get inside so the ceremony can begin," Gemma said.

The four went into the chapel, where they would wait for Ashlyn and stand beside her and Reid as they spoke their vows.

"What should we call you?" Harry mused. "You won't be Lady Dunwood anymore."

"She'll be Her Grace," Arthur said testily. "A duchess."

"But she'll be family," Harry protested. "Even if she'll also be our headmistress."

"I think around the other boys you should address me by my

rank," she said. "It wouldn't do for you to be too familiar, simply because I'm married to your brother." She smiled. "However, when we're with family or it's only us in private? I hoped that you'll call me Ashlyn."

"I like that. Reid and Ashlyn." Harry grinned cheekily at her.

Arthur offered her his arm and his younger brother did the same. She slipped her hands through each and they led her inside the chapel. The music began and as Ashlyn came down the aisle, her gaze never left Reid. He stood waiting for her and she knew she was marrying the most handsome man in all of England.

And he was hers. As she was his.

They reached the altar and Reid said, "Thank you, my brothers, for delivering my bride safely to me." He couldn't tell who beamed more at his words, Ashlyn or the boys. He laced his fingers through Ashlyn's and they faced the clergyman, repeating their vows of love and fidelity to one another as their close friends and her students and staff looked on.

When they were pronounced man and wife, Reid turned toward her. Speaking so softly that only she could hear, he said, "You changed my life in every way imaginable, my love. I am a better man for loving you—and having your love."

With that, he gave her a tender kiss, full of the promises they'd made to one another, showing her that from now on, everything they did would be done together. As man and wife.

In love.

THE END

About the Author

Award-winning and internationally bestselling author Alexa Aston's historical romances use history as a backdrop to place her characters in extraordinary circumstances, where their intense desire for one another grows into the treasured gift of love.

She is the author of Regency and Medieval romance, including: Dukes of Distinction; Soldiers & Soulmates; The St. Clairs; The King's Cousins; and The Knights of Honor.

A native Texan, Alexa lives with her husband in a Dallas suburb, where she eats her fair share of dark chocolate and plots out stories while she walks every morning. She enjoys a good Netflix binge; travel; seafood; and can't get enough of *Survivor* or *The Crown*.

www.ingramcontent.com/pod-product-compliance
Lightning Source LLC
Chambersburg PA
CBHW071437200726
48294CB00002B/678
* 9 7 8 1 9 6 1 2 7 5 3 9 3 *